The Sunday Only Christian:

Still Divas Series Book Three

The Sunday Only Christian:

Still Divas Series Book Three

E.N. Joy

URBAN CHRISTIAN

www.urbanchristianonline.com

Urban Books, LLC
78 East Industry Court
Deer Park, NY 11729

The Sunday Only Christian: Still Divas Series Book
Three Copyright © 2012 E.N. Joy

ISBN 13: 978-1-60162-740-7
ISBN 10: 1-60162-740-8

First Printing December 2012
Printed in the United States of America

10 9 8 7 6 5 4 3 2 1

*This is a work of fiction. Any references or similarities
to actual events, real people, living or dead, or to real
locales are intended to give the novel a sense of reality. Any similarity in other names, characters, places,
and incidents is entirely coincidental.*

Distributed by Kensington Corp.
Submit Wholesale Orders to:
Kensington Publishing Corp.
C/O Penguin Group (USA) Inc.
Attention: Order Processing
405 Murray Hill Parkway
East Rutherford, NJ 07073-2316
Phone: 1-800-526-0275
Fax: 1-800-227-9604

The Sunday Only Christian:

Still Divas Series Book Three

E.N. Joy

Other Books by This Author

Me, Myself and Him
She Who Finds a Husband
Been There, Prayed That
Love, Honor or Stray
Trying to Stay Saved
I Can Do Better All By Myself
And You Call Yourself a Christian
The Perfect Christian
Ordained By the Streets
Even Sinners Have Souls (Edited by E.N. Joy)
Even Sinners Have Souls Too (Edited by E.N .Joy)
Even Sinners Still Have Souls (Edited by E.N. Joy)
The Secret Olivia Told Me (N. Joy)

Dedication

I don't do romance. Once upon a time I used to write secular books, which included erotica, but there was no romance. Either the books were hot like fire and full of lust and temptation, or they were as cold as ice, full of vixens and drama. There was none of that in-between stuff called romance. But all that changed with *The Sunday Only Christian*. Mrs. Brenda Jackson, I would have never been able to make this story as romantic as I did had I not decided to pick up your books and learn from the best. There is no Hatersville in this part of Ohio. Nothin' but love for you. Keep schoolin' 'em!

Acknowledgments

I don't know how far I would be in my success as an author if it was not for the support of my grandparents, Oliver and Barbara Edwards. Thank you so much, Granny and Gramps, for reading ALL my books.

For my husband, Nick "Bang" Ross, you wouldn't let up until I penned and self-published my first book. Now with over twenty-five published writings later, outside of the gift of writing itself from God, I owe it all to you. Thanks for the push and for believing in me. Thank you for supporting me even when sometimes I felt you were the enemy. But I realize now that without the necessary pressure and constructive criticism you gave me, I would have settled for just doing the best I could. Thank you for making me do ALL that I could in a spirit of excellence. I love you like crazy, man!

For my mother-in-law, Gwen Marsh, I think I'm out of words to dedicate and acknowledge you with. None are sufficient. The role you have played in my life is something I absolutely never foresaw almost sixteen years ago when I met your son. Your son has become my husband. Your daughters have become my sisters. Your mother, "Mama" (God rest her soul) my grandmother. Your siblings my aunts and uncles, cousins, etc. . . . But most importantly, your God my God. And it is your godly advice and wisdom, along with my sister-in-law's, Nicole Ross Byrd's, prayers and spiritual guidance, that has helped me breathe when I thought

I was going to take my last breath any minute. The biblical story of Naomi and Ruth makes so much more sense to me now. I love you, Ma.

For my four beautiful children; I have worked and prayed endlessly to make sure that you are nothing like the person who I was, and ten times better than the person I am today. Whenever I feel like giving up I picture your smiles—I hear your laughter. I remember that my work is not done in raising you in the Word. You make me better. You make me feel like going on. I thank God for you.

Last but not least, ReShonda Tate Billingsley, Victoria Christopher Murray, and Pat O'Gorge: I watched you and studied you. You all have that special writing style and that special something that makes readers race out to the bookstore for your next project. If I could just do this old school—without measuring utensils—and take a dash of ReShonda Tate Billingsley, a touch of Mrs. O'Gorge, and a pinch of Victoria, I'd have the perfect meal to serve up to my readers. Thanks for your inspiration over the years.

It's much easier to act like a Christian at church than to be one at home.

—E.N. Joy

Chapter One

"I up and left him for another man, so what on God's green earth would make him want to take me back?" Deborah had been asking herself this question the entire drive to the book signing. And now, as she parked outside of the Barnes & Noble on 356 in Pickerington, Ohio, she still had no answer. Dreadfully, she knew her answer lay inside that one-level bookstore, in which the smell of flavored caffeine from the little Starbucks in the front corner of the store would assault her nose from the moment she stepped inside.

Sitting in her car, stalling, she dug in her purse and pulled out the postcard she'd come across in the hair salon last week. She double-checked the date of the book signing on the postcard. She was hoping she'd gotten her dates mixed up and that the book signing had been yesterday. That way she wouldn't have to risk the embarrassment and humiliation of rejection; if, in fact that's what was about to happen: her being rejected.

"Ughh," she gasped. There was no mix-up. Today was the day.

Next Deborah allowed her eyes to scroll over to the time of the signing. If there was a God and He had her back and wanted to prevent her from being disgraced and her ego from being shattered to pieces, there would definitely be a mix-up with the times. She would have missed the signing by an hour or two. All that would be left once she went inside would be a couple of unsold autographed copies of the *New York Times* bestseller and a handful of promotional bookmarks.

She looked down at her watch. She chuckled at the fact that she could very well be the only person she knew who still bothered to wear a watch. Most people relied on their cell phones to keep up with the time. It was 7:45 P.M. No mix-up in the time department. According to the postcard, the signing was from six to eight.

Deborah had deliberately waited to catch the tail end of the event. If she was going to be shamed with rejection, it sure wasn't going to be in front of a full crowd of fans. It would only be in the presence of those few still milling around, trying to get him to read a chapter or two of their own works in progress, and then provide feedback, of course. Then there were the couple of people who would monopolize a great deal of his time, asking questions about the process they need to take in order to become published. Both kinds of people would be the ones who never even bothered to purchase his book. She'd seen it a million times. But no matter who or how many people were still lingering around, did Deborah really want to get rejected in front of even one?

"Perhaps I should just sit here and wait; catch him coming out," Deborah pondered. "No. No. I should go in there and act surprised that he's even there. I could pretend as though I just happened to be in the bookstore on the day of his signing." That last idea wouldn't be too farfetched. After all, Deborah did own her own literary consulting agency. She did book editing and some agenting. To find her in the bookstore would be normal—believable.

Five minutes went by as she sat in the car wracking her brains on how she was going to approach the man who, if she were him, would never ever talk to her again. She'd played him to the left, right, front, and back. And for what? For a man who fed her a fairytale that he'd marry her and they'd live happily ever after. They'd go start a new life in Chile where he played professional basketball and he'd make sure she had the world. It all sounded good to Deborah. And it was good, until she found out that they couldn't live happily ever after together until he got a divorce from his wife; a wife who Deborah had been none the wiser of—in the beginning anyway. But that was neither here nor there. Right now she had to focus on exactly how she was going to play this thing out.

Pulling her keys out of the ignition and grabbing her purse, Deborah, in an attempt to be a little more optimistic, thought that maybe things wouldn't turn out to be so bad. Besides, since when had she become this Debbie Downer, so to speak? When had she started thinking the worst of everything? Maybe she should have been asking herself why on God's green earth wouldn't this man want to take her back. And that's exactly what she thought as she got out of the car and closed the door behind her. But she hadn't even taken two steps before those negative thoughts resurfaced.

"A girlfriend! A fiancée! Heck, even a wife!" Deborah said out loud as the thought reached down and punched her right in the gut. Those certainly were things that would make him not want to take her back. So much time had passed since she'd walked out of his life, or rather flew out of his life, anything was possible. Heck, he could even have a kid by now. After all, she did.

One minute she'd been on the perfect date with Mr. *New York Times* Bestselling Author, then the next minute her first love had swooped back into town and into her life, convincing her to join him on a plane to Chile to start a new one with him. And just like that, like that episode in *Sex and the City* when Carrie got on that plane to Paris with Mikhail Baryshnikov's character, Deborah had done it. Carrie had left what could have been with Mr. Big and Deborah had left what could have been with Mr. Perfect.

"I can't do this. I can't." She turned to head back to her car and that's when a loud horn scared the bajibbies out of her. "Oh, God!" Deborah screamed as the car came within inches of hitting her. The driver looked just as petrified as she did. "I'm so sorry. So sorry," Deborah apologized.

The woman in the car, with her hand grabbing her chest, nodded. Once again, Deborah let out a verbal apology that the driver accepted with a second nod and then drove off.

"Lord have mercy, I almost got killed over thoughts about this man. No way am I turning back now." And just like that, after a life-altering moment, Deborah found the courage to strut inside that Barnes & Noble like she owned the place; or at least had a great deal of stock in it. With her medium-brown complexion now glowing with excitement, she batted her thick eyelashes, ran her fingers through her shoulder-length hair, then strutted like a fashion model on a New York runway during Fashion Week.

"Hi, welcome to Barnes & Noble," a clerk stacking books at the Summer Beach Read table greeted Deborah. "Can I help you find anything?"

"As a matter of fact, you can," Deborah said confidently. "I'm here for a book signing—Mr. Lynox Chase's book signing. Can you please point me in the right direction?" Deborah asked, knowing in just a matter of minutes, her God of second chances just might give her a second chance at love. For real this time.

Chapter Two

Deborah didn't know how to feel after hearing the clerk's words.

"I'm sorry, ma'am, but Mr. Chase sold out about an hour into his signing," the clerk said with pride, as if she were his publisher, agent, or something and not just a store clerk. "Folks had been lined up long before he even arrived. We practically could have sold out of his books before he ever even showed up had we a cash register outside to ring the folks up." She shot off a half laugh/half snort. "He hung around, autographed copies, read from his book, and did a Q and A; then he left." She shrugged as if to say, "Sorry about your luck."

Deborah felt sorry all right. And no matter how much she tried to hide it, she was certain it had shown all over her face. Instead of feeling sympathy, the clerk continued to pour salt in the wound. "And you should have seen him." She blushed. "He's exactly what you'd expect someone with the name L.C. who wrote a book titled *The Fantasy Fairytale* to look like." She sighed and her eyes took a mini vacation to la-la land. "Tall, dark, handsome, exuding confidence with a bit of conceit. And you should have seen his—"

"Trust me," Deborah shot, cutting her off, "I'm sure I've seen his . . . his . . . whatever you were gonna say. Anyway, thanks for your help." Deborah turned on her four-inch heels. In her peacock strut of an exit, she tripped, nearly falling to the floor. "Dang shoes," she fussed, wishing she'd never taken a chance—on the shoes or seeing Lynox.

The highest heel Deborah had ever worn was three inches. But for some reason she just had to have those Mary Jane–looking tan suede pumps with red bottoms that some booster had carried into the hair salon. Not for some reason—for one reason. It was moments after she'd picked up the flyer about Lynox's book signing when the middle-aged, clean-cut man had entered the salon rolling his very own makeshift department store. With the flyer in hand, Deborah had been visualizing an encounter with Lynox after not seeing him for over two years. Those shoes just seemed to be the cherry on top of the vision. Deborah could picture Lynox drooling at the mouth, among other places, upon seeing her long, slender legs in those babies. They would make him forget all about their crooked past, and dream about their straight future.

"One hundred seventy-five dollars," the booster had requested of the shoes. A small price to pay, Deborah thought, for the opportunity to be in the arms of the most suave, debonair man she'd ever met in her life. Not to mention caring. Not to mention a man who could have loved her like she'd always dreamed of being loved.

A small price to pay out of her pocketbook anyway. Her conscience tapped her on the shoulder and reminded her, though, that there was never a small price to pay when it came to sin. And it just might have been a sin to buy those shoes from that booster for $175 after seeing the department store sticker on them that clearly read $800.

Heck, but he's worth it, Deborah had concluded after giving the man a hundred dollar bill and four twenties, then telling him to keep the change. But now, as two teenagers pointed and giggled at her near fall, as she felt the clerk's eyes burning a hole through her back, burning up the pages of a story she'd fantasized about all week, she felt none of it had been worth it; certainly not those dang-on shoes.

With nothing left to lose, Deborah kicked off the shoes in anger, and embarrassment, and as she exited the store, pitched them in the trash bin. There were no good memories attached to those shoes, probably the same way Lynox had no good memories of his and Deborah's short-lived romance.

"Ouch! Ouch! Ugggghhh!" Deborah roared out in pain after feeling a large shoe come crashing down on her bare foot. The pain was excruciating. She immediately looked down at her battered toe and let out an expletive. She was immediately embarrassed and conflicted by the Holy Spirit, but that didn't stop her from wanting to look up at the person who had just stomped her foot and call them an expletive or two.

She knew that's exactly what she would have done had she dared look up at the person; so, instead, she focused on her injury while she hopped around on one foot while holding the other in her hand. It hurt so bad that tears began to stream down her face. Now she was really embarrassed. Here she was just a-cursing and a-crying, hopping around, looking like some crazy woman. She wanted to bury her head in the sand. But instead, she just kept it down, squeezing her eyes shut, hoping to stop the pain. Hoping to stop the tears. Deborah just couldn't distinguish which tear represented which type of pain. Was it the physical pain from her throbbing foot, or the pain from her throbbing heart?

"I'm . . . I'm so sorry, ma'am. I'm so sorry," the pain inflictor apologized.

"Sorry?" Deborah shouted, her eyes still squeezed closed. "Do you think the word 'sorry' is going to make me feel better? Do you?" Deborah cried, opening her eyes and eyeing her foot, on which the big toenail was ripped down to the skin.

"Please, let me take a look at it," the very sympathetic male voice requested.

"Why? Are you a doctor or something?" Deborah snapped, trying not to gag from the grossness of her toe.

"No, but—"

"Then there's no need for you to look at it, now is there? Seems like what you need to look at is where in the heck you're walking." Deborah meant to say the word "heck," but that certainly wasn't what it sounded like had actually come out of her mouth. That darn cursing demon was rearing its ugly head to the tenth power. She buried her head even deeper in shame. This was not how a Christian woman was supposed to be acting, supposed to be talking.

"Look, I said I'm sorry. If there's anything I can do—"

"Yeah, there's something you can do; watch where you're walking." Since Deborah was already looking down, she allowed her eyes to roam over to the man's feet. "And maybe get a license for those big boats before you go sailing them across someone's feet. How about that?"

The voice that had initially been kind and concerned suddenly changed to match the nasty tone in which Deborah was shooting off. "Look, lady, I said I'm sorry. And besides, who goes walking around barefoot anyway?" He looked at the words printed on the outside of the store's door. "Besides, it says right here"—he pointed—"shoes and shirt must be worn. Looks like you need to learn to read, and I find it ironic that you can't, seeing that you are at a bookstore."

Not only had this jerk just smashed her foot, but now he was insulting Deborah's intellect. Oh she was not about to have that. Saved or not, she was not going to take any mess from anybody. "Look, you piece of work . . ." Deborah rose up and began before that same clerk talking to her in the store hurried outside to see what all the commotion was about. She immediately put her head back down. She definitely did not want that clerk seeing her in that condition. She probably looked like a raccoon from crying.

"Is everything okay out here?" Deborah heard the clerk ask.

Assuming the clerk would come running to her aid, Deborah shifted her focus directly to the ground, just knowing she'd see the clerk's little feet come running over to check on her. Deborah instantly forgot all about the pain in her foot when her blood boiled over to realize that instead the clerk had gone running over to the perpetrator's side.

"I'm the one out here in pain and you're running up next to him and asking him if everything is okay?" Deborah spat at the clerk. She looked up and was about to give the clerk a dirty look when, not thinking, she decided to add a cherry on top of her tantrum sundae by stomping her foot. "Ouch!" She howled out in pain as she once again hobbled over and grabbed her throbbing foot.

"I . . . I was just coming back for my rolling briefcase when this woman came barreling out of the store barefoot," the man said. "I accidentally stepped on her foot."

The clerk paused and looked down at Deborah's disgusting-looking toe with the nail practically hanging off, then replied to the man, "I'm sure she'll be okay. Let's head back inside and locate your briefcase."

That's it! Deborah was going to give both Mr. Foot Stepper On-er and that clerk a piece of her unsanctified mind. She didn't care if she embarrassed and humiliated herself more than she ever had in her entire life put together. Deborah's eyes went from her foot to the man's feet, then drove from his feet up to his knees. Next her eyes went from his knees, to his midsection, to his chest, and then to his face.

Deborah had managed to keep from falling inside the store when she tripped in those four-inch pumps. She'd managed to keep from falling as she hobbled around outside on one foot while holding the other in pain. But now, as she looked into those all–too-familiar eyes, she landed flat on her butt.

"Deborah?"

"Lynox?"

Chapter Three

"You really didn't have to wait. I'm sure you had much better things to do than sit here in the urgent care lobby waiting for me." Deborah gave her best shot at trying to sound undeserving and humble about Lynox having followed her to urgent care, and now two hours later, after she'd gotten her toe cleaned up, still waiting to make sure she was okay. In actuality, her insides wanted to burst she was so moved. She honestly had not expected him to still be waiting for her, especially after how nasty she'd been to him for stepping on her foot. Of course, that was before she realized it was him. And that all of this had been a divine encounter, perhaps. But then again, it could have been purely bad timing and a bad case of the klutz.

Lynox stood. "I didn't mind waiting. I'm accustomed to waiting." He raised an eyebrow and Deborah thought about how long he'd waited for her to come around and show an interest in him. "I figured it was the least I could do after practically taking your big toe off." He looked down at Deborah's bandaged foot. "I didn't recognize your feet were the ones I'd slammed down on. Heck, I didn't recognize you." He stared at Deborah's hair.

"Oh, yeah. I've had my sisterlocks out for a while now." She ran her hands through her natural hair. After wearing it in sisterlocks for years, while in Chile she'd gotten them cut off. Finding someone to tighten

her locks every four to six weeks had been next to impossible, so she had decided to cut them off and let her
hair grow out natural. After coming back to the States,
she found a wonder salon called Synergi Salon. It was
in Whitehall, which was just a little over a half-hour
drive from Malvonia. And the way those women up in
that shop specialized and worked with natural hair, it
was well worth the drive.

"I guess you hadn't recognized me either." He rubbed
his facial hair. "Decided to let my facial hair grow out."
His once clean-cut, brown-skinned face was now covered in waves of hair.

"Well, actually, I was too busy focusing on my foot."
She watched his hands massage the hair down the
sides of his face down to his chin. "But the facial hair;
it's becoming." And Deborah was becoming a little
hot just picturing her own hands running the course
of his face. Feeling embarrassed that Lynox might be
able to detect the flushing of her blood in her cheeks,
she cleared her throat and said, "Anyway, like I said,
thanks for waiting."

He shrugged. "Like I said, it was the least I could do."
He then looked over at the reception desk. "That and
pay the bill that is. I sort of saw to it that your bill gets
charged to my credit card."

"You didn't have to do that," Deborah replied, but
she was glad he did. Being self-employed, in her case,
meant no insurance. A doctor visit in her home meant
payment arrangements with the provider in order to
cover the bill. She'd thought about getting medical
insurance, but it was just so expensive, and she rarely
ever needed medical care. Her baby's father had paid
all her medical bills in relation to having his child, so
that hadn't been a financial burden she had to bear.

"Oh, but I did," Lynox stated. "And please, if you have to make any future visits as a result, please let me know what the bill is and I'll reimburse you."

Deborah knew when to accept a blessing. "I'll do that." And she left it at that.

There was silence as the two just stood there basically looking over each other's shoulders as if they were afraid to look each other in the eyes. The tension was so thick, a regular knife could not have cut through it. Oh, no—a chainsaw was needed to cut through this type of tension.

"Seeing you back at the bookstore . . ." Lynox swallowed. "I was shocked. The last I recall you were living over in Chile." Lynox left it at that. He was going to add, "with your ex," but tried to remain as cordial as possible, even though over the years the thought of how Deborah had dumped him for that LeBron James wannabe made his blood boil.

"Yeah, well, I was, but now I'm back. As a matter of fact, I've been back for several months now."

"Is that so? I'm surprised I hadn't run into you until now." He smirked before adding, "Literally running into you."

"Ha-ha. Tell my big toe that joke," Deborah snarled.

"I'm sorry. I guess that was in poor taste." He looked down at her foot, which was donned in those hospital booties with the rubber grips on the bottom. "Does it hurt much?" He'd managed to wipe the smile off of his face and become serious—very serious. He asked her those words as if it wasn't her toe that he was questioning about, but her heart instead.

"Ummm, so-so. The doc gave me a little something. Once the goodies wear off, though, no telling."

"Hmmm. I know how that can be; pain that is." He looked into Deborah's eyes. "Especially the kind that just won't go away no matter what you do to try to get rid of it."

For some reason, Deborah felt as though Lynox was no longer talking about the kind of pain from jamming a big toe. And just when she thought he couldn't look any deeper into her eyes . . .

"Do you know what I mean? Huh, Mrs. Culvins or Culiver or whatever your name might be now?" He tried to recall the last name of the basketball superstar she'd run off to marry. Not wanting to lose his cool, and feeling a wave of heat coming on, Lynox knew it was time to go. "So, like I said, you get any more bills, send them my way." Lynox turned and walked away.

The last time Deborah had seen Lynox, she was walking out of his life. Now was she going to just stand there and let him give her the ol' eye for an eye? No. Heck no! "Lynox, where can I find you?"

He stopped, but he didn't turn around to face Deborah. He turned his head so that his chin was over his left shoulder. It was as if just seeing her silhouette in his peripheral vision was enough.

Deborah worried that she'd sounded too desperate, so she quickly added, "Where can I find you just in case I do get any more bills?" Deborah wanted to shoot herself in her good foot. Was that the best she could come up with? What was keeping her from being real and just telling him that she wanted to see him again? She wanted him again, not that she ever really had him before. She'd had a nice grip on him though, before her ex had hit the scene. It was a nice enough grip for her to know that if she'd held on long enough, right now he'd have no trouble guessing her last name: Mrs. Deborah Chase.

"LCfantasywriter.com," Lynox shot over his shoulder.

"Excuse me?" Deborah's face twisted up. Was he really doing what she thought he was doing? He might as well have just told her to Google him.

"LCfantasywriter.com," he repeated, knowing darn well he'd said it clearly the first time. He didn't mind repeating it, though, as a slight grin barely spread across his lips. Fearing Deborah might see it, he turned back forward and continued. "That's my Web site. There's a contact form. Hit me up there if you need to." And then he strolled through the double doors, which automatically opened for him like they knew he was the mega national–bestselling author he was. And the doors closed right in Deborah's face like she was that groupie chick who was trying desperately to get to him but couldn't.

"No, he didn't just send me through the Web site route," Deborah said softly to herself. She let out a "tsk" sound before she herself began marching out the door. "I wish I might give him the pleasure of having me stalk him virtually. He thinks it's cute trying to turn the tables on me?" Deborah huffed, remembering how once upon a time it was Lynox who had tracked her down via Internet. "Well, I'm going to show him cute."

Deborah made it to her car, started it, and just as she threw it in reverse to back out, she looked up and saw Lynox. She was parked up front in the parking lot and he was parked a few rows back, getting into his larger-than-life Hummer, which fit his larger-than-life persona. Even before he was a bestselling author with a book that had held the number one spot on every best-sellers list since it had come out three months ago, he had this superstar quality about him. Now, who he was always meant to be and had always had the confidence to know that he would be had only been validated. But all Deborah wanted was to validate who he was meant to be with: her. And that hadn't turned out so well. Just when Deborah was about to mentally throw in the towel she reminded herself that this was only round one. She'd been in longer bouts with the devil and had prevailed. Surely she could take on Lynox—a man of flesh and blood.

With a fresh wind of confidence blowing upon Deborah, she smiled at herself in the mirror while backing out and saying to herself, "If Mr. Lynox Chase wants a chase, then that's exactly what I'm going to give him." Unbeknownst to Deborah, she wouldn't have to chase him down too long. She'd run into him again soon—sooner than she thought.

Bam!

The sound—the jolt. "Oh my God!" Deborah's car came to an almost violent halt. She turned around in her seat and looked behind her. "You've got to be kidding me," she said upon seeing the rear end of her car smashed into the driver-side door of Lynox's Hummer. "Jesus." Deborah immediately pulled back into her space and got out of her car.

Lynox didn't get out of his; he simply said through his rolled-down window, "Your toe, my vehicle." He leaned his head out to see Deborah's white paint mixed in with his black paint. "Guess we're even now."

Chapter Four

"Lynox, I'm so sorry. So sorry." With her hand over her mouth in shock, Deborah walked between the two vehicles to observe the damage. Besides her paint and a small ding on Lynox's truck, his vehicle looked as if it would be okay. The back end of her car was another story. "Man, what is that tank you're driving made out of? Look what it did to my car."

"Pardon me?" Lynox chuckled, now taking the liberty to exit the car. "Don't you mean look what you did to your own car?"

Remembering that this was all her fault, Deborah calmed down and now placed her hand on her forehead. She felt a headache coming on. "What were you doing behind me anyway?"

"I was bringing you these. Thought you might need them." He held up the infamous pair of four-inch red-bottom heels. "The clerk back at the bookstore gave them to me when she gave me my briefcase."

Deborah felt like a vampire and that those shoes were like looking at a cross or a string of garlic or something. Bad luck was all those shoes had been. She didn't want them. She didn't want to see them. She turned away from them.

"And if you don't mind me asking"—he held his hands up—"'cause I can see how I left my briefcase"—he laughed—"but do tell me, how does one leave a pair of shoes in a bookstore?"

All of a sudden Deborah wanted the shoes back. She didn't want him standing there, making a mockery out of this entire situation she'd tried to orchestrate like something out of a fantasy romance novel, only to have it turn out like a bad episode of the old sitcom *Three's Company*. She snatched the shoes out of his hands with an attitude.

"Hey. Shouldn't I be the one who's mad?"

"Lynox, look at my car." Deborah pointed to the huge dent in the rear of her car. "That tank of a truck you're driving is barely damaged. My entire trunk is practically smashed in."

"Oh, calm down. It's not as bad as it looks. I'm sure your insurance company will have it in and out of a shop and back to rolling in no time. Speaking of which, I think we better exchange insurance information. Perhaps call the police even." Lynox looked at the dent in his door and brushed his hand across the white paint that now mixed with his vehicle's black paint. "You dinged me up pretty bad."

"At least all you got was a ding." Deborah ran her hand across her own bruised-up vehicle.

"Yeah, well sometimes what looks like a little ding can go much deeper." Lynox looked away from his vehicle and at her. "It can be far worse on the inside than what it appears to be on the outside."

There was a pause after Lynox said those words. Deborah could feel him staring at her, so she looked away from her vehicle and her eyes locked with his. His electric eyes; God were they intense to Deborah. They spoke volumes, volumes more than what his words could ever mean.

Realizing that once again Lynox perhaps might not just have been referring to the ding in his door, but the ding Deborah might have left in his heart, she stood up erect, her eyes still locked with his. "I'm sorry, Lynox. Really, I'm sorry." And it wasn't just her backing into his vehicle that she was sorry about. Deborah was sorry that she'd made Lynox pursue her for so long. She was sorry that once she finally let him catch up with her she led him to believe that the two could really have a future together.

She hadn't deliberately led him on though. Deborah had really been feeling Lynox. What single woman in her right mind wouldn't have been feeling this man with his tight fade and sculptured body? When Deborah had first encountered Lynox, she had way too many demons she had to be delivered from before she could involve him in her life. And, unfortunately, the two had a common denominator in their lives who went by the name of Helen.

Helen was a member of Deborah's church, New Day Temple of Faith, and she also just happened to be someone Lynox had gone out with on a date or two. But that wasn't the biggest of Deborah's issues. Not only did Helen know Lynox, but she knew Deborah's demons as well, up close and personal. After all, Helen had been that stranger sitting next to Deborah in the abortion clinic years ago when Deborah got a late-term abortion when she was well into her second trimester. Helen had been so taunting that day in the clinic and then years later when she visited New Day and then joined.

Sure, Helen had had the procedure done too, but she'd tried to make herself feel better by making Deborah feel worse. Helen had only been a "little bit pregnant" while Deborah could feel her baby moving inside of her. Helen wasn't showing at all while Deborah was visibly pregnant. Helen never let up on making the comparisons between the two, deeming Deborah far worse of a person than she was.

Helen's taunting had worked. By the time Helen got finished with her, Deborah had felt like a murderer who needed to be on death row. And it ate Deborah up inside that Helen might tell Lynox about the dirty deed. It was just too much. But thank God for knowing just how much His daughter could bear and for how long.

Getting delivered from her past and receiving both self and God's forgiveness hadn't been easy for Deborah. But nothing was too hard for her Lord and Savior. She came through it all with no scars, ready to receive the joy of life. That joy had included a relationship with Lynox. And just when she'd allowed herself to let go of her past and live in the now, her first love and ex-fiancé came sniffing around.

Elton resurfacing in her life was just confirmation that the devil may be defeated, but he certainly wasn't destroyed. Satan had influenced Deborah's mind to believe that if she and Elton got back together again, they could right their wrong. The baby she'd aborted at Elton's urging and with Elton's dime, she could recreate. So basically, the devil convinced her to repeat her past sin of fornication with Elton, even after she found out he was married. So when she turned up pregnant a second time, living in the fantasy that God was giving her back the baby she'd aborted, she kept this child. Not only did she keep the child, but she gave up her life in Malvonia to move to Chile as Elton's mistress, on his promise to divorce his wife and marry her. Now only the devil could convince a college-educated, professional, Christian woman to do something so stupid. And only God could pull her through it. And once again, He had.

She wanted to right her wrong with Lynox so badly. But with the way things were going, she couldn't figure out if God was putting her in a position to do so, or if Satan was up to his old tricks again.

"You have to believe me, Lynox, I really am sorry." Deborah stood there on the verge of tears as she apologized to Lynox.

He sighed, closed his eyes, and then opened them again. "Deborah, I forgive you."

Deborah exhaled. *Yes, this is all God.*

"I'm probably just being selfish about this entire situation. It's clear that you're worse off than I am. I mean, look at your car and look at mine."

Deborah's shoulders fell. "Cars?" Deborah snapped. "We're talking about cars here?"

Lynox looked confused. "Well, yeah. What else would we be talking about? You just backed into a vehicle that cost more than some people's homes."

Deborah shook her head and quickly wiped her moist eyes. "Just forget it. Here . . ." She walked back to the driver's door, sat in her seat, then reached over into her glove box and pulled out her insurance card. She then grabbed her purse, took out a scrap piece of paper and a pen, and transferred her insurance information onto the paper.

She got back out of her vehicle, and headed back toward Lynox. "There—take it." She practically shoved her insurance information into Lynox's chest. "I don't even know why I bothered. Just have your insurance company contact mine. I'm sure they'll take care of everything. Now if you don't mind, would you please move your vehicle from behind mine?"

Lynox absolutely did not understand where Deborah's little tirade was coming from. He'd known Deborah to be a strong, no-nonsense type of woman who was about her business. That's what had attracted him to her. But he had no idea where this side of her was coming from. It was like he was missing something.

Lynox held the paper in his hand, looked down at it, and then looked at Deborah. "If this is the way you want to handle it, then that's what I'll do. I just thought you and I could work this out."

Regretfully, Deborah replied, "You know what? I thought the same thing too. But it looks like I was wrong." Deborah got in her car and watched as Lynox, looking confused as ever, got into his car and moved out of Deborah's way. Now if only Satan would get out of her way, things would be just fine.

Chapter Five

It was times like this when Deborah wished Mother Doreen still lived in Malvonia. Even though Mother Doreen was just a phone call away, it wasn't the same as having her confidant there right next to her to lay hands on her, and touch and agree and pray together about her situations.

"I could always call Pastor," Deborah said to herself as she sat on the couch eating pizza, her encounter with Lynox still on her mind.

"Call Pastor."

Until she heard the little voice of her two-year-old son mimicking her, Deborah had almost forgotten he was even there. She looked down beside her at his sauce-covered face, and smiled. She placed her half-eaten slice of pizza back in the box and scooted him over onto her lap.

"Why is Mommy sitting here driving herself crazy about a man when she's got the perfect little man sitting right here next to her?"

"Perfect little man," he repeated.

"You're enough for Mommy to deal with. What makes her think she needs to add to the situation?" By this time, the two-year-old's attention had turned to the animated movie on the television screen. But still, Deborah continued talking as if she were having a conversation with an adult.

"What do I need a silly old man for anyway? All it could possibly bring into our lives is drama. And right now, I don't mind living a drama-free life. I don't need no man, especially the likes of Lynox Chase, interrupting things. He's too arrogant. Too cocky. There's nothing wrong with being confident, but he sometimes goes a little overboard. The Bible says we shouldn't think more highly of ourselves than we actually are." She sighed. "Let's just face it, kid; it would have taken nothing short of a miracle for me and Mr. Chase to ever get back together again anyway."

The ringing doorbell was what finally tore Deborah away from the one-sided conversation with herself.

"Just a minute," Deborah called out, placing her son back on the couch from her lap and then getting up.

It was early evening, but evening nonetheless. Walking over to the door, she had absolutely no idea who would be knocking at this hour without calling first. She hadn't missed any church or church functions, so there was no way a New Day member was doing a drive-by to check on her. In a split second, suddenly Deborah was hopeful. Maybe it was Lynox. Never mind all that mess she'd just rambled on about not needing a man in her life. She'd only said those things to make herself feel better. She hadn't meant them. Her mouth might have said them, but her heart had nothing to do with it. And God knew her heart.

Yes! That's exactly who it was at her door. It was Lynox. He'd probably been staring at the piece of paper with her information on it all night, wanting to use it for something much more than just giving it to his insurance company. Deborah could only hope.

By the time Deborah made it to the door, she'd pumped herself up to believe that, without a doubt, Lynox was on the other side of that door. *Who else could it be?* she asked herself. *God, you are still in the mira-cle business,* Deborah thought as she anxiously asked, "Who is it?" when she really wanted to swing open that door and jump right into Lynox's arms.

"Can you open up?" the male voice on the other side of the door replied.

It was a man's voice. That was good.

"It's the police."

Not good.

"Thank you so much, ma'am. I really appreciate your cooperation," the officer said as he tilted his hat and exited Deborah's house.

"No problem, Officer—no problem at all." Deborah closed the door behind the officer and then looked down at the citation in her hand. She then looked up to the ceiling. "Are you finished yet, God? Are you fin-ished humiliating me?" she yelled, but then lowered her voice after realizing she might wake up her sleeping child.

Initially not knowing what the officer's business was with her, she'd asked him if it was okay for her to take her son up to bed. The officer didn't have a problem with it, so Deborah did just that. Upon returning to the living room was when she'd learned just why the officer had come to her home.

"Do you know a"—the officer read from some type of notepad—"a Mr. Lynox Chase?"

"I do. Of course I do. I just ran into him today," Deborah replied.

"And that's exactly why I'm here—the fact that you ran into him." Deborah was still slightly clueless as to what the officer was getting at. "With your car, he says you backed up into his car."

Now Deborah got it, but she couldn't believe it. Had Lynox really called the cops on her after they agreed that they'd allow their insurance companies to handle things? "Well, I uh, did," Deborah started with a stammer. "But we took care of everything. We decided that we would allow our insurance companies to take care of the matter."

"Yeah, well, all I know is that I got a call about the accident and that I needed to come here to take a report. Get your side of the story."

Deborah stood there feeling like a criminal. Like she'd been involved in a hit-and-run and now the cops had chased her down. She wrapped her arms around herself for security purposes. She felt so open, vulnerable . . . and guilty. "There is no side. I backed into him while I was pulling out of my parking spot."

The officer began to jot things down on the notepad he'd pulled out. "And were there any damages that you noticed your car had done to Mr. Chase's vehicle?"

"Well, yeah, there was a dent and a little paint. Nothing major. My car suffered the bulk of the damage. My car insurance rate is probably going to go up because of this."

Unsympathetically and robotically, the officer jotted down something else and then looked to Deborah. "Did anyone get hurt?"

Deborah paused. Why did it seem like she was referencing every other question to her and Lynox's past relationship? Would she be lying if she told the officer that no one had gotten hurt? Obviously someone had gotten hurt: Lynox. She'd done a hit-and-run on him; backed right into his heart, left a ding, a little remnant of herself, and then ran off as if there had been no damage done. There had been damage, though, to both her and Lynox.

The entire time she was in Chile being kept by Elton while he "handled things with his wife," Deborah
couldn't stop thinking about Lynox. She couldn't stop
thinking about whether she'd made a mistake by end-
ing what she'd had with him in order to start something back up with Elton. But one of the main reasons
she'd decided to leave Malvonia and board that plane
in the first place was because, with all her and Elton's
fornicating on his short trip back to the States, she'd
ended up pregnant.

She hadn't been on birth-control pills because she
had vowed to God that she would never have a need for
the Pill as long as she was a single woman. She would
never violate her temple again the way she'd done with
Elton all those years ago when she'd aborted their
growing, kicking, moving baby from inside her womb.
She vowed to never put herself in such a devastating
situation again. But those vows and promises had obviously been made in the heat of the moment: Sunday
morning down at the church altar after high praises
and a moving Word from God.

Just like with some other Christians come Sunday
morning when the spirit was high, praise and worship
were doing their thing, and the pastor was preaching
the Word of God like there was no tomorrow, Deborah
had made promises and commitments that at the time
she felt like she could keep. But come Monday through
Saturday, somehow that encounter with God had long
been forgotten. All those promises and commitments
were thrown out the window by using sayings like "God
knows my heart" to make a person feel better.

A Sunday only Christian. That's what Mother Doreen
had once told Deborah that type of behavior described.
"You know what I'm talking about, child," Mother Doreen had said. "A Sunday only Christian is that person

who is only a Christian come Sunday morning. But Monday through Saturday, they ain't thinking about living righteous and holy or living according to God's Word. It's easy to be a Christian come Sunday morning. But what say you about the other days of the week?"

Had that been what Deborah was? A Sunday only Christian?

"Excuse me, ma'am." The officer had interrupted Deborah's thoughts. "Was anyone hurt?"

"Yes, yes," Deborah said sadly.

"So was an ambulance called?"

Deborah didn't respond. She just allowed her mind to roam off into its own thoughts again.

"Ms. Lewis, was an ambulance called?"

"Ambulance?" Deborah shook her head and snapped back out of her zone.

"Yes, you said someone got hurt. Was an ambulance called?"

Deborah stared at the officer for a moment with a puzzled look on her face before everything began to register. "Oh, that kind of hurt. Oh, no, no. No one was physically hurt. No, Officer, not at all. I'm sorry, I must have misunderstood. No ambulance was called. No one was physically hurt."

The officer shot Deborah a tight, concerned eye. "Hmmm. I see." He went about erasing something then looked back up to Deborah. "Is there anything else you can think of that I might need to put in my report? Because I'm going to be honest with you, sounds like this is pretty much all your fault."

"All my fault?" *But I'm suffering some damage too here,* Deborah thought. Once again her mind had traveled back to her and Lynox's relationship versus the incident the officer was referencing. "I mean, is it really all my fault that Mr. Chase has God-awful bad timing?

That he just popped up out of nowhere and wouldn't go away? He was just there. What else was I supposed to do?" Deborah looked at the officer desperately for answers.

For the first time, the officer showed some emotion sympathetic toward Deborah. "Are you saying that Mr. Chase wasn't just making his way by, that he was basically just sitting there idle?"

"That's exactly what I'm saying," Deborah said with plenty emotion as she began pacing and using her hands to emphasize her words. "How was I supposed to know he'd just pop up and wouldn't go away?" Now she was talking about Elton. His timing, too, had been awful. He'd shown up right when God had made her over, fixed and cleaned her up, and she felt ready to present herself to a man. Not just any man, but Lynox. But like a thief in the night, Elton had sneaked in and claimed her as his—saying, doing, and promising all the right things. "What was I supposed to do? I had to go. I had to leave."

If she hadn't agreed to get on that plane with Elton she would have been left in Ohio to repeat history: pregnant by Elton while he ran off to play ball. She was not going to let that happen again. She couldn't. She didn't. "He tried to block me." Lynox had tried to block her—keep her from leaving with Elton. He'd used his own heartfelt opinion and scripture, but Deborah went anyway.

"He was blocking you?" the officer questioned, now scribbling something down very quickly. "Now that changes things, Ms. Lewis. That changes things greatly." He put the notepad away. "I'll file this report and it should be available within the next forty-eight hours," the officer had told her before thanking her for her co-operation and then leaving.

Looking upward, Deborah prayed the words to God, "Lord, if you're not done making me feel like an idiot when it comes to Lynox, please give me a sign so I can at least be prepared for some more foolishness!" And on that note, Deborah stomped off to her bedroom to lay it down for the night, having no idea that she had asked God for a sign, and now she was about to receive it.

Chapter Six

It had been two days since the police had been to Deborah's door, and over those past two days, Deborah had been simmering in heat. "I can't believe that man called the police on me after we agreed to let our insurance companies handle everything," she'd repeated more times than she could count.

The entire situation was taking over her thoughts; so much so that she was doing a crappy job on the book she was editing for a seasoned author who was paying her darn good money. In her spirit she knew she'd have to redo the last fifty pages she'd done, as it had not been her best work. Doing her best work meant being able to focus. And in all honesty, ever since picking up that flyer promoting Lynox's book signing, she hadn't been able to focus on anything but that man. But since actually seeing him in person, her loss of focus had been to the tenth power.

"What time will you be back to pick up little man?" Deborah's mother asked as she took the boy from Deborah's arms, then mumbled to the child, "Come to ya Ganny Ban Banny."

Deborah smiled as Mrs. Lewis took her son from her arms. She smiled because he was smiling. His smile was the only thing that could break up and shatter anything negative that was building itself around Deborah. Whoever knew so much strength and power could be found in a child's smile?

"Fute snack," the little boy said to his granny, knowing she kept boxes and boxes of the fruity, gummy treats at her house just for him.

"I shouldn't be too long, just an hour or so," Deborah, still smiling, said as she rubbed her son's chunky cheek.

"Just an hour?" Mrs. Lewis kissed her grandson on the forehead. "Ganny Ban Banny only gets an hour with her boy?" Mrs. Lewis made an exaggerated sad face, poking out her bottom lip. Her caramel-brown forehead wrinkled; otherwise, it was as smooth as a bowling ball. Deborah, knowing she was the spitting image of her mother, didn't mind aging one bit, knowing she'd wear age as well as her mother did.

"Mom, you keep him almost every day. You see him all the time," Deborah reminded her mother.

Even though Deborah worked from home, that was not an easy feat with a small child. Talk about not being able to focus and losing concentration; try attempting to do that with a terrible two demanding so much time and attention. So several times a week for about two or three hours, Deborah's mother would keep the boy for Deborah while she got caught up on her work from the days she'd gotten behind while the child was there.

"I know, but a grandmother can never see too much of her grandkids. And he's my only one." Deborah's mother kissed the boy again.

"Hmm, you say that now." Deborah sucked her teeth and twisted her lips. "Trust and believe, Mother, the time is coming when you'll still love him to death, be glad that he comes over and visits, but be even more elated that he gets to go home."

"Umm, umm." She rubbed her nose against her grandson's. "Never."

"Anyway . . ." Deborah dropped to the floor the bag with the baby's things in it. "I should only be an hour or so. What I have to do shouldn't take long." *Shouldn't take long at all,* Deborah thought. All she had to do was go to the library, patiently wait for Lynox to finish up his reading, and then check him up and down, from left to right. Deborah knew she might never regain her focus if she didn't confront Lynox.

She wasn't sure if Lynox still lived in his same house. Besides, she was afraid if she showed up on his doorstep, he'd call the police and have her arrested for stalking or something. She didn't put anything past the man at this point. So she visited his Web site he'd given her, and found his tour schedule. She made it a point to be at his next local event, which was at the library.

With the exception of the actual book release, most authors' tour schedules started out of town; then they worked their way back home. Lynox's three-month tour had wound down and now he was doing a lot of local signings and readings. The reading tonight was the last event listed on his calendar for now. So Deborah felt it was her last opportunity to do what she needed to do.

"Well, don't think you have to come rushing back," Mrs. Lewis told her daughter. "He can even spend the night if you want."

"We'll see, Mother," Deborah said, only to appease Mrs. Lewis.

Ever since Mr. Lewis's passing several years ago, Deborah's mother had spent time doing whatever she could to keep busy: taking craft classes at Jo-Ann Fabric, going to bingo regularly with one of her dearest and oldest friends, and volunteering in nursing homes. Once Deborah returned from Chile with her baby in her arms, Mrs. Lewis had been filling most of her time tending to him. Deborah knew this was to keep her mother from feeling lonely.

Deborah gave her son one last kiss, then gave her mother one too before she was off on her mission. By the time she arrived at the library the moderator was taking the last question directed at the bestselling author.

"Was it easy getting an agent and getting a book deal?" a gentleman in the audience had asked Lynox just as Deborah stepped in the door.

A few people turned around and looked at her, but then turned their attention back to the guest author. Lynox, on the other hand, stared at her until she was comfortable in the nearest seat. She wasn't technically comfortable—a little nervous about the pending confrontation—but no one could really detect it.

"For those of you who might not have heard," the moderator spoke, "the question to Mr. Chase was whether it was easy getting an agent and a book deal." She then turned to Lynox and smiled. "Go ahead, Mr. Chase."

"Well truthfully," Lynox started, "I always knew I had a bestseller on my hands. I felt it when the book was just an idea in my head. I felt it when I was writing it and I felt it even more so after I completed it. Some might say I'm a pretty confident man, so in all honesty, I thought there wasn't a sane agent or publishing house that would turn me down." He buried his eyes deep into Deborah's. "I was wrong. I tracked down one of the, in my opinion, best literary agents in the world. I mean, I felt as if I had the best product, so I wanted the best representation for my product."

Now it was visible Deborah wasn't all that comfortable in her seat as she began shifting around both her bottom and her eyes. She knew where the story was heading, but was unsure as to exactly where it would end up.

"Like I said, I was as wrong as Kanye West was for interrupting that Taylor Swift girl's acceptance speech," Lynox continued, receiving a chuckle from the attendees. "She rejected me flat out." With his eyes still pinned on Deborah he said, "I thought I had her there for a minute; thought I had convinced her that she'd never find anyone else out there like me. She entertained me for a while but then, like I said, she just flat-out rejected me. Guess something better came along she felt she needed to direct her attention to. Couldn't give me the attention that would be required in order for this thing to work—to be as successful as it could be. As it is now." Lynox took a deep breath. "But I eventually found an agent willing to work with me. And as they say"—he picked up a copy of his book—"the rest is history."

There was a thunderous applause as Lynox wrapped up.

"I bet that agent who rejected you is kicking herself right about now," an audience member shot out.

"Hmmm," Lynox said. "I'm not sure. But you can ask her if you'd like."

Once again, his eyes focused on Deborah and she wanted to die. This man was not about to do what she thought he was about to do.

"She's right there." Lynox pointed to Deborah and every eye in the room followed to where he was pointing.

He did it! He actually did it, Deborah thought.

Once again, Deborah felt embarrassed and humiliated. *God is not my friend!*

Chapter Seven

Was it possible that like a true earthly parent, there were times when God had to be Daddy and not friend? For Deborah, was that time now? A friend would have warned her and told her, "Girl, don't you go to that library and try to check that man. You better let God handle it." Or in this case, if it was God speaking He would have said, "You better let me handle it, vengeance is mine"—something.

But that hadn't happened. God had not stopped her, on either occasion, from getting in her car and going to see Lynox. He had not stopped her when she'd gone to the bookstore and He had not stopped her now. And now here she sat, mortified, with accusing eyeballs stinging her very being.

"A he, he, he, he, he." Deborah tried to play it off with a fake laugh. "Isn't Mr. Chase just the comedian?" She glared at Lynox, her eyes forcing him to play along—to take back his comment—or else.

"I've been told I have quite the sense of humor," Lynox commented. "But there was nothing funny about the way you crushed me when you rejected me."

Here we go again, Deborah thought as she realized that once again Lynox was probably alluding to their relationship versus his manuscript submission. Well Deborah was tired of it; sick and tired of it. If this joker had something to say . . . if he was holding some vendetta against her, then he needed to just spit it out. He needed to stop hiding behind an illusion of words and just say what was on his mind. And what better time than now? Heck, he'd already put her on Front Street. She might as well take them to their final destination; then she could sever any dealings with this man once and for all. And just to think, this all started when she initially wanted to perhaps get back into his good graces. Now she couldn't get far enough away from him.

"Rejection? So you're not too good with rejection, Mr. Chase. Is that it?" Deborah stood, taking control of the room. "So what hurt the worst? When I rejected your manuscript, or when I rejected you?"

There was an echo of gasps throughout the room. There were some heads turning, eyes bucking in surprise, and some whispering once everyone realized that what was going down was far from fiction. It was a real, live lover's quarrel going down right before their very eyes. And it was a fact that reality television was a growing addiction, so this kind of thing was right up some of these folks' alley.

"Is that why you called the police on me and had them showing up at my door like I'm some common criminal?" Deborah spat.

Lynox said nothing. He'd learned a long time ago that if he allowed a person to do all the talking, there was a chance that they'd end up making his case for him.

Deborah, falling right into his trap, continued. "You're mad, angry, jealous, and bent out of shape because you chased after me for so long, and then just when you thought you'd caught me, you had a blow to that big ego of yours when I sought interest in someone else. Oh that probably just ate you up inside, didn't it? Mr. Lynox Chase, not getting what he wants. Mr. Lynox Chase having to walk away with the 'L.'"

Lynox still said nothing. This just fueled Deborah on even more. She had the complete stage. It was like Deborah was a third-grade bully who was actually the size of a sixth grader. And there stood some defenseless classmate who was actually the size of a first grader. And all the other kids were gathered around to witness the pooch go up against the pit bull. Deborah was eating it up as if she wasn't the child of God she was supposed to be. She was eating it up like Satan in all his beautiful glory before he got kicked out of heaven.

"Running into me again outside of that bookstore just brought it all back up again, didn't it?" Deborah said boastfully. "And then over at the urgent care. You weren't trying to return my shoes. You were just upset that I hadn't tried to come crawling back to you, begging to give you and me—us—one more chance. You were just using the shoes as an excuse to talk to me again. Then you tried to make everything seem like it was all good after that little fender bender. But once you got home, your blood got to boiling all over again. It was payback time in your mind. So you sicced the cops on me just so we'd have to deal with each other again." Deborah laughed snidely as she now stood face to face with Lynox. She crossed her arms, a sign that she was done, that the floor was all his for his comeback.

Yet and still, Lynox said nothing.

Deborah felt like she had the "W"—the good old-fashioned win. "Got nothing to say for yourself, huh, Mr. Chase?" She sucked her teeth. "Figured as much." Deborah let out a harrumph, rolled her eyes, and felt like she'd gotten the weight of the world off her chest.

"Are you finished?" Finally Lynox spoke.

Deborah was stunned to hear his voice. She'd been used to just hearing her own for the last five minutes. "Huh? What?"

"I wanted to know if you were finished talking so that I could now speak. Ladies first, and I didn't want to interrupt."

Deborah swallowed hard. Her stomach began to rumble with nervousness. What could he possibly have to say? Nothing was what Deborah had hoped. The plan was that she'd come there and say everything she had to say and walk away feeling some sense of closure. But for some reason, she felt as though she'd just opened a whole new mess of things. "Uh, yes, I am, uh, finished." She tried to muster up a look of confidence, but it wasn't looking so good. "The floor is all yours." With a wave of her hand, she presented the floor to Lynox.

"Well, if you really want to know the truth, I have no vendetta against you. Vengeance is mine thus sayeth the Lord." Lynox looked up and then looked down again at Deborah. "And I think He's doing a pretty good job at it if I do say so myself." He chuckled, which made Deborah feel a couple inches shorter. He then continued. "I wanted to give you your shoes because I had a date later that evening and didn't want to have to explain why I had a pair of four-inch stilettos in my car." He raised an eyebrow and a few members of the audience laughed. "And I called the police because when I tried to file a claim with my insurance company, the first thing they said was that a police report needed to be filed. It was done out of protocol, not because I'm going to claim I have whiplash and try to sue you for injuries. So see, Ms. Lewis, you were all wrong about the situation. But if you don't mind, with your permission I'd love to use your theory in my next book." Again, members of the audience laughed.

Deborah was losing count of how many times she'd felt like a fool when it came to Lynox. It was clear now;

she'd made a mistake. She'd left Lynox for Elton and there would be no second chances when it came to picking up where they'd left off. So now all there was left to do was pick up her face and take off.

"I hate to put an end to this little dramatization," the moderator said, "that I honestly don't think was planned, but who doesn't love a great improv?" She chuckled and so did some others. "But we're already over time. We've got to give this meeting room up. So if there's nothing else . . ." She looked from Deborah to Lynox and waited for some type of response.

"No, there'll be nothing else," Deborah said. "It's over." She looked into Lynox's eyes. "It's over." This time who was alluding to something else? Deborah slowly began to walk away as folks began to gather their things. The walk to the door was long and painful. The closer Deborah got to the door, the farther away it seemed. She couldn't get out of that room fast enough.

"Actually, there is one more thing," Deborah heard Lynox say just as she made it to the door. His voice seemed to be right up on her now, as if it was haunting her.

"Oh, God, now what?" she looked up to the heavens and mumbled, debating whether to stop. Hadn't she had enough? She didn't know what else God had in store for her, but figured she'd take her punishment now, so she turned in order to see the final blow coming. "What, Lynox? What is it? Let's just get it over with so that we never have to see each other—"

Lynox cut Deborah off—with his tongue. Not with words falling from his tongue, but literally with his tongue as he planted the most passionate kiss on her she could ever remember receiving. The kiss seemed to go on forever as the room froze.

When Lynox finally removed his mouth from Deborah's he asked her, "What is that you were saying?"

Deborah, all starry eyes, finished her sentence. "Again."

"So we never have to see each other again?" Lynox questioned.

"No. Again. Kiss me . . . again."

And that's exactly what Lynox did. He took Deborah into his arms and gave her the kiss she'd read about in fairytales—that she'd seen in the most romantic movies ever. But could this all be real? Could Lynox be her true knight in shining armor, riding into her life on a white stallion to rescue her from single, saved, sexless sistahood? She didn't know, but what she did know was that she wanted the kiss to last forever. Not even the thunderous handclaps roaring throughout the room could interrupt the tender kiss.

As the participants moved out of the room, Deborah and Lynox remained lip locked as they heard someone say, "Now that's what I call a book signing."

Chapter Eight

"Thanks for agreeing to come have coffee with me," Lynox said to Deborah, who sat across from him at the coffee shop they'd gone to immediately after leaving the library.

Deborah smiled. "No problem." And it was no problem indeed. Heck, little did Lynox know, she would have gone to the moon with him if he'd invited her.

"I just felt we really needed to talk and explain some things without an audience."

Deborah chuckled. "I agree." She took a sip of her coffee. "And about that; I really am sorry for the way I just showed up at your book signing with my ammunition on my back like that. It's just that the more I thought about the police showing up at my door, the angrier I got." She thought for a minute. "Then again, I'm not sure if it was just anger, or a little mixture of disappointment. I mean, you'd agreed that we wouldn't call the police, and take care of it ourselves through our insurance company. So I guess I kind of felt like you lied to me; led me on to believe we were going to do one thing, then changed your mind and did something else."

Lynox sat there nodding, taking in Deborah's every word. "Umm, hmmm. I could see how that could disappoint you—even hurt you." He exhaled. "I know what it's like to feel like you are being led in one direction and then swoosh . . ." Lynox used his hand to drive a straight path toward Deborah, but then when his hand got close to her, he turned it quickly as if making it do a U-turn.

Deborah was about to take a sip of her coffee but then she paused. "Wait a minute, are we talking about something else here?"

Taking a sip of his own coffee and looking at Deborah over the rim of his cup, Lynox shrugged his shoulders.

Without ever taking that sip of her coffee, Deborah placed the cup back down on the table. "Okay, look, if we're going to do this—really move beyond the past— we're going to have to talk about it."

"I agree," Lynox said. "So talk." He spread his hands as if giving her the floor to speak.

Deborah decided that she wanted to hear what Lynox had to say and then base what she needed to say as a response to him. "Me? Why can't you go first? I went first at the library." They both thought about her comment and then laughed.

"I guess you're right. I'll go first."

"No, no, no." Deborah rested her hand on Lynox's. "Let me, because this is long overdue." In that instant, she wanted to say what needed to be said to him a long time ago; what she would have said to him that day at the bookstore if everything had turned out all right. She didn't want to wait and end up being a coward and backing out. "I'm sorry. I'm sorry the way I ended things with us when I ran off to Chile. I made a mistake. It was a huge mistake." Deborah figured right here she'd allow Lynox to get a word in edgewise if he wanted.

He cleared his throat, then decided to take Deborah up on her unspoken offer. "And at what point did you realize you'd made a mistake?"

"From the moment that plane took off," she said without hesitation. "But it was too late. I felt like I was at the point of no return. I couldn't turn back and listen to all the 'I told you so's.'"

"Now that really hurts." Lynox looked down and kind of slumped in his seat.

"What?"

"The fact that you felt you couldn't come back to me, and if you did, I was gonna hit you with an 'I told you so.'" He shook his head. "I just thought we were better than that. I thought I'd made it clear how much I wanted you in my life, no matter what."

"And you did, Lynox. Really you did. I felt it. When it came to you, once I just let everything go and let you in, for the first time since I could remember both my head and my heart had agreed on something. That something was that you were a great man."

Lynox sat upright again. "Well, I guess LeBron was just greater." He pretended to be swooshing a basketball.

"Stop it now, Lynox." Deborah raised an eyebrow at his jealous schoolboy antics.

He put his hands up in defeat. "Okay, I'm sorry. My bad. I know your boy is probably over in Chile winning up all types of championship rings with his skills. So consider my calling him LeBron as a compliment."

From the first moment Lynox had laid eyes on Elton, which was when he'd interrupted Lynox and Deborah's date at a restaurant, Lynox had always thought the cat was too flashy for his own good. The expensive clothes, the jewelry, just seemed a bit much for Lynox's taste, and he thought Deborah would have had better taste as well. But she seemed to be drawn to that life. He couldn't imagine what in the world would have made her leave all that behind. But he was about to find out.

"Actually, Elton is not over in Chile winning all kinds of championship rings." Deborah's tone became somber. "He's dead."

Lynox's eyes grew as large as the saucers he and Deborah's coffee cups sat on. "Oh, no. Are you for real?"

Deborah nodded. "Yes. Remember that big earthquake they had over in Chile a couple of years ago? Well, unfortunately, Elton was one of its casualties."

"Awww man." Lynox washed his hands down his face, feeling bad that he'd just spoken ill of the dead. "I . . . I . . . I didn't know. You must have been devastated—left over there in a foreign country all alone."

Deborah twisted her lips and almost angrily said, "Harrumph, I was alone from the moment we got there. I hate to say it, but it made no difference with Elton dead or alive—I was alone."

"But you knew going into that, that the life of a ball player is crazy busy."

"Yes, I knew that, and I didn't mind that the majority of his time was dedicated to the game. What I did mind was the minority that was leftover still wasn't dedicated to me." Deborah took a sip of her coffee but not before quickly slipping in the words, "But that was dedicated to his wife instead."

Lynox nearly spit out his last sip of coffee when he heard Deborah's last words. "Did you say . . . did you say 'wife'? Elton had a wife over in Chile." Lynox tried to hide his smile, but a small portion crept out. "That dude was more than just a ball player; he was a player to the highest. Dang, I take back all the bad stuff I said about that dude. He had skills. I mean, you have to in order to be able to come back to the States, steal the woman I love from right up under me, convince her to pick up and move to another country, while you have a wife over there making you *pastel de choclo*." Lynox began laughing.

As Lynox laughed, Deborah's eyes began to fill with tears, but Lynox hadn't noticed until her first tear actually dropped.

"Oh, Deborah, sweetheart, I'm so sorry." Lynox got up from his side of the table and went and scooted in next to Deborah in their booth. "I didn't mean to make you sad. I was just joking around. I know—I know. It was in poor taste." Lynox picked up a napkin and began dabbing Deborah's tears away. "I'm sorry."

Deborah turned and looked at Lynox. "Please don't apologize. No man has ever said something that sincere and genuine to me and meant it."

Now Lynox was confused and it showed on his face.

Deborah could see the puzzled expression on his face, so she clarified things for him. "You said 'the woman I love.'"

Still, Lynox had a look of confusion on his face.

"You said that Elton came and stole the woman you love," she said, still looking deep into Lynox's hypnotizing eyes, and placing her lips so close to his that when she spoke he could feel her breath on his own lips. "Lynox, do you still love me?"

Chapter Nine

Pulling into the garage after spending two hours talking to Lynox at the coffee shop, Deborah felt that not even all the coffee in the world could give her back her energy. Nothing could provide the boost she'd need to pick her up out of the dragging funk she now found herself in. Her body felt lifeless and her mind drained. She didn't even know how she'd managed to get home without having to pull over to the side of the road and just sit there and let her body figure out what it was going to do with itself.

Her body hadn't been tired or feeling worn out. She'd been getting plenty of rest, but all it had taken was just a few words out of Lynox's mouth to zap every last ounce of energy from within her.

She'd asked him if he still loved her. Why did she have to go and do that? Why did she have to go and try to move things along so fast? Why couldn't she have just let nature take its course and then one day, out of nowhere, Lynox could have told her how much he loved her . . . or "liked her a lot"? But no, Deborah had to, like she'd been doing up to this point, take things into her own hands. It would have been too much like right for her to sit back, wait, and let God do His thing.

Deborah never was good at waiting. The patience of Job she did not possess. She could wait for some things. Like in church on Sunday morning; she could wait for Deacon Lowe, whenever he was called on to

lead the body of Christ in prayer, to finish up his twen-
ty-minute prayer. He'd pray the same stuff over and
over, and then go off on a tangent somewhere and pray
for his cousin in Tucson who just found out that her
old college friend had a child with a best friend whose
mother had a bad case of eczema that had her scratching her arms all day. She had no problem on Sunday
morning at church waiting for the same twenty people
who came down to the altar every single Sunday to get
prayed for and to touch and agree with the pastor, min-
isters, or elders. On Sunday she didn't seem to have a
problem waiting at all. It was those other days of the
week she had an issue with.

Today, a Thursday, had been no different. Deborah
just couldn't wait to find out if all this time Lynox had
been thinking about her, feeling the same way about
her as she him. So she just came right out and asked.
Maybe she wouldn't be feeling as bad as she felt now if
his reply had been something other than what it was.

His reply had sent a surge of power through her body
like never before.

"Deborah Lewis, I never stopped loving you," had
been the words Lynox replied.

Just to hear him say that, Deborah would have
practically broken her ankle, got her big toe crushed,
slammed into Lynox's truck, had the police show up
at her door, and made a complete idiot of herself in a
room full of strangers all over again. All the drama she
had been through all week in the name of Lynox had
not all been in vain. God was her friend. In the end,
He'd seen to it that Deborah had gotten exactly what
she wanted; with several obstacles and tests to pass,
that is. But she had gotten her guy.

Oh, but did God have jokes, Deborah surmised by
the end of the evening. Because it was the end of the

evening when everything changed. It was toward the end of two hours of talking when Deborah realized in all her talking she'd forgotten to mention to Lynox one very important factor in her life. And she probably never would have even thought about it had Lynox not brought the subject matter up.

"And just so you know . . . because I know eventually you are going to ask," Lynox said to Deborah. "That's just how women are," he said with a knowing look on his face. "The date I had the other night, the night you hit my car—the date I mentioned back at the library who I didn't want to find your shoes in my car . . ."

"What date?" Deborah feigned dumb; all the while she really had been waiting for the opportunity to ask Lynox about that date, if things were serious between him and the woman.

"Oh, please. Don't play with me." Lynox laughed. "You know you couldn't wait to ask me about that. But I'll save you the trouble. It was nothing. It was our first date and it was our last."

"Oh, couldn't concentrate on the date thinking about me, huh?" Deborah joked.

"Modest aren't we?" Lynox played along but then continued. "Actually she was a really nice lady. Had her own house, car, career, two degrees in finance, a nice savings, and good credit. You know—qualities most men would love for one woman to have. But there was something she didn't have . . ."

"Looks?" Deborah began to pat her hair as if complimenting her own.

"Why, Ms. Lewis, I never knew conceit was one of your characteristics."

"Oh, now you know I'm just messing around with you. I know I'm not all that." Deborah dropped her hand. Lynox caught it.

"Oh, but you are all that—and then some." And Lynox meant every word of it when he said it. Deborah could feel it. "Anyway"—he pulled his hand away—"she looked aiiiiiggghhht," he exaggerated the word. "Not that she could hold a candle to your beauty." Lynox smiled. "But that wasn't it. As a matter of fact, it wasn't what she didn't have. It was what she did have." Lynox stared off.

"And what was that?" Deborah asked and then took a bite of her slice of cheesecake she'd ordered.

"A kid. She had a kid."

Deborah's eyes bucked and she began choking on her food.

"Are you okay?" Lynox asked. "Here—drink some water." He reached for Deborah's glass of water, which had remained untouched until now. He handed it to Deborah, who then gulped half the glass down in just a couple of swallows.

Coughing, Deborah was beating her hand on her chest, as if she could knock the cheesecake that was stuck in her throat down her pipes. Between the beating and the water, it finally made its way down.

"You all right?" Lynox asked with uncertainty.

"Yeah, I'm good." Deborah took another sip of water. "Just went down the wrong pipe is all."

"Oh, good. You scared me there for a minute." Now Lynox sounded relieved. But with all the drama, he'd forgotten he'd been in the middle of telling her why he broke it off with his date. But Deborah hadn't forgotten.

"So you were saying about the date . . ." Deborah pressed.

"Oh, yeah, that. Well, like I said, she had wonderful qualities, but she had a kid. I'm not and never have been the kind of guy who wants a readymade family.

I've always had the dream of the white house, picket fence, dog, cat, lovely wife, and kids . . . of my own. Not my kids and his kids; 'him' being the man she was with before she was with me. I mean, come on, any man who is honest with himself will admit that there is just something about a little reminder, walking around the house, of the person who had his woman before he got to her. As shallow as it sounds, for me, that's the deal breaker—a woman with kids from another relationship. I can't do it. I won't do it. Not to mention the baby daddy drama that could possibly come along with the relationship. I mean, men aren't nearly as catty and petty as women . . ." He looked to Deborah and put his hands up. "No offense, but you know there is far more baby momma drama between women than there is baby daddy drama between men. But whatever the case, it's not my cup of tea." He lifted his cup. "Or my cup of coffee." He winked at Deborah then took a sip.

That's when all the life in Deborah's body made a quick exit. How had she talked to this man for two hours and never mentioned the fact that she had a child? Her little man, besides God, was the most important part of her life. That should have been one of the first things she had delighted in telling Lynox, but she hadn't, and after hearing him be so adamant about never dealing with a readymade family, how in the world could she possibly tell him now? She couldn't . . . and so she didn't.

Yes, her son was the most important person in her life, but even before him, Lynox had captured a piece of her heart. That piece of her heart along with the rest of it wanted Lynox—even after his comment about not wanting a woman with kids.

"But I'm different," Deborah had said to herself out loud on her drive home. She and Lynox had history.

Surely he could make an exception for her. She knew that if the tables were turned, she would for him. And if she was reading into things correctly, he felt the same strong connection with her that she felt with him. "For God's sake the man said he loves me." Well, how Deborah saw it, if he loved her, he'd love her son, who was just a mini extension of her. So even though she couldn't and didn't bring herself to mention at the coffee shop the fact that she had a child, she knew eventually she would have to. When? Now that was a whole other dilemma.

Deborah's cell phone vibrated. She had turned the ringer off at the coffee shop to avoid any loud interruptions. She picked up her phone and looked at the caller ID. She tapped herself upside the head to punish herself for forgetting to do something. "Hi, Mom," she answered the phone. She'd forgotten to call and check in with her mother, and that was after telling her she'd only be gone about an hour.

"I guess you decided to let my baby stay the night with his Ganny Ban Banny after all, huh?"

That wasn't a conscious decision Deborah had made. She'd simply forgotten to go pick him up after her evening with Lynox. But there was no way she was going to tell her mother that. "Uh, yeah, Mom. I figured I'd just let him stay. Sorry I didn't call."

"It's okay. No worries. And don't rush to come get him in the morning. Get as much work done as you need to. See you tomorrow, honey. Good night." And her mother was off the phone just that quick; and the way things looked now, her and Lynox's relationship had been over even quicker.

Deborah threw herself back on the bed and exhaled deeply. She then looked over at the picture on her nightstand of her holding her son on his first birthday.

Tears began to pour out of her eyes as she thought about how she'd forgotten all about her son twice in one evening. *What kind of horrible mother am I?*

She turned and buried her face in her pillow, using the fluffy object as a silencer for her crying.

"Oh, God! What am I going to do?" she cried into the pillow. She never thought in a million years she'd be torn over an issue between her son and a suitor. She'd just wanted to reconnect with Lynox so badly that she never even thought about how he'd feel about her having a child. That was obvious, considering she didn't even think about telling him about her son. Her only focus had been getting her guy. Well, she had gotten her guy all right. But now, would she be able to keep him?

Chapter Ten

"Lynox. Hi. How are you?" Deborah answered the phone. She'd been in the middle of editing a manuscript.

"I am more wonderful than I have been in about . . . hmmm . . . two years," he said through the phone receiver.

"Is that so?"

"My dear, that is very much so."

Deborah could hear a smile in his voice. It was contagious. So much so that it not only put a smile in her tone, but one on her face as well. "Thank you for taking time out of your schedule to sit and talk with me yesterday. I really needed to hear a lot of the things you said. And more importantly, there were a lot of things that I needed to say."

"Well, I hope you were able to say them all, because from this day forward, I want to forget all about anything in the past. From this point on, I don't want to talk about anything or anyone from the past; or anything or anyone that will even slightly remind us of the past. That includes both Helen and Elton. I don't want even a remnant of those two in our future. Agreed?" Lynox paused for a response from Deborah.

This conversation was not going as she had planned. Maybe that's because Deborah's intention was to call Lynox instead of him calling her. When she called him, she would have been ready to tell him that she had a child and that if that was the deal breaker for him, then there wasn't even a need for them to move forward. They could both walk away now before things went any further than coffee and a kiss. But that's not what had happened. Lynox had called her first and took lead of the conversation. Now Deborah felt all she could do was follow.

"Agreed. But there is—" Deborah started before Lynox cut her off.

"No buts. When you add the word 'but,' it crosses out something or everything that you've just said. I don't want anything crossed out. I mean it. Fresh soil this time. Nothing or no one is just going to walk into our lives and try to throw a monkey wrench into our relationship. Sooooo, with that being said, what are you doing for dinner tomorrow night?"

Deborah knew this was the moment. This was the moment when, in spite of Lynox being in the lead of the conversation and in spite of the direction in which it was going, she should have spoken up. She should have used her God-given authority and taken control of the conversation. She should have boldly told him, "Yeah, I have a son, so what? He's a part of me. So if you want me, then you have to want him too. We're a package deal, baby. Take us both or leave us both." But instead what Deborah said was, "What time are you picking me up for dinner tomorrow night?"

"So now that we've covered all of the old business on the agenda," Deborah said as she stood behind the podium conducting the New Day Temple of Faith singles ministry meeting, "is there any new business anyone would like to discuss?"

The twenty-seven female members and eight male members looked to each other, mumbled in the negative, and shook their heads.

"Okay, very well then," Deborah said as she closed her notebook, preparing to close out the meeting in prayer. She looked out among the members who began putting their things away in preparation to leave. She felt proud that the ministry had grown so and that she had been able to maintain a steady membership since returning from Chile and taking back over as leader.

What Deborah was even more proud of was that the ministry had consistently had between eight and ten male members. From the inception of the ministry, it had been difficult to get men to join. They had assumed that a singles ministry wasn't anything but a bunch of women who sat around bad-mouthing all the men of their past while trying to figure out how to get one in their future. Ironically, that wasn't too far from the truth. But things had changed drastically since the ministry's earlier days. Maybe that's because God had done some drastic things in some of the women's lives. Whatever the case, God had now blessed the ministry with men. And the men seemed to be just what the doctor ordered so that the ministry could function decently and in order.

With the male of the species now among them, the women thought twice before going on a man-bashing tangent. They were also more mindful of the way they discussed past relationships. It was one thing to put their business out there in a room full of women, but having men around seasoned the women's tongues a little bit more.

The men were also able to provide some valuable input. They were able to allow the women to see how they sometimes saw things. Having the male perspective enabled the women to see a lot of things differently. It often allowed them to see themselves for who they really were, prompting them to begin to make some serious changes in their lives.

Just the thought of the men and all the past valu-able information they'd provided to the ministry made a light go off in Deborah's head. "Uh, excuse me." Deborah cleared her throat. "Before we go, I'd like to throw something out there for both the single men and women out there who have children." She thought for a minute. "I guess this could go for the single men and women out there who don't have kids as well."

Deborah now had everyone's attention again, so she continued. "For those with kids, have you ever met someone who was really into you but not that into your kids?" Right off the bat Deborah heard some groans and murmuring. But she continued with the second part of her questions. "And for those of you without children, have you ever met someone who seemed to have all the qualities you were seeking but had something you weren't—a kid?" There were more groans, murmuring, and now a few sour faces.

"I thought I had met the perfect man," a sister in the ministry called out. "He had all the right stuff." She then poked her lips out and rolled her eyes. "But then I found out that he had the wrong stuff, which was two kids." She held up two fingers and once again rolled her eyes with disgust. "Not just two kids, but two baby mommas to go along with them."

"But wait a minute, don't you have three kids?" Deborah asked her.

"Yes, but I still have the right not to date someone else with kids," she replied.

This time a brother spoke up. "Now that doesn't seem fair. Why should he have to deal with you and your three kids and you not deal with him and his two?"

"He doesn't have to," the woman replied. "That's the thing. We all have a choice. Now if he chooses to date a woman with kids, it's his right to do that or not to do that. Why shouldn't I have that same right? Are you trying to say that if a person has kids, by default they have to be okay with getting involved with a person who has kids? That's crazy," she declared. "I know me. I know that I'm not the baby-momma-dealing kind of chick. I don't do babies' mommas. I don't do raising someone else's kids. If I know these things about me, then why should I subject him and his children to it? I think by me being truthful with myself and knowing I'm not built for that type of relationship, I'm being more fair to him and his children than I possibly could be."

"Preach, sister," another female said with a triple snap of her fingers.

The brother bowed out gracefully with, "I never looked at it that way, sister. You have a very valid point. Kudos to you for knowing your limits and sticking with them."

"Amen," the woman said. "Because you don't want to go forcing someone to have to deal with your kids if they've already made it clear that they ain't cut out for that type of party. Because at the end of the day, you'll know in your heart that you are with someone who, deep down inside, really ain't feeling your kids. And for all you know they could snap off on 'em. That could turn out to be ugly for everybody. So not that I'd ever snap off on somebody's kids or a baby's momma, but why even put myself in that situation to be tried?"

"I feel you, sister," another man spoke up. "But . . ."

By now, Deborah was still taking in all that the woman who'd just spoken had to say. She'd made so many valid points; points that only made it clear to Deborah what she had to do. She had to break things off with Lynox.

Chapter Eleven

Deborah stood and looked at herself in the mirror. She took a moment to thank God for her clear, smooth skin. She'd seen so many commercials for various acne products, she could only imagine how many people were out there struggling with the insecurities of being acne prone. It didn't seem like much to be thankful for, but in Deborah's eyes, it was.

She fingered the silk handmade blouse she'd gotten from Chile. Elton had paid almost $500 for it. That's what he did whenever he felt bad for not being able to see or talk to her for several days—sometimes weeks. When he finally did come around, he was bearing gifts. The thing was, he always expected some type of intimacy in return. Deborah went from feeling like the trifling mistress, to the kept woman, to the high-priced whore.

Deborah molested the soft material, which was designed with bright-colored shapes of different sizes. "Harrumph," she said out loud. "All he put me through; I was worth it." And that comment had shut her conscience up before it could tell her that she needed to take that shirt off and put on something that didn't remind her of her sins. But the blouse was just too cute for all that. Maybe how she'd come about the shirt had been a sin, but wearing it certainly wasn't one. In Deborah's opinion, it would have been a sin not to wear it.

"I gotta go potty."

Deborah turned and looked to see her little guy standing in the doorway. He had been quietly in his room playing with his toys while Deborah got ready.

"Mommy's big boy has to go potty?" she asked.

"Umm hmmm." He nodded.

Deborah walked over to her son and scooped him up in her arms. She placed him on her hip while she cupped her arm around his bottom to keep him in place. That's when she realized he'd already gone potty—in his underwear. "Oh, no!" Deborah shouted once she felt the moisture soaking through the sleeve of her blouse. Following that was the big "D" word with the word "it" after it. Deborah's angry outburst startled her son and he began to cry. "Oh, Mommy is sorry. I didn't mean to scare you." She sat him back down. "Mommy didn't mean to yell." As she began to remove her son's clothing she whispered, "God forgive me for cursing at my baby."

Once Deborah got her son's clothing off of him, she scooped him back up. He was still crying and sniffling. "Mommy's sorry, baby boy." Deborah's phone rang, so holding her child in one arm, she swooped the phone up with the other. She knew it was her mother telling her she was coming around the corner and to have her grandson ready.

"Yes, Mother," Deborah answered the phone without even looking at the caller ID.

"I think I prefer to be called daddy," Lynox joked with a deep voice.

"Oh, Lynox?" Deborah was completely caught off guard as she balanced her twitching and whining son in one hand while trying to keep the phone to her ear with the other.

Noticing the flustered tone of Deborah's voice, Lynox asked, "Did I catch you at a bad time? You sound a little antsy."

"Oh, no, I'm just—" Deborah was cut off by the wail her son released.

"Is that a kid?" Lynox asked, his tone laced with curiosity.

Deborah looked at her son, closed her eyes, and bit her lip. She had to think fast. Once again, this was not how things were supposed to go down. Yes, she was going to tell Lynox about her son and then break things off with him, but she was going to do it face to face during dinner. But once again, Lynox had taken the lead and just messed up everything.

"It's a kid . . . on TV," Deborah partially lied. She looked at her son and put her index finger over her mouth while her eyes pleaded with him to stop crying. Lucky for Deborah it worked.

"Oh, well, I guess the televisions these day do more than just look like real life; they have a heck of a sound system, too. Anyway, I was just calling to tell you that I left my house a little early because I thought there might be traffic. But wouldn't you know I'm making great time. So I just wanted to let you know that I might show up a little early, if that's okay?"

Deborah looked over at her clock. She then looked down at her son and repositioned him over her shoulder. "Uh, well, uh . . ." *Think. Think. Think.* Her mother was due to arrive to pick her son up, but what if Lynox got there before her? *I knew I should have just dropped him off over at my mom's and met Lynox out,* Deborah scolded herself. She knew better than to have a man come pick her up at her house anyway. That was one of the first things she'd been taught in the singles ministry. It sounded good in the church classroom when she was hearing it. Now that she was at home out in the world, like she often found herself doing, she was playing by her own rules.

"Umm, well uh . . ." Why did those seem to be the only words of choice Deborah could manage to come up with? "I guess it would . . ." Her words trailed off as she placed her son at her feet. She was going to tell him that she guessed it would be all right, but it wouldn't have been.

"Ohhhh, I get it, still getting beautiful for me, huh? Although I don't think it is possible for you to get any more beautiful than you already are," he complimented her. "So, I'll just kill some time stopping off at a bookstore or something. You know—do an author drive-by, go see how many of my books are on the shelf—blah, blah, blah."

Deborah exhaled a deep sigh of relief and said, with nervous laughter, "Yes, I know how it is. Plus, I do wanna look my best."

"No problem. I'll see you at our scheduled time. And you better be lookin' good."

"I will. I will," Deborah replied and then ended the call. She wanted to pass out on the bed, but she couldn't. She didn't have time. She had to finish changing her son's clothes, and unless she wanted to smell like "tinkle," she had to change her clothes too. "Okay, fella, let's go get you together," she said to her son.

Deborah took a step and then paused. She looked down at her $1,000 pair of shoes. Another "I'm sorry" gift, compliments of Elton. She was disgusted. She wasn't disgusted at the shoes or the sexual act she performed with Elton after he had given her the shoes. At this moment, she was disgusted with what was under the shoes. "Please tell me you didn't," she said to her son, who offered her an "I'm sorry" smile. *Like father like son.*

But her child didn't have to say anything. When Deborah lifted her shoe, beneath it was a pile of brown, stinky, mushy stuff.

"The baby boo-boo," her son said in the third person.

Before Deborah could even catch herself, the big "S" word shot from her mouth, causing her son to break out in tears again.

Unbeknownst to Deborah, the "S" word was a perfect analogy of what she was about to find herself in . . . or already had found herself in—literally.

Chapter Twelve

"How's your steak?" Lynox asked Deborah.

Deborah was too busy off in la-la land. She had been operating under a spirit of rush for the last hour and just couldn't manage to reel herself back in, calm down, relax, and get it together. She had rushed to get her son cleaned up and changed. She had rushed to get herself cleaned up and changed. She'd rushed to clean up the mess off the floor. Rushing was bad enough alone, her heart rate increasing the faster she tried to go. But add panic on top of that, and it's a high blood pressure moment waiting to happen.

As the clock had ticked and Deborah continued to rush, she realized her mother hadn't arrived yet. She was obviously running a few minutes behind. That wouldn't have been so bad if Lynox hadn't been due to arrive in just a few minutes.

Initially Deborah had felt safe in only allowing a half-hour window in between the time she'd asked her mother to pick up her son and the time she'd told Lynox to pick her up for dinner. Thirty minutes was plenty of time for her mother to pack up her son and be long gone before Lynox ever even pulled up. But she never banked in a million years on her mother, who was always prompt, being late.

"Ma? Where are you?" Deborah had called and asked in a panic once she realized Lynox—who she learned not only liked to be on time, but early—was due to arrive at her house in ten minutes.

"I'm sorry. I'm running a little late," her mother apologized through the phone receiver. "Your Aunt Magnolia called me talking about nothing. But you know how hard it is to get that woman off the phone." She laughed. Deborah didn't. She just sat there looking stoic, tapping a nervous foot.

"So are you en route?" Deborah asked, looking down at her watch.

"Oh, yes. I'm just around the corner. I was about to call you as a matter of fact."

"Good!" Deborah exclaimed. Realizing she might have sounded overexcited to be getting rid of her son for the night, Deborah said more nonchalantly, "Because I know how you are about spending time with your grandson, so I don't want you to miss a minute."

"Oh, don't worry. You let my baby know that Ganny Ban Banny will be there in a minute."

"All right. Thanks, Mom." Deborah exhaled. "Thank you so much."

"Now you know you don't have to thank me. What kind of grandmother doesn't love spending time with her grandkids?"

"I don't know, Ma, but she's certainly not you. See you in a minute." Deborah ended the call and smiled, feeling all warm inside for the love her mother had for her son. It was surprising to Deborah how good of a grandmother her mother was to her son. In Deborah's opinion, her mother couldn't have even been nominated for Mother of the Year, let alone hold the title.

Deborah couldn't remember, for the life of her, her mother ever being that excited to spend time with her when she was a little girl. Deborah had been on the high school drill team and not once had her mother ever even come out to a game to see her perform. She never sat down with her and did homework with her—even ask her if she had homework. And not once did Deborah ever recall her mother attending parent/ teacher conferences. What Deborah did remember, though, was her mother fussing, cussing, screaming, and hollering all the time.

"Oh, that's just how black folks raise they kids," Deborah's Aunt Magnolia used to tell her whenever Deborah was upset and would talk to her about it. "That's how your grandmother raised us. Black people handle they kids; yell, whippings, whatever it takes. It's them white folks that do all that time-out stuff. Yo' momma's mouth might get on your nerves now, but once you all grown up, you'll understand why she had to raise you the way she did. It'll make you strong. Can't make it in this world being all soft."

No matter what explanation Aunt Magnolia told her niece, Deborah still hated living on pins and needles not knowing when her mother was going to go on one of her yelling and hollering tangents. Deborah had made a promise to herself that if she ever had kids, she would not yell and cuss at or around them the way her mother had. She had done pretty good up until tonight. Tonight, she had broken her promise to herself. Tonight, she had both yelled and cussed. With so much going on, it was like a dam had broken and Deborah had just erupted. In doing so, she'd created a tension in the atmosphere that her young child had easily picked up on.

Instead of loving on him and coddling him the last few minutes she had with him before her mother came to pick him up, she sat there with him nervous and tense. He picked up on it, too, as he tried to stay clear of her, and played over on his blanket covered with toys. When the doorbell rang, both Deborah and her poor child jumped. She answered the door and couldn't ship him off with her mother fast enough. She couldn't even recall if she'd kissed him good-bye. And that was the very thing she now sat thinking about. Her mind was so into trying to remember if she had kissed her son good-bye that she hadn't even heard Lynox ask her a question. So he repeated it.

"How's your steak?" This time Lynox reached over and patted Deborah on the hand.

His touch, not his query, pulled her out of her daze. "Oh, I'm sorry. Did you say something?"

Lynox pulled his hand away, sat back, and just stared at Deborah for a moment. Finally he said, "I know what's going on here."

"You do?" Deborah immediately sat erect in a panic. Had he read right through her? Was it something she'd said or done that blew her cover for being a mother . . . for being part of the readymade family he so detested?

"Sure I do. I've known all along. I was just waiting for you to tell me."

Deborah breathed out a huff of air. "You have?" Deborah felt so relieved that she knew her blood pressure had just dropped a few notches. She didn't have a history of high blood pressure, but here, lately, she'd given it a lot of reasons to go up.

"Sure I have," Lynox said with a serious tone. "But how do I bring something like that up?" He shrugged. "I mean, I'm not a woman, so I have no idea what it's like. Yeah, I have my personal opinion about the issue. Always told myself no way would I ever date a woman who has had one."

Deborah looked downward, figuring it was coming. That once again Lynox had taken the lead and now, instead of her being the one to tell him it was over between the two of them, he would be telling her. For Deborah, though, at the end of the day, it didn't matter who told who. The fact was . . . it was about to be over.

Chapter Thirteen

"Who told you? How did you find that out?" Deborah nearly shouted.

"Shhh." Lynox put his index finger over his mouth, then looked around to see how many restaurant patrons were giving them dirty looks because of Deborah's rude outburst. There were just a few. "Look. Maybe I shouldn't have said anything—not in here anyway. I'm going to have the waitress wrap up our food so we can go talk about it elsewhere." And Lynox did just that; all the while Deborah sat in her chair steaming—smoke coming out of her ears and nose.

Once Lynox paid the bill and the waitress returned with his credit card and their boxed food, he escorted Deborah out of the restaurant. "Let me put these in my car." He held up the food. "As a matter of fact, let's go sit in my car to talk."

Deborah didn't speak. She just agreed by following Lynox.

"It's the gold Lexus over there." He pointed to his second car. The Hummer was a gas guzzler so he didn't drive it regularly. Not only that, but it was at the body shop having the door repaired.

Lynox unlocked his car with the remote and then walked to the passenger side to let Deborah in. She didn't even say thank you. She just slipped in and looked straight ahead—as if she couldn't even look Lynox in the eyes.

After walking around to the driver's side, Lynox got in, still holding their food. He looked at the markings on the tops of the boxes and handed Deborah the one that belonged to her. "Here you go."

Deborah accepted it, knowing darn well she no longer had an appetite.

"You calmed down any?" Lynox asked, looking over at Deborah.

"I just want to know who told you. That was my business to be telling."

"Does it matter who told me? The fact of the matter is that I know and I'm okay with it."

Deborah turned slowly and looked to Lynox. "Are you really? You don't think any differently of me? You don't think I'm some monster? Because that's exactly what I felt like." Deborah, by burying her face in her hand, tried to hide the shame that was creeping up on her. "I mean, what kind of woman denies her baby . . ." Deborah got choked up, but then got herself together and finished the sentence. "Life? That's basically what I did."

"No, I don't think you are a monster. Having an abortion had to be hard enough."

"What? Abortion?" Deborah hadn't thought about the late-term abortion she'd had almost seven years ago. That was until Lynox just mentioned it. At first, when he told her that he knew what was going on with her—why she was so distant—instinctively she thought he'd found out she'd given birth to a child, but instead he'd learned that she'd taken the life of a child.

"In all the times we've been talking and telling each other about ourselves, I could tell you were trying to find just the right time to tell me about it. But is there really a right time to tell someone something like that? I have to admit that at first I felt a certain kind of way about it. But, sweetheart, that's your past. And like I said before, I'm not going to let anyone or anything from the past keep us from a future together."

Although Lynox had spoken with such compassion and sincerity, the entire time Deborah had just been sitting there seething with one thing on her mind. "Who told you? I still want to know how you found out."

And now, as she sat there in his car, those were still the only questions at the forefront of her thoughts. Still looking straight ahead, and almost robotic, Deborah asked, "Lynox, who told you about my abortion?"

"Does it matter who told me? What matters is that it's out in the open. So now when you're with me, you can be open and free. There's no black bubble hovering over us anymore. It's been burst." In an attempt to lighten the mood, Lynox took his index finger and poked the air as if he were bursting a bubble. He smiled at Deborah, but she was still stone faced forward.

"It matters to me," Deborah replied.

"Well, it shouldn't." Now Lynox was getting a little upset. That was evident by the tone of his voice. "What should matter is that I'm okay with it and we can move on in this relationship."

With a quick snap of her neck, she was now facing Lynox. "Oh yeah? And who made you God? Since when did you need to be all right with the sins of my past in order for me to be able to live free? Huh?"

Lynox was caught off guard by Deborah's tone with him. He knew she was a strong, independent, headstrong woman, but her tone was on the verge of complete nastiness. "I apologize. That's not what I was trying to insinuate." Lynox was the one who now turned his face from Deborah and looked straight on.

Instantaneously Deborah realized her ugly side had seeped out. That was a side of her she hoped Lynox never would see. That was a side of her she tried not to let anyone see—at least the people who knew her well.

Now when it came to the clerk at the grocery store who had an attitude of her own, or the person who took her order at the fast food restaurant and got the order wrong, or the customer service rep she was on the phone complaining to, she didn't mind if they saw that side of her. But she never wanted her church friends or the people she worked with to know she was even capable of being so callous. But most importantly, she never wanted Lynox to see that side of her. So she quickly toned it down.

"I'm sorry, Lynox. I didn't mean to snap off on you like that. It's just that you have no idea how long it took me to get delivered from the shame and guilt of that abortion. And to just hear you talk about it . . . it brought up bad memories. That's all." Deborah turned her head away like a wounded puppy and looked out the passenger-side window.

"It's okay." Lynox accepted her apology. "I can only imagine what you're going through. And maybe I should have just waited and let you tell me. It's just that I could see something was eating at you, and I figured this was it."

Deborah remained silent. Lynox paused for a moment and then said, "Was I right?" He sounded a tad doubtful.

Now facing him, Deborah asked, "What do you mean were you right?"

"Was that what was bothering you, or is there something else?"

Deborah swallowed and began looking out of the window again. Her mind was racing 1,000 miles per hour and so were the beats of her heart. God was open-ing a window for her to climb through and tell Lynox the truth, the whole truth, and nothing but the truth. The question was, would she crawl through it . . . or close it?

Chapter Fourteen

It was Easter Sunday. Deborah loved Easter Sunday, not only because that was the day Christians celebrated the resurrection of Jesus Christ, but it was also when all the youth got to open service with prayer and song. She loved watching her little guy stand at attention among all the other children in the church and sing about how Jesus loved him. But what really did it for Deborah was the play the young adults and children put on every Easter.

Deborah entered New Day and headed straight for children's church to sign her son in.

"Praise the Lord!" Sister Helen, who was the children's church leader, greeted her. She and all of her size-fourteen curves made their way over to Deborah for a sisterly church hug. Her brown skin and round cheeks were just a-glowing like she had a halo over her head reflecting light on her face.

"He's worthy," Deborah replied, leaning in and hugging Helen.

About three years ago, when Sister Helen first started attending New Day, one would have never imagined the two women could ever be so cordial to one another. After all, Helen had done nothing but taunt Deborah by holding Deborah's secret over her head. Helen had been the stranger in the abortion clinic who placed her hand on Deborah's pregnant stomach and felt the baby kick inside. She then watched Deborah walk into a room, and when she came back out, she wasn't pregnant anymore.

The fact that Helen was there to get an abortion too didn't matter to her. At least she wasn't terminating a baby that, with the help of medical technology, could possibly live had it been born the day of the abortion. What Deborah was doing was far worse than what she was doing was how Helen saw it. That line of thinking was what made Helen feel better about having her own abortion. And four years later when she encountered Deborah again in the New Day sanctuary and was reminded of the sin of her past, she used that same line of thinking. Every time Helen saw Deborah she said something slick to make Deborah feel awful, guilty, and shameful. Deborah would fold up into a shell, not even putting up a fight—afraid that if she said the wrong thing to Helen or even looked at Helen wrong, her past secret would be exposed.

But to God be the glory that Deborah was able to come up out from under that stronghold that had her mind twisted. To God be the glory that Deborah was able to break the shackles and chains that had her caught up in bondage. And to God be the glory that she was able to seek and receive forgiveness from both God and herself.

Once Deborah was delivered, healed, and set free from all the heavy weight of the abortion, she found the holy boldness to finally stand up to Helen. She somehow managed to remain Christ-like in their confrontation, and lo and behold, God had touched Helen's heart to receive Deborah's words.

Deborah learned that day that sometimes when a person sets other people free, they can end up getting set free as well in the process. So not only was Deborah free to walk around church without fear of her past being exposed unless she was ready to expose it through testimony, but she was also able to date Lynox freely: the man who Helen had taken an interest in first.

And dating Lynox was just what Deborah was doing, considering that she still hadn't told him the truth about her son and broken things off with him.

"Bye-bye, Mommy," Deborah's son said, waving, then heading off to join a couple of other toddlers who were playing with blocks.

"Bye, son. Be good," Deborah told him before signing him in and then moving out of the way for the next parent.

Making her way into the sanctuary, Deborah was in awe. The decoration committee had done a superb job. There was white sheer draped from corner to corner. Lifelike doves and olive tree branches were hung about. In the middle of the altar was a huge cross with a crown of thorns where Jesus' head would have been. There were nails eight inches long driven into the cross where Jesus' wrists and feet had been nailed to the cross. Just the thought of what Jesus had gone through on that cross brought shouts about the sanctuary.

"Thank you, Jesus!" Deborah cried out before she had even made it to her seat. "You're worthy. Worthy is the blood of the lamb."

"Yes, God," others mumbled as pretty much everyone in the sanctuary was moved by the atmosphere.

Because of the high emotions of the saints, church was running fifteen minutes behind schedule—man's schedule, that is. Because as far as the order and direction of the Holy Ghost, everything was right on time.

Eventually, the children were introduced as, one by one, a different youth mounted the pulpit in order to fulfill their assignment. First a teenage boy opened up in a mighty prayer. Second, a young lady read scripture. Next, twin sisters welcomed first-time visitors, then after that the youth choir sang two song selections and all of the young people from the dance ministry ministered in dance.

God could certainly use children to deliver His message and His Word, because New Day Temple of Faith was having an awesome time in the Lord, with children leading the way.

"And now," Sister Helen started as she took the stage, "we introduce you to the children of New Day Temple of Faith in their reenactment of the life, death, and resurrection of our Lord and Savior, Jesus Christ."

There was thunderous applause for the ministry that the saints felt in their spirits the children were about to bring forth. And the youth brought it all right. They did a phenomenal job. They had the adults on the edge of their seats as if they were learning of the Bible story for the first time. The youth closed out with a young man and girl sharing a monologue, telling the saints how much Jesus loved them. And they all exited singing "Yes, Jesus Loves Me," Deborah's son included.

"That's my baby boy," Deborah cried as she stood and clapped.

While being carried away in Helen's arms, her son spotted her and began waving and shouting, "Mommy!" Members who noticed the exchange laughed.

Helen shifted the young boy higher on her hip and smiled while she held a little girl's hand.

Deborah just shook her head. God was an awesome God. Helen had been a thorn in Deborah's side, her nemesis and her worst enemy. The two had shared the horrific experience of getting abortions together. Now they shared the admiration for the second chance God had blessed Deborah with: her son.

Helen had taken to Deborah's son as if he were her own. At first Deborah thought Helen was being phony, or maybe trying too hard to mend things between them. It wouldn't be out of the ordinary for Helen to try extra hard to redeem herself through Deborah's eyes by acting too nice and not really meaning it. People did it all the time. But Deborah just felt genuineness about Helen. And her son loved her to death. All he ever talked about after church was how Miss Helen this and how Miss Helen that.

As Deborah sat back down, she smiled at the turn of circumstances. But no sooner had Pastor approached the pulpit to give the Word, than Deborah's smile had turned upside down. She immediately lifted her head up and looked toward where Helen had exited the sanctuary with her son. *What if . . .*

Deborah's mind began to run so rampant with what ifs that she actually broke a sweat. What if Helen had been faking all this time? What if Helen had been playing her all this time? What if instead of her cordialness being genuine, Helen had been doing nothing more than the old adage of keeping her enemies closer? What if all this time she still had ill feelings for Deborah? Still wanted Lynox and . . .

And told him about the abortion? Deborah thought. She shook her head and snapped her fingers. That was it! That's how Lynox found out about the abortion. Somehow Helen had found out that Lynox and Deborah were kicking it again, Deborah presumed, and then jealousy rose up. *She's probably been following me,* Deborah thought. *Wouldn't put it past her. She's just crazy enough.*

All types of scenarios ran through Deborah's mind. And the more over-the-top her thoughts, the hotter her head got. All this time Deborah had thought Helen had changed, but in all actuality, she'd just been sitting in the cut waiting for the kill—waiting to strike on an unsuspecting Deborah.

Deborah made a mental note that just as soon as service was over, she was going to go pull Helen to the side and tell her about herself. But the longer church service went on, Deborah lost her patience. Before she knew it, she'd gotten up and exited the sanctuary, making a beeline straight for children's church. Sunday, Monday, Tuesday, Wednesday, Thursday, Friday, Saturday. It didn't matter what day of the week it was—nothing Deborah was about to do or say would make one think she was a Christian. It was about to be on and poppin'!

Chapter Fifteen

"Sister Deborah, is service over already?" Helen said once she looked up and saw Deborah entering the classroom.

"You can cut out all the phony talk with your words laced with syrup. I'm on to you, sista." Deborah pointed as she strutted toward Helen.

Helen was taken aback. She and Deborah had been pretty cool, gotten over all their hurdles, so she had no idea what could have brought on Deborah's attitude. Just a while ago, when Deborah had checked her son into children's church, she had been sweet as cotton candy. Now she was as sour as a box of Lemonhead candies. "Pardon me?"

"You heard me. The jig is up," Deborah snapped. "You have been acting like everything was kosher all this time, when all along you've still had it out for me. For once, you see me about to be happy again and you think of what could have been." Deborah walked up close to Helen, pointing an accusing finger. "You want my life, don't you? You wanna be me, huh? But you can't be me, so that's why you mad at me."

"Do you know what you sound like up in here?" Helen calmly asked Deborah. "Lil' Kim, that's who."

There was a chuckle coming from the corner of the room. It was the children's church assistant, Unique. Both Deborah and Helen shot Unique a cutting look.

"What?" Unique asked, raising her hands in confusion. "That mess was funny and you know it, Helen."

With her attention back on Helen, Deborah said, "There is nothing funny about someone trying to sabotage your life."

"Look, I have no idea what you are talking about, but trust me, I think you've got the wrong one." Helen went to walk away, but was stopped when she felt a pull on her shoulder.

Everything in Deborah knew she should have just let Helen walk away and kept it moving herself. Gone and prayed about it. Taken it to the altar or something. The Holy Spirit even tried to warn her by bringing a scripture—Psalm 37:8, Amplified Bible—to the front of Deborah's mind:

Cease from anger and forsake wrath; fret not yourself—it tends only to evildoing.

Deborah quickly buried it deep down in the back of her mind and proceeded without caution.

"Don't try to run away from the situation and act stupid," Deborah said, her hand still on Helen's shoulder. "You know exactly what I'm talking about." She dropped her hand to her hip. "You just couldn't stand to see me with him, could you?" Deborah seethed through her gritted teeth. "After all this time, you still want him, don't you? Well forget about it, because he's mine!"

Deborah's voice had risen by several decibels since entering the room. The children appeared to start getting a little fearful.

"Look, if there's something you need to say to me, then we can get together and talk later." Once again, Helen tried to walk away. Once again she felt a pull holding her back. And yet again, she found Deborah's hand on her shoulder.

Although Helen had been maintaining her composure, even Unique could tell she was about to snap.

"Check this out," Unique interrupted, making her way in between Deborah and Helen. "I don't know what the beef is about, and I don't care. What I do care about is two grown women 'bout to set it off in a room full of kids. This ain't *Dance Moms* or *Basketball Wives* reality shows."

Deborah looked around the room and for the first time realized that every child in the room had been watching her.

Unique continued. "Ain't it bad enough y'all clownin' in God's house? Let alone in front of God's children." Unique rolled her eyes and walked away mumbling the words, "And you call yourself a Christian."

Feeling slightly embarrassed that she'd been acting this way in front of the children, Deborah slowly slid her hand off of Helen's shoulder. She was not about to back down though. "I don't have the time to be meeting up with you like we're old friends catching up. Can you just step outside the room and talk to me for a minute?"

Helen thought for a minute while she stared at Deborah. She then looked around the room. Whatever was on Deborah's mind was heavy. It was obvious she was not about to let it go. Helen would have preferred to talk about it some other time, and not on church premises, but she had a feeling Deborah was not about to let it go until she got it off her chest. And since Helen didn't want the kids to witness any more drama, she agreed to take the conversation outside of the classroom—for the sake of the children.

"Sure." Helen brushed past Deborah, leading the way outside of the classroom. Once she was to the door, Helen moved to the side and allowed Deborah to exit before closing the classroom door. Just as soon as she turned around, Deborah was all up in her face.

"You told him, didn't you?" Deborah dived right in with the questioning. "You thought if you told him, he'd be so disgusted with me that he would never want to be bothered with me again. That way he'd be all yours."

Just when Helen thought Deborah couldn't get up in her face any closer, she did. They were nose to nose and Helen could feel Deborah's breath hitting her face. She took a step back toward the door, but Deborah took one forward.

"But guess what, sweetheart?" Deborah continued. "He doesn't want you."

Finally, Helen put her hand up. Her intention wasn't to "give Deborah the hand," but Deborah was so close, it seemed that way. Helen was just trying to use her hands to ask Deborah to calm down and tell her who and what she was talking about. But Deborah took it as an insult, and before Helen knew it, there was a stinging on her hand from where Deborah had slapped it away.

"Don't you ever put your hands up in my face," Deborah spat. "I don't know who you think you are. You may have Pastor and everyone else fooled. Heck, you even had me going all this time. But I know the real you. You're the same jealous, conniving Helen who walked into New Day's doors three years ago."

By this time, Helen was so upset and frustrated that her eyes began to water from nothing but pure anger. She was angry that not only was Deborah winning the battle between the two of them, in which Helen had no idea why she was fighting, but her spirit was also winning the battle over her flesh. Helen's flesh wanted to yoke up Deborah by the throat and mop the halls and walls with her. But Helen's Spirit Man was overpowering and kept her flesh under subjection.

"I am so not moved by those tears," Deborah said callously. "You should have thought about all this when you were running your trap to Lynox."

"Lynox? Lynox?" Helen's mouth dropped open in disbelief. "Is that what all this is about? Deborah, are you serious?"

"Oh, quit acting like you didn't know what all this was about, you phony heifer. Now that I done pulled your ho card, you ain't so hard after all, huh?" Deborah was taking advantage of the fact that Helen wasn't coming at her all crazy. Realizing that Helen's bark had been worse than her bite all along, Deborah kept pushing. "But like I said, in spite of what your intentions were, he still wants this." Deborah ran her hands down her body.

"And he can have *that*," Helen spat. "I don't want no Lynox."

"Oh yeah? Then why did you tell him?" Now it was Deborah putting up her hand, not allowing Helen the chance to speak. "Oh, I know, like I said, so he'd dump me and then you'd have an opening to crawl and sliver through like the serpent of a snake you are." Deborah's words were laced with so much venom, she hoped her words alone would poison Helen and make her drop dead right there where she stood.

Helen just laughed right in Deborah's face though. She couldn't help it. This was all too much for her. "Girl, you are crazy and you need Jesus. Now go on back into that sanctuary and go find Him." On that note, Helen turned back toward the door to enter the classroom.

"Oh no, you don't." Deborah jerked Helen back around, gripping her arm. "Did you or did you not tell Lynox about"—Deborah moved in close to Helen's ear and whispered—"the abortion?"

Helen jerked away. "You doing all this . . . You trippin' about something that happened years ago?"

"Answer me! Did you tell him?" Deborah spat, spittle landing on Helen's face.

Helen paused for a moment and then replied, "Yeah, but it—"

"I knew it! I knew it was you! How could I have been so stupid to think that all this time you had changed? Well, thank God He opened my eyes up to you. You ain't nothing but the devil in disguise and I don't want my child around you ever again." Deborah nudged Helen out of the way. She opened the classroom door, walked in, scanned the area for her son, and then immediately scooped up him and his belongings.

"Mommy, I playing. No, Mommy. I play," her son cried out.

"Don't do this, Deborah," Helen pleaded as calmly as she could.

"I didn't do it, Helen, you did."

"Please just let me explain." She looked down at Deborah's son, who looked fearful and upset. "Let him stay. You and I can go talk later and you'll see that you're making a mistake. You're overreacting."

"The only mistake I made was forgiving you and thinking we could be cool. But I will not make the same mistake twice. Deuces." Deborah threw up two fingers and swished out of the room with her son in her arms. "And to think I thought she had changed," Deborah said about Helen as she headed back to the sanctuary, none the wiser that God was saying the same exact thing about her.

Chapter Sixteen

Once Deborah returned to the sanctuary, she got settled and turned her attention immediately to the Word
Pastor was giving. It was as if she hadn't missed a beat.

"Hallelujah!" Deborah had shouted out when Pastor
said something she agreed with. "He's worthy!"

"Yes, He is, Sister Deborah. Tell 'em again," Pastor
said from the pulpit.

"He's worthy!" Deborah shouted out again.

"Again!"

"He's worthy!"

"Again!"

"He's worthy!" By now, the woman sitting next to
Deborah had taken the liberty of removing Deborah's
son from her lap as Deborah stood up with lifted hands
raised in the air. "He's worthy! God you are so worthy
to be praised. Hallelujah. Worthy is the blood of the
lamb. Glory." Tears began to fall from Deborah's eyes
as she looked at the ceiling. "You're worthy, God. So
worthy." She began jumping up and down, praising
God. Two altar workers made their way over to Deborah. "Hallelujah. Glory. You're worthy. You're worthy."
The next thing everyone knew, Deborah broke out in
tongues. "Ah ba yo se ba ha yo se ye ma ya toe," she
rambled.

"That's right, praise Him. Praise Him," one of the altar workers said as she held her arms out around Deborah, but still giving her room to be free in the spirit.

"Thank you, Jesus!" Deborah would shout out every now and then between tongues. "It could have been me. It should have been me." At that moment, Deborah thought that had it been her and Elton together that deadly day over in Chile when the earthquake hit—had God answered her prayers and given her another woman's husband—she could be dead and buried right about now. "You thought of me, God. You thought of me."

Tears streamed down Deborah's face as her tongues began to silence and she could only whimper. She let out a couple more thank-yous before she returned comfortably to her seat. It took her a few seconds to recall that her son was no longer in children's church—that she had retrieved him and brought him back into the sanctuary with her. Just as soon as she began looking around for him, the woman who had been sitting next to her and had taken her son from her arms returned to her seat. She returned without Deborah's son in her arms.

"I took him to children's church," the woman whispered in Deborah's ear as she sat down. "He seemed a little frightened and I wanted you to be able to be as free in the spirit as you needed to be. Don't worry; he was glad to be with all the kids. Nearly jumped out of my arms to get to Sister Helen." The woman smiled. "Must be that warm, sweet spirit of hers. Kids love that." The woman then turned her attention back to the service at hand.

Obviously, the Holy Ghost that had touched Deborah was touching a lot of other folks too. There was shouting and running around the church. The saints were just glad to be free. Glad to be free all because their Lord and Savior had laid down His own perfect and sinless life for them. *For my jacked-up, sin-filled one,* Deborah thought.

She covered her eyes with her hand and shook her head. She couldn't understand for the life of her why anyone would be so kind and selfless as to die for her: the woman who had just acted as ugly as anyone could . . . and right in the house of the Lord. She felt she didn't deserve God's love, not with how she acted. Never mind her sins of the past. She'd received God's forgiveness and had moved on without guilt or shame. She wasn't the person she used to be. But what about the person she was now? Was this person any better?

"Now, now. You just go ahead and release," the woman next to Deborah said as she patted Deborah's back, sensing Deborah had a little bit more releasing to do.

Deborah was crying uncontrollably. She was so upset, so upset, with herself. After all God had done for her, after all God had brought her through, this was how she repaid Him? This was how she showed Him how grateful she was? By yelling, screaming, cursing, and acting out? Not only in God's house, but in front of her son, in front of other people's children?

For a moment, Deborah tried to justify her behavior just moments ago by telling herself that it was all Helen's fault; that she had no business running her mouth to Lynox. Had it not been for Helen's actions, then she wouldn't have acted the way she had. But what about the other times she'd snapped and lost it? The times that had nothing to do with Helen?

"I'm going to do better, God. I promise," Deborah mumbled to herself as she wiped her tears. "I'm not going to turn into how my mother used to be." She wiped all her tears away and then sat up straight, bound and determined that from this moment on, her actions and her attitude would be pleasing to God. She would control what came out of her mouth and the tone in which it flowed. And Deborah's first test would be when she had to face Helen when she picked up her son from children's church after service.

"I appreciate you going to get my son from children's church," Deborah said to the woman who had sat next to her during church service. "I just didn't have the strength." Deborah hadn't told a complete lie in the house of the Lord. Physically, she had the strength to get up, walk down the hall, and carry her son out. What she didn't have the strength to do was to face Helen— not right now.

"It's no problem." The woman sat Deborah's son down next to her. There were just a handful of people left in the sanctuary, as service was over and everyone was anxious to get home and start digging into Easter Sunday dinner. "I know how it can be when you go into the spirit. You come out feeling like you've run a marathon." The woman laughed. "Well, I better get to getting. My husband is probably at home fit to be tied waiting on me to get there to serve up Easter dinner. The man only been in church and read the Word enough times for me to count on one hand, but want to celebrate Easter Sunday with a big ol' meal. But, I'm still praying for him. Been married ten years, trying to get him to go to church for seven of 'em. But I realized all I can do is pray, the rest is up to him and God. Only God can truly change a person, and that's only if they want to be changed." The woman smiled and patted Deborah on the shoulder. "Now you have a blessed Resurrection Sunday."

Deborah just sat there taking in the woman's words, the part about only God being able to change a person and that was only if they wanted to be changed. So now the million dollar question for Deborah was: did she really want to be changed?

Chapter Seventeen

"I would have picked you up, Deborah," Lynox said after kissing Deborah on the cheek as she entered the museum lobby.

"Oh, no. That's okay. I had to come out for something anyway, so it all worked out." That something she had to come out for was dropping her son off to her mother's house. She didn't think she could deal with the stress of another close call of Lynox arriving before her mother had picked up her son. "So anyway; where's this wonderful exhibit you're going to treat me to?"

"Ahh, it's on the second floor. And it looks like it's going to be a pretty nice turnout." Lynox started walking toward the elevator, slightly pressing his hand against Deborah's back to move her along.

She loved his touch. It was so calming. It was like medicine for Deborah. Perhaps that's all she needed to make things well in her spirit—to keep her relaxed and from getting out of line every now and then . . . a simple touch.

"So you said this is the guy who designed your book cover for you?" Deborah asked, knowing she needed to get her mind off of Lynox's touch quickly before naughty desires of him touching her all over in that elevator manifested.

"Um, hmmm." Lynox nodded and pushed the up button. "I was lucky to be able to get him to design it before he got all big and famous and stuff."

"I'd say he was the lucky one to be able to design for someone who was already big and famous."

"Oooooh, you know just what to say to a man." Lynox brushed a finger down Deborah's cheek.

She closed her eyes and once again took in his touch. Just when her mind roamed to thoughts of other places he could possibly touch, the elevator doors opened. Several people exited, making room for Lynox and Deborah to hop on. Thank God, not everyone got off the elevator. Deborah could only imagine purposely stopping the elevator mid-floor and pouncing on Lynox like she was a lioness and he was her prey—had they been on the elevator alone, of course.

The couple rode the elevator up to the second floor and then followed the crowd to the local artist's display. After oohing and ahhing over it, congratulating the artist, and then viewing a couple more pieces, Lynox and Deborah left the museum.

"Thanks for joining me," Lynox said as they walked down the museum steps. "I told you I wouldn't keep you long."

"A man who keeps his word; what more could a lady ask for?" Deborah smiled.

"Since the evening is still premature—"

Deborah stopped walking and laughed.

"What? What's so funny?" Lynox wanted to know.

"Premature? Can you just say 'since the night is still young'? I know as an author, when you're writing, you try to find words that aren't so clichéd. But when you're talking, especially to me, you don't have to do that."

Lynox laughed, not realizing he'd carried over his writing techniques into his everyday vocabulary. "I guess that did sound kind of crazy, huh?"

"Uhhhh, yeah." Deborah started walking again.

"Well, Miss Lewis, since the night is still young, what do you say we cop a squat over at the benches by the fountain and talk for a few?"

"I'd like that; besides, these dogs could use the rest." Deborah looked down at her one-and-a-half-inch pumps she'd purchased from Payless. Ever since her fiasco in those stilts she'd purchased hot in the salon, she'd been careful about the height of her heels. And even though these shoes weren't high at all, the arch wasn't made for the shape of her foot. They were starting to feel a little uncomfortable.

The two headed over to the bench and sat down.

"Here, put 'em right here." Lynox patted his lap.

Deborah looked around, having no idea what he was talking about.

"Your feet—you said they were bothering you. Let me see what I can do about that."

"Are you serious? You want to rub my feet?" Deborah was surprised.

"I just want to rub your feet, not suck your toes." He laughed. "Why you say that like I'm a pervert or something?"

"No, it's not that—not that at all. It's just that, well . . ."

"You mean to tell me you've never had a foot rub before?"

Deborah shook her head in embarrassment. "I'm one of those women who do not allow anyone to touch their feet. I don't even get pedicures. I take care of my feet myself."

"What? Are you serious?" Lynox pulled his neck back, astounded. "Even I get pedicures, manicures too. You have no idea what you're missing. Woman, there are just some things you need to let go and let other people do for you. You deserve it." He looked into her eyes. "Let ol' Lynox give you what you deserve."

Deborah squirmed where she sat, deciding not to respond to his latter remark, for fear it may lead them down a path she'd promised God she'd only go with her husband. "I get manicures. It's the feet I can't let somebody else touch. That just seems so private and intimate."

"You don't like privacy?" It was the way Lynox asked; like he wanted all the privacy with her he could possibly have without giving her a bad reputation.

"Well, yeah, but—"

"You don't like intimacy?"

She blushed. "Yeah, but—"

"Then hand them over." Lynox held out his hands, which waited for Deborah's feet to rest in them.

Deborah looked at him like he was crazy. "You are dead serious, aren't you?"

"Woman, if you don't give me those feet . . ."

Deborah giggled like a schoolgirl while she blushed. She went to lift one foot and then changed her mind and returned it to the ground. "I can't. You'll never look at me the same if I show you my feet. They're like Myra's feet on that episode of *Martin*." Both Lynox and Deborah burst out laughing. "Or like the girl in the movie *Boomerang* with Eddie Murphy."

"Oh, no." Lynox laughed even harder. "Not Hammer-Time."

The two kneeled over in laughter until their stomachs hurt and tears were falling from their eyes. Right while Deborah was still laughing, Lynox scooped her feet up into his lap, removed her shoes, and began his massage.

"Lynox! No!" Deborah shouted, trying to stop laughing. "Stop! My feet! Tickles!"

"Just relax, silly girl. Relax and enjoy." He winked. His wink was like a switch that had turned off Deborah's silly behavior, but had turned her on nonetheless.

"Oh, my God. I can't believe you're touching my dogs."

Lynox looked down at Deborah's feet and examined them. "I wouldn't say they were dogs. Puppies maybe, but definitely not dogs."

"Give me my feet." Deborah tried to pull them away, but Lynox had a pretty good grip on them. After some tugging and pulling from both parties, Lynox prevailed and proceeded to give Deborah a foot massage.

"Does that feel good?" Lynox asked.

"Does it ever," Deborah confessed, now completely relaxed and okay with the fact that a man was rubbing her feet.

The two sat in silence while Lynox continued to rub her feet. He decided to speak once he could see that Deborah was good and lost in herself. "About our conversation the other day," he started.

"Huh?" Deborah's eyes were closed and her head was resting back.

"Our conversation the other day in the restaurant, you know, the one about the um . . . procedure you had back in the day."

Deborah's eyes flipped open.

"Relax." Lynox could feel the sudden tension in her ankles. "I just wanted to reiterate that everything is all good. You got a little heated, so I'm not sure if you were clearly hearing me. But I'm good." He fingered her toes as if he were about to say, "This little piggy went to the market." Instead he said, "We're good. Right?"

Deborah nodded. "Yeah, we're good," she said while thinking, *but Helen and I are far from good.* "And since you decided to bring it up, I know Helen is the one who told you."

"Yeah, I figured you'd figure that out."

"And believe me, it wasn't hard."

"I think she was just trying to sabotage what you and I had. You know I never thought she had all her marbles."

"I know she was trying to sabotage our relationship."

Lynox finished up his massage and began to place Deborah's shoes back on her feet. "But that was so long ago. You said she still goes to your church, right?"

Deborah sucked her teeth. "Yes, she does." *Unfortunately.*

"Well hopefully church has worked for her and she's gotten herself together. I don't know. I haven't seen or talked to her since back in the day when I first met you." Once Lynox had placed Deborah's shoes on her feet, he tapped them, letting her know he was all done and that she could remove them from his lap.

Deborah froze, though, not able to move. "Wha . . . what do you mean you haven't seen or talked to her?" Deborah let out a nervous laugh as she ultimately placed her feet on the ground and sat erect on the bench. "You would have had to have talked to her in order for her to have told you about the . . . you know." Deborah swallowed . . . hard.

Lynox shooed his hand in Deborah's direction. "Oh, she told me that a long time ago, like I said, when we first got together. I knew she was just telling me in an attempt to get me to look at you in a different light. She said a lot of horrible things. The girl was obsessed. But I wasn't about to go running back to you, telling you what she'd said." Lynox thought for a minute. "Well, at one point I was going to, but then you asked me not to talk about her badly around you. I respected you for that. And I respected your request. So I let it go."

Deborah felt sick to her stomach. She couldn't believe she had jumped all over Helen about something she'd said years ago, before they'd made amends. "But why didn't she just say that?" Deborah mumbled to herself, thinking back to how when they were at church Helen confessed to telling Lynox about the abortion. Why hadn't she just told Deborah it was back when they were certified enemies? But then Deborah realized Helen had tried to tell her, but she was being too hotheaded and out of control to allow her to get her words out.

"Why didn't who say what?" Lynox asked, confused.

Deborah looked at him with this pitiful expression on her face. "Never mind. I was just thinking out loud." Deborah stood. "Look, Lynox, I have to go."

Lynox grabbed Deborah's hand. "No. The evening is still premature," he joked.

"Yeah, and so were my actions." Deborah sighed. "I'm sorry, I have to go. I have so much on my mind right now I wouldn't be good conversation. I'll call you tomorrow." Deborah squeezed Lynox's hand and headed back to her car.

Her erratic behavior had gotten her in trouble. She had to stop losing it and flying off the handle the way she did sometimes. "God, please fix me!" she pleaded as she arrived at her car. Hopefully He would, but for now, she had to fix things with Helen herself. But how?

Chapter Eighteen

"Sister Deborah, you're here," the pastor of New Day Temple of Faith greeted Deborah when she looked up from her desk and saw her standing in the doorway. "Come on in and have a seat." Pastor Margie stood and pointed at a chair at the opposite side of her desk. "Sister Helen isn't here yet." Pastor Margie looked at her desk clock. "Probably stuck in traffic or something because she's usually always on time."

"Good, I'm glad she's not here yet," Deborah replied as she walked to the chair and sat down. Once she got comfortable, she looked up to see her pastor giving her a reprimanding look. "Oh, no, Pastor, I didn't mean it like that. I meant I'm glad she's not here yet because there is something I'd like to say to you first."

Pastor relaxed her facial muscles and then got comfy in her own chair. She then looked directly at Deborah, giving her her complete attention.

"Well, first of all, I just want to apologize for the way I acted this past Sunday in children's church," Deborah started. "I was completely out of line. Fussing, yelling, and carrying on like that toward Sister Helen was just totally uncalled for, and in front of those kids."

Pastor raised an eyebrow and allowed Deborah to continue without saying a word.

"Even when Sister Helen suggested we meet somewhere else to have the conversation, I was too stirred up to oblige. I wanted to put it all out there right then and there. Going out into the hallway wasn't sufficient either. I should have composed myself, cooled off, and just talked to her at another time like a grown woman. I'm sure Jesus was looking down on me wishing He could have a do-over at Calvary for my sake." Deborah wiped a falling tear and then began to imitate what Jesus might have said that day. "I'll get up on that cross for mankind; everybody except for this broad named Deborah Lewis. She's a lost cause." Deborah hunched over and began to cry, shoulders heaving up and down.

Pastor Margie leaned back in her chair, rested her chin in her hand, then looked out the row of windows to the right of her that faced the church parking lot. She inhaled, thought for a second, then exhaled. Finally she turned her attention back to Deborah. "So, you said this all happened this past Sunday?"

Deborah looked up at her pastor with a question mark on her face. "Uh, yes."

Pastor Margie was silent for a moment, but then spoke again. "Did anything else happen?"

Deborah now wore two question marks on her face. "Well, uh, no. I don't think . . . Pastor, didn't Sister Helen tell you all of this already?"

"Actually, she didn't. When you called requesting I set up a meeting with you and Sister Helen, I wasn't too certain what it was going to be about. I mean, I know you two have a history during which you've had issues, but in my spirit, I truly felt the two of you had grown in Christ and were moving beyond it."

"We were, but . . . then I . . ." Deborah couldn't get her words out. She was still shocked about the fact that Helen hadn't gone running straight to Pastor to tell her about the incident. Deborah was sure the first thing Helen would have done was to try to get her removed as a leader of the singles ministry. Deborah really wouldn't have blamed her. Her behavior had not been conducive to that of a church leader. But Deborah loved holding the title and she'd hate to have to deal with the humiliation of having it taken away from her. That's why she called the meeting with Pastor. She wanted to take the initiative to come explain herself—fight for her position in the church if need be. And to patch things up with Helen, of course. But now here she was finding out that she'd, in fact, opened the can of worms herself.

"Sorry I'm late."

Both Pastor Margie and Deborah turned to see Helen entering Pastor's office.

"Oh, no, you're fine," Pastor Margie said as she stood and immediately pointed to the chair next to Deborah. "Come on in and take a seat." Pastor Margie sat at the same time Helen did. "Sister Deborah here was just telling me about a little incident that took place in children's church on Sunday."

Helen instantly buried her head in the sand.

"I'm surprised you hadn't shared that information with me first." Pastor Margie's eyes were planted on Helen, who was avoiding all eye contact. "After all, you are in charge of that ministry and what goes on in it, Sister Helen. What I'm even more surprised about is that one of the parents hasn't said anything to me about it. You know how kids are; they tell it all. And had a parent come to me, I would have been blind and in the dark about what was going on under the roof where I'm pastoring." Pastor Margie continued reprimanding Helen. "Sister Helen, you have been placed as leader of the children's church, which means I myself, God, and parents hold you in a higher regard than almost any other position in the church."

Deborah squirmed a little. She didn't know how she felt about the pastor sitting there and basically saying

that Helen's position in the church was more important than hers. But on the other hand, she was glad that
she wasn't the one Pastor was tearing into right now.
Although her time could very well be coming.

"I'm so sorry, Pastor," Helen replied regretfully.

"I understand you might have some kind of loyalty
to Sister Deborah. I know you two have a history, have
been mending your relationship, and you probably
didn't want to risk jeopardizing how far you two have
come. But you have to realize that your loyalty is to
your assignment, those children, those parents, and
more importantly, to God. If He puts you in charge
over a few and little and you can't protect that, how can
He trust you with increase?"

"I get it. I understand, Pastor, and I apologize. It
will never happen again," Helen said, and that's when
Deborah felt it was finally time she step in to take some
of the heat. After all, she was the one who lit the actual
fire.

"She's right, Pastor," Deborah said. "It won't happen
again, because I will never, ever behave like that again.
Not to Sister Helen or anyone else for that matter. I can
honestly say that from the bottom of my heart. I realize what I did was absolutely un-Christ-like, and that's
why I wanted to have this meeting today. I wanted to
apologize to you, Pastor, for tainting God's house like
that." Deborah looked to Helen. "And I want to apologize to you, Sister Helen. You have been nothing but
good to me and my son. When we agreed to put the
past behind us, that is exactly what you did. I, on the
other hand, let it come crashing back into my life like
a deadly wave. It just took me under and I submerged
myself in it. I did exactly what the devil wanted me to
do. Satan set me up to fail, and I failed—miserably. But
I promise you, the past is the past—for real this time.

If you will forgive me for my behavior, I'll work hard to redeem myself in your eyes."

Pastor just sat back and looked at Helen as if saying, "The ball is in your court."

Helen stared down at her fingers she was nervously twiddling. After a moment she looked up at Deborah. "It wasn't my place to tell Lynox about the procedure. But that was back when you and I had issues. You have to understand that I was hurting back then. Hurt people hurt other people. Back then, I would have felt like I'd accomplished something by seeing your reaction. But now it just hurts me to see how much pain I caused you."

"First of all," Deborah replied, "I didn't realize that you'd told Lynox so long ago. As you know, I'd left the country, so he and I hadn't talked in a while. And now that we finally are talking—and one of the first things he tells me is that he knew about the abortion—I lost it. I knew it had to be you who told him. But I didn't even take it into consideration that you'd told him so long ago."

"Well, that explains a lot on my end as well. I couldn't understand why you were saying something about it now. But, granted, that was still something that wasn't my business," Helen said. "From the sounds of it, you are maybe trying to hook back up with Lynox again. I hope I didn't do anything to mess things up for you and I wish you both the best. And that's real talk."

"I know it, Sister Helen. I know." Deborah got up and hugged Helen, who returned the hug.

Helen said to Deborah, "Do you forgive me?"

"I forgave you a long time ago," Deborah told Helen as she pulled out of the hug and took Helen's hands into hers. "The question is, do you forgive me?"

"With the love of Jesus, I certainly do." Helen squeezed Deborah's hands, released them, and then stood. "Unless you want to whoop on me some more, Pastor," Helen joked, "I'm going to head out. I have class later this evening."

"Oh, yeah. That's right, you're taking those classes required by the state for you to start your own childcare business. How's that going?"

"It's going really well." Helen smiled. "I just can't wait until I'm all finished so I can work on the next phase of licensing. Speaking of which, Pastor, when you have time, do you mind coming out to this building I found that I'd love to turn into a childcare facility? I'd like you to walk around the building with me, pray and touch and agree that I get that building. I've already asked a couple of other saints to join me."

"I don't mind at all. Just let me know the date and the time." Pastor Margie was glad to.

"Thank you, Pastor, for everything." Helen gave Pastor Margie a hug and then headed for the door. "Stay blessed, Sister Deborah."

"You too," Deborah replied. Once Helen was gone, Deborah exhaled and said, "I guess I better get going myself." She walked around to her pastor. "Thank you, Pastor, for taking the time out of your schedule for me. I really appreciate you and all you do." Deborah hugged her pastor and then she, too, headed for the door.

"Not so fast," she heard Pastor Margie say right as she stood at the doorway.

"Yes, Pastor?" Deborah turned around with a puzzled look on her face. As far as she was concerned, everything that needed to be said had been said. She and Helen were, once again, operating on a clean slate.

"Can you come back in and have a seat?" Pastor Margie nodded toward the door. "And close that, would you?" She then sat down in her seat.

Deborah, still a tad confused, obliged her pastor's request and then sat back down. "What is it, Pastor? What do you need to tell me?"

"It's not what I need to tell you. It's what you need to tell me."

"I don't know what you're talking about." And Deborah really didn't know what her pastor was referring to. Confusion was evident on her face.

"Can I be real with you right now?" Pastor Margie asked.

"That goes without saying, Pastor."

"Good. Real talk, that little song and dance you put on for Sister Helen, that sappy apology, that was all good. But what I need you to do is sit there and tell me what's really going on. In other words, be real and keep it real."

As far as Deborah was concerned, Pastor Margie was showing a whole lot of attitude for a white woman. But God didn't care anything about color. What it all boiled down to was that Pastor Margie had seen right through Deborah's original little song and dance. Now it was time for the remix.

Chapter Nineteen

"I have to tell him. I absolutely have to tell Lynox this time," Deborah told herself as she paced back and forth in front of her living room couch. Her son sat on the couch playing with an electronic toy and watching *Yo Gabba Gabba!* on the Nick Jr. television station.

Her mother was on her way to pick him up. She was scheduled to arrive at the house a whole half hour or so before Lynox. Deborah would have taken him to her mother's, but it was bingo night, so her mother said she'd swoop her grandson up afterward. Deborah knew she was cutting it close, but trusted God to be on her side. In spite of herself, somehow God always ended up on Deborah's side. Although Deborah was waiting for the day God would show up and say to her, "You know what? The devil can have you. I'm tired of playing with you. I'm going to give Satan the 'W' on this one." But for some reason, God never got tired of Deborah. He never gave up on her, always remaining on her team . . . no matter how dirty she sometimes played the game.

"Mommy, basketball," Deborah's son called out, requesting she give him the mini-sized basketball that rested on top of his diaper bag.

"No, baby. Mommy can't have you pulling out toys all over the place. Your Ganny Ban Banny will be here shortly to pick you up. You can play basketball at her house. Okay?"

"Okay, Mommy," her son said, basically just mimicking her, but still pointing to his basketball.

Deborah went and sat down next to him. "Oooh, look at *Yo Gabba Gabba!*" Deborah tried her best to distract him and get his mind off of that basketball or any other of his favorite toys other than the one he was playing with. She could keep up with that one toy, but feared if he started pulling others out, she might accidentally leave a toy out for Lynox to see. How would a supposedly childless single woman explain toys in her house? She'd spent the last hour making sure that nothing was out in the open that revealed a toddler lived there. The last thing she wanted was for Lynox to be tipped off before she got a chance to tell him about her son. He might not even stick around long enough to wait for an explanation.

Deborah had invited Lynox over for sweet tea and a little somethin' somethin' to put in their bellies. She didn't prepare an all-out full-course meal. She had no idea how long Lynox would hang around, if he would hang around at all, after she told him she had a son— that she was that readymade family he wanted nothing to do with. Times were too hard to be cooking up a big meal only for it to go to waste once Lynox told her he never wanted to see her again and walked out the door. That was the worst thing that could happen anyway. And it was pretty much inevitable. Lynox had made it clear how he felt about women who already had kids.

Refusing to think about the negative, Deborah sang and clapped along with her son to the show on the television. The doorbell ringing interrupted the playtime. "Ganny's here." Deborah shot up and looked down at her watch. "And she's right on time." Galloping across the living room, Deborah picked up the diaper bag and then went and opened the door. Upon opening it, her eyes bucked, and instinctively she slammed the door closed again.

"Oh my God! What is he doing here?" she whispered. She would have yelled it, but her voice was barely working. Her brain was hardly working. Her heart, her limbs, her lungs. She could hardly breathe.

"Ganny!" her son shouted as he hopped down off the couch and went running to the door. Once he reached the door and right as his little hand reached the knob, Deborah fought out of her mental paralysis and scooped him up into her arms.

"No, no, no, son. That's not Ganny," she told him. "God, that is so not your Ganny." Deborah just stood there holding her son nervously, clueless as to what her next move should be. The one thing she wasn't clueless about, though, was that she could not leave Lynox standing out there on her front porch. "Oh, God help me. Please."

Once again, right when Deborah had had things all planned out, Lynox, marching to the beat of his own drum, got everything all out of tune.

The doorbell rang again.

"Think, Deborah, think," she said to herself. But what was there to think about? She didn't have time to think. Lynox was going to think she was crazy if she didn't open that door. So, with no other options, she walked her son back over to the couch, sat him down, then went and opened the door. "Lynox, hi, glad you're here. You're early." Deborah tried so hard to remain calm, but the fact that Lynox kept taking it upon himself to show up early was bothering her. Had she had nothing to hide, maybe it wouldn't have gotten under her skin so much. But that wasn't the case. She had plenty to hide.

"No, I'm right on time," he begged to differ. "Your text said you'd see me at eight-thirty."

"No, I'm sure it said nine o'clock," Deborah insisted.

"No, I'm sure it said eight-thirty." Lynox reached in his pocket. "See, I still have the text." He pulled out his phone, pulled up the text on his screen, and showed Deborah. "See, eight-thirty."

She felt so stupid, because lo and behold, the text read eight-thirty, which only meant one thing: she'd sent her mother and Lynox the wrong texts. If she'd sent Lynox the text telling him she'd see him at eight-thirty, that meant she'd sent her mother the text saying she'd see her at nine. It would be another half hour before her mother arrived. Now what in the world was she going to do about her son for the next thirty minutes?

Chapter Twenty

"Is that the new Coach purse or something?" Lynox pointed to the diaper bag Deborah still had on her arm.

"Oh, oh, this." She grabbed the diaper bag. Nervously she pushed it under her arm and behind her back so that he couldn't see it, but he'd already seen it.

"Yeah, tha . . ." His words trailed off once he noticed the little fella sitting on the couch. "And that." He pointed, stepped around Deborah without waiting for an invite inside her house, then walked over to the couch. He pointed at her son as if he was an alien. "Who's this little guy?"

"He's my son," was what Deborah wanted to say. That's all she had to say. That's what she should have said. But that look on Lynox's face, it was confusion, puzzlement, but behind it all was a look of fear.

Please don't let this child be this woman's baby. She could tell that those were his exact thoughts.

This is not how he was supposed to find out. Those were Deborah's exact thoughts. She didn't want to be found out. She wanted to tell the truth on her own. There was a difference. It would be the difference between her still having a chance with Lynox or not.

"He's a little boy I babysit." *Did I just say that?* Deborah couldn't believe it herself, but yes, she'd just said that.

"Oh." She watched—she heard—Lynox let out the hugest sigh of relief she'd ever heard. "Cute little kid."

He then looked at Deborah strangely. "But what's he doing here? I thought we had a date."

"We did." Deborah nervously walked over to her son and picked him up off the couch. "I mean we do. It's just that—"

"Mommy," her son said, looking up at her.

"Mommy, yes, that's right, his mommy hasn't made it here to pick him up. She's late. Soooo, uhhh, he had to stay late. His granny's coming to pick him up instead. She should be here any minute." All of Deborah's nervous energy was only making her more nervous. But she was nervous. And worried. Worried and nervous. She didn't know what she'd do if her son called her Mommy one more time. "Hey, uh, Lynox. You know, I hate to ask, but I uh, forgot to pick up the sparkling cider from the store. Would you mind . . ."

"Oh, well, not at all, I suppose. But I'm good. Water will work for me. Kool-Aid. Whatever you've got."

"No, no, no!" Deborah yelled without realizing she was yelling. "Cider. I really wanted that cider. I . . . I . . . I can't invite someone into my home and serve them water. Not you anyway. I know you're used to the finer things in life. You drive a Hummer for Pete's sake."

"Which, by the way, I got back from the dealership. The door looks like n—"

"Oh, good, wonderful," Deborah cut him off. She had to. It was a must that she hurried him out of there before her mother arrived. Getting a two-year-old to keep quiet was one thing, a grown-up woman was another. "Let me grab you a five from my purse." Deborah walked over to her purse with her son still in her arms and began fumbling around with one arm in an attempt to retrieve the money. The next thing she knew, Lynox's calm, gentle hand was on top of her shaky one. She looked up at him, almost squinting her eyes, praying to God inside that he wasn't on to her or the situation.

"Relax. I know what's going on here."

"You do?" Deborah braced herself.

"Sure I do. I've dated other Christian women before. I'm a Christian too. I believe in God. Got saved when I was a kid and baptized. I kind of strayed away from the church, getting busy with life and all, but I still know who God is and His principles. Now, I can't say that I'm a saint and have abided by them all . . ." He laughed. "But I get it. You're a little nervous about being alone with me—on a date, with this much privacy—and where there's a bed a few feet away. Which explains why you slammed the door in my face . . ."

Deborah was hoping he didn't mention that.

"Got a little nervous, I understand." Lynox put his hands up. "But don't worry. It's not that type of party. I'm certainly not trying to go there with you." He chuckled.

Deborah's face got all twisted up and contorted. Had he just offended her? Why wouldn't he want to go there with her? She was an okay-looking woman. Had a little belly fat that she hadn't been able to get rid of since having her son, but other than that, add another penny or two and she could be a dime.

"Oh, I didn't mean it like that." He had read the expression on Deborah's face. "Of course I want to go there with you. What man wouldn't? What I'm saying is that I won't go there with you. I don't want to mess up dating with mating. 'Cause I really like dating you, Deborah."

Her heart melted into red cinnamon, chocolate, and marshmallow hearts. She stood in the sticky, icky, gooey puddle at her feet, mesmerized. "Lynox . . ." she cooed.

In an effort to avoid a mushy, romance-novel moment, Lynox pulled away from Deborah. "I better get to the store." He turned toward the door.

"Yes, you better," Deborah agreed, although inside she couldn't have disagreed more. She wanted him to stay. She wanted them to talk more and date more, but first she wanted to tell him the truth about her being a mother. Then she wanted to continue dating. But she was scared. She did not want to lose this man. Just one more second with him, minute, hour. Just as much as she wanted to tell him, she didn't want to tell him. Not knowing how he'd react was just frightening.

"And maybe by the time I get back"—he looked at her son—"this little one will be long gone. No offense"—he playfully started scratching his arm—"but kids give me the hives. Guess it's all those little crumbs that I'm allergic to." He winked at Deborah and smiled.

She feigned a smile, but what she really wanted to do was burst out crying. Her lips trembled and her eyes moistened. She couldn't stand feeling this way. It just felt all wrong. Yes, she wanted Lynox in her future, but if she couldn't build their present on an honest foundation, how could things ever truly work out for them? They wouldn't, she surmised, and that's why she had to tell him. "Lynox!" she called out.

"Yes?" He turned toward her and just stared into her eyes.

Just say it. Just say it. Just say it, she ordered herself, then opened her mouth and said, "You forgot the money." She couldn't say it.

"Oh, don't worry about it, pretty lady," he replied. "I got you." And then he left.

He left Deborah standing there now in a pile of deceit and lies. Oh, yeah—and with her son.

Chapter Twenty-one

"If I haven't told you yet, I love what you've done with your hair," Lynox complimented Deborah as they sat on the floor at her coffee table. Lynox had talked her into playing a game of backgammon.

"Thank you." Deborah smiled and patted her hair. "I must say, I do miss my locks though. They were just so easy to manage, especially after having a . . ." Deborah almost said the word "baby." She just almost slipped up and told him that she had a kid.

It wouldn't have actually been a slip-up. After all, wasn't that the reason she'd invited Lynox over in the first place? To tell him that she was a single mother? That she was one of those women on the prowl to find a husband for herself and a daddy for her child? Well, maybe that last assessment was taking things a little too far, but she knew that's how Lynox would see things. But she needed to tell him. God, she needed to tell him, but she just couldn't. Him showing up early had thrown everything off-kilter, and now, so would one more thing.

"After having a what?" Lynox urged Deborah to finish her sentence as he studied the board, being that it was his turn.

"After having had them for so long." Deborah was quick on her feet. If she didn't know how to do anything else in life these days, she certainly knew how to lie. She was living one. But she couldn't help but question whether she'd always been living one.

"It's your move," Lynox told her.

Deborah rolled the dice and then began moving one of her chips.

"Hey, you can't do that." Lynox pointed down at the board. "You have to roll doubles first in order to be able to play.

Stunned, Deborah looked down at the board. Her thoughts had been so far off, she hadn't even realized Lynox had put one of her men on board. "Oh. My bad."

"You dang right it's your bad," Lynox joked, scooping the dice up off the board and placing them in his little shaker cup. "So you're one of those people who make up their own rules in order to win, huh?"

Deborah broke down Lynox's words. Was she that type of person? Even though the Bible told her that in the end the believers win, why was she still trying to play the game of life her own way? Why was she saying the heck with the big set of rules God wrote, she was going to make up her own and still pray to come out on top? Thing was, it had never worked thus far, so why did she think it would work now?

"I thought you said you were some good at this game," Lynox shot off at Deborah. "Woman, I got another one of your men on board. If you keep playing the way you are playing, you are never going to win." Lynox was talking smack. And Deborah was listening, dissecting every little thing he'd said.

He's right, I'm never going to win. Not with the way I'm playing the game—the game of life, Deborah decided within her being. Living this lie was miserable. And no way would she be able to keep it up much longer. She had to do it. And the longer she kept her motherhood status from Lynox, the worse things would seem to him. She had to start letting God lead her. And that's just what she planned on doing—right now.

"Lynox, there's something I have to tell you, and you probably are going to think that I'm a big fat liar. But here it goes . . ." Deborah started before the ringing doorbell cut off her words. A puzzled look crossed her face.

Lynox raised an eyebrow. "Oh, I know that look. That's the look you women make right after you tell a guy that it's okay to come over. That don't nobody know where you live. You just moved here. Then, lo and behold, the baby daddy shows up." Lynox laughed.

Deborah playfully swatted at him. "You so crazy. I don't have no baby daddy," Deborah said as she stood. And at least that wasn't a lie. Since Elton had died in that earthquake in Chile, technically, she didn't have a baby daddy. But what she did have was a . . .

"Baby! You brought the baby back?" Deborah said, horrified, as she opened the door only to find her mother standing there with her son in her arms whining.

"You forgot to pack this boy's Mr. Blankie. He is having a fit. Wouldn't stop all that fussing," Deborah's mother said as she barged through the door.

Deborah looked down at her son and could tell he'd been crying. How could she have been so stupid as to not pack his Mr. Blankie?

"I tried calling, but I got no answer, on either the house phone or your cell."

Deborah had turned the ringer off the house phone and put her cell on vibrate. It was her attempt to avoid that moment when just when she's about to tell Lynox the truth, her phone rings. With just her luck that was exactly what would have happened. But now look what had happened. The doorbell had rung instead. If it weren't for bad luck, she wouldn't have any luck at all.

"Where's it at? In his bed? I'll get it." Her mother started toward the baby's room before she spotted

Lynox sitting on the floor at the living room table. She stopped in her tracks and looked at him with wonderment.

Lynox stood to greet her. "Hello, ma'am, I'm Lynox." He looked at the child he was now seeing for the second time today. "You must be the boy's grandmother." He looked at Deborah's son and said, "You back, little man?"

"I am his grandmother." Mrs. Lewis smiled as she looked from Lynox, to Deborah, then to Lynox again. "I see you know who I am, but I haven't had the pleasure of hearing about you." She turned and shot Deborah a snide look.

"Uhh, Mr. Blankie is in the crib. Go ahead and get it." Deborah walked over and nearly pushed her mother out of the room. She then turned back around to Lynox, who had sat back down at the table without a second thought.

Deborah wanted to die. She wanted to die. She wanted to die. How come every time she was about to tell Lynox about her son, it never played out the way she wanted it to? This was crazy. It was driving her crazy. If the truth didn't come out, she was going to lose her mind.

"Found it." Her mother returned to the living room with Mr. Blankie in hand, and her grandson caressing a corner of it. "All should be well. Now we can leave you two to do whatever it was that you were doing." Deborah's mother winked at her.

"Okay. And sorry about forgetting to pack Mr. Blankie. See you guys later." Deborah rushed them off.

"Nice meeting you, Mr. Lynox," Mrs. Lewis shot over her shoulder at Lynox as Deborah escorted her out.

Finally getting her mother and son out of the door, Deborah closed it, turned around, leaned up against the door, and smiled at Lynox. "Now, where were we?"

Lynox thought for a moment. "You were saying that there was something you needed to tell me, and that I was going to think you were a big fat liar." Lynox had a serious look on his face as he waited for Deborah to come clean.

With Deborah's heart beating faster than she could ever remember, she opened her mouth and said the words, "I lied to you. I'm not good at backgammon at all." Dang it! She'd done it again. Fear of the unknown outcome just would not let her spill it.

"I figured as much." Lynox closed up the board, stood, and then walked over to Deborah. "But don't worry, I have all the time in the world to teach you." He ran his hands through Deborah's hair, then rubbed her cheek with the back of his hand. "You are something special, Miss Lewis."

"I can say the same about you, Mr. Chase." Deborah was falling deep into Lynox's eyes as he put his arms around her and pulled her in close to him. The next thing she knew, Lynox's lips were joining forces with hers. When he finally pulled away, she could barely stand; his kiss had been so exhilarating.

The kiss had swept her off her feet as she felt her feet no longer touching the floor. Then she realized that it was Lynox who had literally swept her off of her feet by lifting her in the air and carrying her over to the couch. He sat her down, then joined her and picked up where they'd left off in the kissing department. Then, just for a second, he pulled away long enough to say, "I'm going to marry you, Deborah Lewis, if it's the last thing I do; watch and see. I've never met anyone like you—any woman who does to me what you do to me. You put my last name to good use and made me chase you. Well, now I've got you and I'm never letting you go—no matter what."

Once again Deborah fell into Lynox's kiss, forgetting about everything else in the world. Unfortunately, that included her son.

Chapter Twenty-two

"So who was the fella?" Deborah's mother asked her. Mrs. Lewis couldn't wait for Deborah to walk through that door so she could hit her with Twenty Questions.

"A guy I've known for a few years now. We lost touch for a minute there, but then I guess you could say we ran into each other a couple of weeks or so ago," Deborah replied nonchalantly. She didn't want to let on to her mother just how big a role Lynox played in her life. That was because, honestly, she didn't know if he would just be making a cameo appearance or going out for the part of the leading man. Although they'd spent a lot of time talking and connecting, there were still so many things unsaid that needed to be said.

"He seemed like a decent fellow. And I see he's been around Ganny Ban Banny's baby. He knew who he was."

Deborah just nodded while she began gathering her son's belongings.

"How does our little guy here act around him?" Deborah's mother inquired.

Deborah was becoming agitated. She didn't like her mother's line of questioning; not that it was out of line or anything. It's just that she knew if she replied, ultimately lies would have to come out of her mouth. She was tired of lying. It was too draining. Too hard to keep up with them. She was already buried in enough of them. Why was her mother bound and determined to pull out a shovel and pile on more?

"Okay," was all Deborah said as she sped up the process of getting out of her mother's house. The sooner
she got out of there, the sooner she could be free of her
mother's questions.

"Does he have kids of his own? You know it ain't just
you two who have to get along, but the kids will have to
form a relationship and get along as well."

"Ma, he doesn't have any kids," Deborah slightly
snapped. She just wanted for her mother to be quiet.
She needed her to be quiet.

"Well, that makes it easier. Now all you have to
worry about is him and the baby bonding. That's very
important you know, especially with you having a man
child. I know single mothers do it every day, but a
boy needs a good male role model. A nice, steady role
model; not a bunch of men in and out of his life. And
that I commend you for, Deb. You've been good about
not bringing a bunch of men around our guy." She
smiled a lit-up smile, then walked over to Deborah and
rubbed elbows with her. "That must mean this Lynox
guy is some kind of special for you to have him around
your son." She winked, still elbowing Deborah. "Come
on, you can tell me. Just how serious are you and this
Lynox guy?"

"Mommy, please." Deborah frowned, then ran her
hand down her face. "We'll talk later. I have to get him
home, get him settled and situated, and then work on
editing this manuscript I have to have done by this
weekend."

"Well, okay. I'll call you later on so you can give me all
the details," Mrs. Lewis relented as she assisted Deborah in getting the baby's things packed up, then walked
them to the door. "Give Ganny Ban Banny some suga',"
she said to her grandson before he and Deborah exited.

Deborah's son closed his eyes and puckered up big for his granny. When his lips touched his granny's he let out a big "Muah!"

"Thank you." Mrs. Lewis smiled at her grandson as Deborah went to step out of the door. "Oh, wait a minute; Mr. Blankie. It's upstairs."

Deborah sighed. "Oh, Ma, I'll get it tomorrow or something. I need to go. I got a lot to do."

"Now you know just as well as I do you ain't gon' get a thing done if that boy don't have his blankie. He ain't gonna do nothing but whine and worry you to death like he did me last evening. I'll grab it right quick."

Deborah let out a huge grunt as her mother hurried off, returning a minute later with the blankie in hand.

"Misser Blankie," her son said with excitement, and then reached out for the blanket upon seeing it in his grandmother's arms. He nearly jumped out of Deborah's arms. His sudden movement caused Deborah to drop his diaper bag, which was more like an open sack instead of the ones with a zipper. Several things spilled over out of the bag. Evidently the lid to his sippy cup hadn't been on tight, because juice spilled out as well.

"Dang on it, boy!" Deborah snapped, then sharply placed him on the ground. "See what you made me do acting all crazy over a stupid blanket. I don't even know why I let you have a blanket. Black kids don't have blankies." Deborah ranted and raved as she cleaned up the mess.

"Deborah, all that ain't even necessary," Mrs. Lewis said as she scooped her grandson up in her arms. "He was all happy and carrying on, now look at him."

Deborah shot a sharp glance up at her son, then focused on him. His little, round face had a huge question mark on it that asked, "Did I make Mommy mad?"

A part of her felt bad. The other part felt justified in having an attitude as she went back to cleaning up the mess. "So what. He's messing my day up. I'm trying to get out of here and he's worried about a blankie. Just stupid."

"Now that's enough!" her mother interjected. "All that yelling and fussing is what's stupid."

"Oh, now yelling and fussing is stupid," Deborah said sarcastically. "It wasn't 'enough' when you fussed and yelled at me when I was younger," Deborah snapped back.

"That's because I didn't know any better. That's how all the black people I knew raised their kids. We fussed, yelled, cussed, made 'em go pick a switch. We did what we thought it took to keep them out of trouble and out of jail. That's how my momma raised me and my brothers and sisters. So that's all I knew when it came to raising you."

"Then I guess I got it honest, because that's all I know in raising mine."

"But now, as your mother, I'm standing here telling you it's not the right way. What I've come to realize is that all that yelling and carrying on, it changes the atmosphere for the negative. It can break people's spirits." Mrs. Lewis looked down at her grandson, who still had a broken look on his face.

"Well, whatever." Deborah wasn't trying to hear it. After wiping up the spilled juice with a couple of wipes and putting everything back in the bag, she snatched her son out of her mother's arm. "Come on. Let's go."

Mrs. Lewis watched as Deborah stomped off. Her grandson, whose head rested on Deborah's shoulders, was staring at her. Mrs. Lewis waved at her grandbaby and smiled. He usually mimicked everything she did. This time, he mimicked the wave, but not the smile. That meant he wasn't all the way broken, but Mrs. Lewis's heart was. And in her heart she knew something had to be done in order to keep her grandson from being completely broken. There was nothing worse than a broken black boy growing into an angry black man. Mrs. Lewis couldn't let that happen. She wouldn't. She had to do something about it. She didn't have a clue about what to do, but she did know it would more than likely include a faceoff with her daughter. But who would be the last woman standing?

Chapter Twenty-three

"Ma, what are you doing here?" Deborah said, opening her front door, surprised to see her mother standing there.

"Can't a mother stop in and check on her daughter?" Mrs. Lewis asked, stepping into the house.

"You mean can't a grandmother stop in and check on her grandbaby?" Deborah rolled her eyes and walked away.

"See, you've got it all wrong. I actually did come here to see you today." Mrs. Lewis looked around. "But since you mentioned it, where is that little man of mine?"

"Napping, thank God." Deborah sighed. "He's been working a nerve. He's just so dang-on busy."

Mrs. Lewis knew her grandson's schedule like the back of her hand. The fact that he was napping wasn't a surprise. It was perfect timing for her to do what she needed to do, or rather say.

"I could barely get any work done," Deborah complained and then began mocking her son. "'I gotta pee-pee potty. Can I have a fruit snack? Apple juice, Mommy. I wanna watch *Ant Bully*.' He was working my nerves every five minutes." She rolled her eyes into the air.

"Well, that's what babies do. You were the same way." Mrs. Lewis walked over to the couch and sat down.

Deborah, standing there holding the door, just watched her mother and shook her head before mumbling under her breath, "Oh sure, Mother, I don't have anything to do today. Come in, sit down, stay awhile." Deborah threw her hand in the air and let it flop to the side as she closed the front door. "So, what really brings you out this way?"

"Didn't I tell you already? I came to see you."

"Oh, yeah." Deborah made a face that said, "Okay, that might be true, but the chances are slim to none."

"Yeah." Mrs. Lewis patted the empty spot next to her on the couch. "Now come sit down. As a matter of fact, how about we go into the kitchen and I'll make some tea or something?"

A peculiar look ran across Deborah's face. "Um-mmm, okay. But I'll make the tea. I don't mind. It is my kitchen." As Deborah led the way into the kitchen, for the life of her she couldn't figure out why her mother was being so extra nice to her. It wasn't like her mother had been mean to her—not in her adulthood anyway. The verdict was still out on whether how she treated Deborah in her younger years was mean or just "how black parents raised their kids." But she was being just too sugary right about now, it seemed.

"What kind of tea do you have?" Mrs. Lewis asked, sitting down in the nook.

"Oh, just regular tea. You know I'm more of a coffee drinker." Deborah retrieved a pan from the cupboard and went through the motions of boiling water.

Mrs. Lewis watched her daughter move about the kitchen as she contemplated how to proceed with her words. "I'm sure our little guy was glad to have his blankie yesterday."

"Yeah, well." Deborah shrugged. "You know how he is with that thing."

"I know how he is about the blanket, but it's how you are about the blanket that gives me pause."

Reaching for the tea bags in the cupboard over the kitchen sink, Deborah paused, turned, and looked at her mother. "What's that supposed to mean?" The slamming cabinet let Mrs. Lewis know the showdown was about to begin.

"Well, how you were saying how stupid it was, yelling and carrying on and stuff."

"Are you really on that again? Mom, did you forget that when I was coming up, you rarely ever talked to me with a civil tongue?" Deborah went to retrieve two cups from the cabinet, slamming those as well. "Instead of, 'Deborah, sweetheart, can you come clean your room up?' it was 'Deborah Janelle Lucas Lewis . . .'" At birth, Deborah had been given both her father's last name and her mother's maiden name because the two had not been married yet. Sometimes she represented herself, especially to clients, as Deborah Lucas, but she mostly went by the name of Deborah Lewis. "'If you don't get your lazy, black self up here and do something with this nasty room with your ol' trifling self, I'ma beat your you-know-what.'" Deborah laughed. Mrs. Lewis didn't. "I mean, really, Ma, you were the boss. No matter how you asked, because you were my mother and the authority over me, I would have done it. But would it have hurt to just make the request a little differently?"

"No, it wouldn't have hurt. And you're right; there was no need to talk to you the way I did when you were coming up. You were a good kid. I know you would have done anything I asked without disobedience."

"You dang right. I was too scared to be disobedient."

"Scared?" Mrs. Lewis twisted up her lips in disbelief. "Now you're going too far."

Deborah stopped midair as she reached for the tea bags. "Ma, are you serious? You were a terror. I never

knew when you were going to snap. I'd get home from
school before you got home from work. I'd always try
to make sure everything was decent and in order, but
you always found something to yell about." Deborah
began mocking her mom's old childrearing techniques
again. "'Who used the last of the toilet paper and didn't
replace the roll?' You would scream . . . and scream . . .
and scream . . . and scream. The empty toilet paper
roll would lead to something else. You'd go on and on
for hours. You'd still be yelling by the time Daddy got
home." Deborah shook her head. "I don't know how he
did it. I didn't have a choice, but him . . ."

"You're just over exaggerating now." Mrs. Lewis
stood with a look of denial on her face. She walked over
to the refrigerator and opened it. "You got any milk? I
take milk in my tea."

Deborah could tell she'd hit a nerve with her mother.
And for some reason, it gave her some type of adrena-
line rush. Her mother had started this conversation,
and now Deborah was hell bent on finishing—and winning—it. "Exaggerating. I wish." Deborah walked over
to the fridge. After watching her mother look for the
milk, which was actually right in front of her face, she
decided to help her out. She handed her mother the
jug of milk. "Your milk." Deborah smiled almost wick-
edly. She loved winning a fight, especially if someone
had picked it with her. "But like I was saying . . ." It
was time for Deborah to go in for the kill. "As bad as I
wanted to have company and sleepovers like some of
the other girls I knew, I was scared to death to do so. I
never knew when you were going to snap off, go on one
of your screaming rages and embarrass me."

"Deborah Janelle Lucas Lewis!" her mother spat.
Now she was the one doing the slamming. The refrigerator shook she'd slammed it so hard. "You cut it out
right now."

"Cut what out? Telling you how it was? Oh, yeah, that's right, from the way this conversation was heading, I think you were supposed to be the one telling me about myself instead of me telling you about yourself."

Mrs. Lewis was found out, and guilt plagued her face. That had most definitely been her intention for coming to her daughter's house.

"Umm, hmmm. Thought so." Deborah snapped her fingers, realizing she'd forgotten to get some saucers out.

"You're really getting off on this, aren't you?"

"On what?" Deborah feigned ignorance.

"On reminding me what a bad mother I was."

"Remind you? Tuh. How can I remind you of something you obviously don't seem to think ever took place? You're sitting here like you deserved some Mother of the Year award."

Mrs. Lewis was silent for a moment. She took in her daughter's words and came to the conclusion that although Deborah could have been a little more diplomatic in her delivery, it was how she felt. It was her truth. It was how she had seen things. And the longer Mrs. Lewis thought about it, she knew it was her very own truth as well.

In all honesty, it hadn't taken her daughter telling her that she used to be a hell raiser in order for her to realize it. Hearing Deborah say it though was like nails down a chalkboard. Over the years she'd looked back on her life and often cringed at some of the things she'd done and said, at the way she used to act. But over the years, in her older years, all that hell raising had taken its toll.

While watching her husband on his deathbed she had thought about how kind, compromising, and compassionate he had always been. He had been so peaceful, so it only seemed natural he'd have a peaceful death as he lay there, free of pain, just ready for the good Lord to call him home. He had left the universe with what he'd put into the universe. But her, on the other hand . . . She imagined some violent, raging death because that's all she'd ever given the universe. So what else did she expect in return? It was then that Mrs. Lewis had apologized to her husband and thanked him for loving her unconditionally over the years. And it was at this very moment that she realized she'd yet to offer the same to her daughter.

"I'm sorry." Mrs. Lewis allowed the words to fall purposely and sincerely from her lips.

Deborah spun around from the stove where she was turning down the boiling water. She was at a loss for words. She'd never—ever—heard her mother apologize. Not for how she'd acted in the past years, anyway. Yes, she'd heard her say she was sorry if she accidentally bumped into her, or if she showed up late for a lunch date or something. But this was different. This was big. But did her mother mean it? Or was she just saying it out of guilt because maybe she felt this was what Deborah needed to hear?

"I'm so sorry for the hell I raised in our home," Mrs. Lewis continued. "I'm sorry if you felt like you had to walk on eggshells or if you were on pins and needles, not knowing what my mood was going to be like from one day to the next."

Deborah could tell her mother was sincere as she stared off. Looking into her mother's eyes, Deborah could see that her mother was looking into the past. She was replaying some of her actions. And she was regretful. Regret covered her face while tears filled her eyes.

"I'm sorry that you couldn't have sleepovers and friends over for dinner. I'm sorry that I yelled, screamed, hollered, and cursed instead of just talking to you like you were a human being." A tear fell from Mrs. Lewis's eyes.

Deborah wasn't moved. She was receiving of her mother's apology, just not moved by it. The reason she wasn't moved by it was because she felt it was too late. She was grown now. Her childhood was done and over with. No do-overs. Her mother couldn't give her what she really wanted, which was a peaceful, tension-free childhood. That's all most kids want, is to be kids without someone telling them it's not okay to be a kid.

"All you think about is playing." Deborah recalled her mother always yelling that to her. All the while Deborah wanted to scream back, "But I am a kid. That's what kids do—they play."

"Life ain't always about fun and games," her mother would tell her. But for a kid, Deborah felt that life should have been about being young and having fun. No, that didn't mean that they shouldn't be taught responsibility as they grew up, but why did the adults always seem to want the kids to act adult like when they were still just a kid? Then they'd yell, *"You ain't grown."* What a contradiction. This confused Deborah to no end as a child. How was an eight-year-old supposed to know when to be a kid and when to act like they weren't in order to please the big people?

The more Deborah thought about it—her mother's old ways—the less weight the apology she'd just received held. The more her mother's voice from the past replayed in Deborah's head, the more it brought back those old feelings Deborah felt as a child. The feelings of having no voice of her own, unable to tell her mother how she felt. But she wasn't that kid anymore. Now she was a grown woman. Now she had a voice, and dang on it, she was going to use it. She was going to speak for all those times that, as a kid, she knew she'd have gotten her head knocked off if she dare spoke back to her mother.

"I hear your apology, Ma," Deborah said. "It's just hard to accept it because I just don't understand why. Why did you have to make our home so dark? I mean, it could be broad daylight, the sun shining and birds singing outside, but when I walked into our house . . . just dark. The mood, the atmosphere. Just dark. And it was because of your spirit that you'd spewed."

"I know, baby. I know." Mrs. Lewis sniffed, then wiped her nose with the back of her hand.

"I could see if you were some angry drunk. But all you drank was tea. So that means that you were just mean and nasty for no reason. And I had to suffer for it."

"I know. And that's why I'm here. Because I don't want your son to suffer."

Deborah was taken aback. "What do you mean you don't want my son to suffer? How is he going to suffer from the way you acted? You don't act like that anymore. As a matter of fact, I'm glad your grandson will never know that side of you." Deborah poured the boiling water into the cups where the tea bags had sat waiting. She then turned the burner off.

Mrs. Lewis stood. "But he's already starting to see that side of me . . . through you." Mrs. Lewis braced herself. She knew she'd just landed a low blow as far as Deborah would be concerned. And if she knew her daughter, Deborah would answer it with a power punch.

"Are you trying to say that I treat my son the way you treated me?" Deborah had turned so quickly to confront her mother, Mrs. Lewis didn't know if her entire body had spun around, or just her head itself. "Are you trying to say I run my house the way you ran yours?" Deborah shooed the air. "Because that's just outright madness." Deborah continued to mumble under her breath as she opened and slammed cabinets and drawers, retrieving sugar and spoons. She looked like a raging dragon. All she needed was smoke fuming out of her nostrils.

"Is this what I looked like all those years ago?" Mrs. Lewis asked her daughter. "Is this what you had to go through? Because if it was, I apologize again. I apologize from the bottom of my heart. I'm an old woman and just sitting in this room being subjected to this type of behavior is breaking me down." Mrs. Lewis stood as if all the energy had been zapped out of her body. She balanced herself on the table with both hands.

Deborah ignored her mother and just continued slamming cupboards and drawers.

All Mrs. Lewis could do was wipe the tears streaming from her eyes and say, "May God break this curse. In Jesus' name." She looked around for her purse and remembered that it was in the living room. She then headed that way to retrieve it.

"Oh, so what about the tea?"

"Sorry to have put you through all the trouble. Just ain't in the mood for it anymore." Mrs. Lewis headed into the living room. She could still hear her daughter mumbling and rambling on, dishes clanking and crashing into the sink. "I know I ain't a religious, church-going woman," she said, grabbing her purse, "but I know this job is too big for me." She looked up before exiting her daughter's house and said, "But ain't nothing too big for God."

Chapter Twenty-four

"It wasn't too long ago that if you had invited me over to your house for dinner, I would have thought it was to poison me." Helen let the forkful of linguini rest just right at her mouth. "You ain't trying to poison me, are you?" She laughed. Deborah laughed too. Even Deborah's son, who was sitting in his high chair, laughed, just to be mimicking the adults.

"Girl, no," Deborah replied. "You done watched too many episodes of *Snapped*." They laughed some more. "I can't say I blame you too much for thinking it though. Heck, had the tables been turned, I probably would have thought the same thing about you. Just to eliminate any concerns, I was just going to invite you out to dinner, but my mom usually keeps my son for me and she and I . . . well . . . Let's just say I didn't have a sitter."

"Oh, I feel you. And I know how it is when mothers try to take their kids out to a restaurant. My sister, Lynn, can never even enjoy the meal she paid for for tending to the kids. Dining out is playtime for those little rug rats." Helen finally ate her bite of food, chewed, and then added, "But I love my niece and nephew to death. I love all kids to death."

Taking a bite of her own food, Deborah chewed and chewed on the words Helen had just said. "I hope you don't mind me asking . . . I mean, I hope I'm not bringing up bad memories, but if you love kids so much, then why did you . . ." Deborah's words trailed off. She almost wished she hadn't started her line of questioning, but decided to finish anyway. "Why did you get that abortion? Why didn't you just have the baby?"

Helen gently placed her fork down on her plate, rested her back against the chair, and thought for a minute.

"I'm sorry. You don't have to answer that. I should have never brought it up." Deborah shoveled a couple bites of food into her mouth.

"No, it's fine. There are not many people I've talked to about this, or people who I even can talk to about this." Helen picked up a napkin, wiped her mouth, then set it back down. "The short version, he used to beat me. The guy who I was pregnant by used to beat me. Then after he'd beat me he'd make up with me by having sex with me. It was usually by force. I ended up pregnant. As much as I loved kids, I knew if I had that baby, I would be making a horrible mistake. Plus, I thought there was a chance that since it was his seed growing inside me, that it might turn out to be a monster too. I couldn't let that happen. And as you know, I didn't let that happen." Helen took a bite of garlic toast. "He never knew about the abortion. I told him I miscarried. It tore him up, thinking his unborn child had died. So for the next couple of years he tried to get me pregnant. Whenever my period came, he'd beat me for not being pregnant. So, I prepared myself to expect a beating at least once a month, because I knew I'd never get pregnant." Helen took a sip of her ice-cold lemonade, then casually said, "Because I got on birth control after the abortion. I couldn't take a chance on ever getting pregnant again by him. Thing is, he had no idea I was even on the Pill. And once I realized he was on this mission to get me pregnant again, I made sure he never found out."

Helen let out a nervous chuckle. "I even thought about having my tubes tied it was so bad."

"Helen, that's awful." Deborah cringed. "But what if the next man you dated wanted children? Did you think about that? Is that what made you have a change of heart?"

"Nah, that wasn't it. He told me that he couldn't live without me. He'd kill himself if I ever left him, but not before killing me." Helen mocked him: "'If I can't have you, nobody can have you.' And I believed him. I believed I would spend the rest of my miserable existence with him."

"So, are you with him now?"

"No. He ended up beating up this dude in a wheelchair and getting sentenced to a year and a half in jail. That gave me eighteen months to pack me and my son up and move away."

"Your son? But I thought you got an abortion." Deborah was confused.

"Yeah, that was my second pregnancy with him. We'd already had one together." She smiled when she mentioned her son. "I don't regret having my Baby D though. He was far from a monster, but so had his daddy been when I got pregnant with him. His father had changed over the years though. Like I said, he'd turned into a monster. I couldn't risk giving birth to a monster. I'd gotten lucky the first time, but who was to say I'd be so lucky the next?"

"You . . . you have a son?" Deborah repeated more so to herself, then said to Helen, " But I've never seen him."

"That's because my mom ended up raising him. My head was so messed up dealing with my ex and then the ex after him. I was being hurt, so I wanted to hurt people, and unfortunately, the only person around to take out all my pent-up aggression on was my son. So, my mom stepped in. He's grown now. Doing very well. In college, working, got his own place with a roommate. He's visited the church once or twice. If I can talk him into a third, I'll be sure to make introductions." Helen smiled, then took a sip of her drink.

Deborah just sat back in her chair, dumbfounded. She would have never known Helen had such a story. But what really got to her was that Helen was being so forthcoming with her story.

"Helen, thank you for being so transparent," Deborah said.

"Oh, child, please. You know the saying, if I don't tell it, the devil will. It's all part of the testimony, sista. All part of the testimony. Don't know who it's for, but I know it's going to help somebody out some day."

"I'm sure it will," Deborah agreed—as long as that somebody wasn't her. Although she had no intention of judging Helen based on her testimony, she knew that she'd never get so far gone that her mother, of all people, would have to step in and help her with her son. And that little intervention mess her mother had tried to pull the other day, Deborah would charge it to her head and not her heart. Her mother was jumping to conclusions. She feared that all her ways were going to start rubbing off on Deborah. But as far as Deborah was concerned, she wasn't nearly as bad as her mother had been, and never would be. And again, not to judge Helen, but she wasn't as bad as her either. So all was good in her book. But had she fast-forwarded a page or two, she would have realized that, no, she wasn't as bad as her mother or Helen; she was worse.

Chapter Twenty-five

"Ganny Ban Banny missed her baby," Mrs. Lewis said as she walked into Deborah's house and scooped up her grandson. She then proceeded to cover him with one kiss after the next, and he loved it, too. Those three days without Mrs. Lewis seeing her grandson had taken their toll on her.

"Thanks for coming by, Mom," Deborah said, closing the door. "He's been asking about you. That boy knows he loves and missed his Ganny Ban Banny."

"Oh, yeah?" Mrs. Lewis asked. "Well, what about his mother? Does she still love me and did she miss me too?" Mrs. Lewis began playfully batting her eyes while making a puppy-dog face.

Deborah rolled her eyes up in her head and tried not to let her girlish smile slip out, but it did. "Yes, Momsy. I still love you and I missed you too." Deborah walked over to her mother, hugged her, and then gave her a kiss on the cheek. She didn't like fighting with her mother. And she was urged to make up with her when a scripture, Ephesians 4:26, came to her mind and wouldn't leave:

Be ye angry, and sin not: let not the sun go down upon your wrath.

Well, Deborah had let the sun go down three times before making amends with her mother. She couldn't allow a fourth. "So can we call it a truce?" Deborah waited for her mother to respond.

Mrs. Lewis placed her arms around her daughter. "Truce, baby girl." She kissed her on her cheek. "You know I was only trying to help you, don't you? I didn't mean to offend you with anything I said the other day. I just don't want to see you angry and in pain like I was."

"I know, Mom. I know. And I'm sorry that I keep bringing up the past. You were as good a mother as you knew how to be. You did the best that you could." Deborah shrugged.

"Yeah, I did the best that I could. And I know a lot of mothers who use that as an excuse for the way they raised their kids. But I believe in my heart that there is a big difference between doing the best that you can and doing all that you can. I didn't do all that I could to be better, Deborah. But see, you have an advantage over me. You have something that I didn't."

"What's that?" Deborah asked.

"You have God." Mrs. Lewis smiled. "You know I never was into church. Never had time for it. Can't say I've ever really had a personal relationship with God. But I'm glad that you do. And if your God is what makes you better than me, than to Him be the glory."

"If you think that much about God, then why don't you come visit my church?" Deborah saw a window of opportunity for witnessing and decided to climb right through it.

"Oh, I'm too old to be starting up a new relationship with anybody," Mrs. Lewis countered. "But you keep doing what you doing and you'll be okay." She looked down at her grandson. "Whenever you think of snappin' off, especially around him, just think about how it used to make you feel when I did it to you. Don't ever want that feeling for your son. I didn't want that for you. When I gave birth to you and held you in my arms for the first time, I would have tried to kill anybody who dared try to hurt you. Then when it came down to it, I was the one who ended up hurting you." Mrs. Lewis was on the verge of getting emotional.

"Come on, Ma. Cut it out." Deborah put her arm around her mother and rested her head against her.

"I'm sorry—I'm just saying. I want you to be better and do better than me. You got that?"

"Yes, ma'am." Deborah stood straight and saluted her mother's orders.

"Don't get fresh now." Mrs. Lewis playfully swatted Deborah's behind.

"Ouch!" Deborah faked an injury.

"Yeah, like that little swat hurt that ba-dunk-a-dunk of yours."

"Ma! No, you didn't." A dropped jaw and smile covered Deborah's face.

"Yes, I did. What? I'm telling the truth. You got a big ol' butt. Especially since after having that baby. But don't be ashamed about it. Runs in the family." Mrs. Lewis leaned in and said to her daughter, "Now that I don't mind saying you got from me."

Both women burst out laughing. Deborah's son followed suit.

"You think that's funny?" Deborah said, squeezing his cheeks. "You think Mommy having a big ol' butt is funny?"

"He does, and Granny is about to see to it that he has a big tummy. If you don't mind, I'd like to run and get him some ice cream right quick. Maybe stop off at the park for a spell, too."

"I don't mind at all. That will give me an opportunity to work on my book."

"Oh, my. You finally dusted off that book you started all those years ago and got to working in it again." Mrs. Lewis was both hopeful and excited.

"Oh, no. I didn't mean my personal book. I meant a book I'm editing for someone. I haven't thought twice about that book I wrote since I last put it down."

"Well, maybe you just ought to." A little disappointed, Mrs. Lewis looked around until she spotted her grandson's diaper bag that Deborah always had packed and ready just in case. "I mean, you working on books that end up on *New York Times,* you might as well put that same effort into your own book. You get a chance to go on them fancy, long book tours like some of them other big-name authors do. You deserve it. You've been in this book business a mighty long time. It's long overdue you see the other side of it." She picked up the diaper bag and headed to the front door.

Deborah bounced her shoulders up and down modestly and said, "Yeah, well, I don't know. I'll have to see."

"Well, you know I'm here to support you no matter what. I'd love keeping my grandbaby while you go see the world on those book signings."

"Trust me, Mom, those book signings are overrated. It's not all that, especially once you run out of family, friends, and cousins to come buy a book." Deborah laughed.

"If you say so. But you're young. A change of scenery might do you some good." Mrs. Lewis opened the door. "Speaking of a change of scenery." A huge smile covered her face and she looked back at Deborah. "I'm sure you'll like this view." Mrs. Lewis stepped to the side, revealing an unexpected caller standing outside the door.

Deborah's eyes bucked. "Lynox . . ."

Chapter Twenty-six

"What are you doing here?" Unfortunately, Deborah wasn't as pleased as her mother was to see Lynox standing on her doorstep.

Lynox was all smiles, bearing a brown paper bag with an aroma that immediately invaded the front living room. "I know how busy you've been the last few days," Lynox started. "You've barely even had time to take a break to eat. I know this because I've asked you out to eat twice and you've declined because of your workload. So I figured if you couldn't come out and join me for a meal, then I'd bring it to you."

"Oh, my," Mrs. Lewis said. "What a sweet, sweet gesture. Isn't it, Deb?" Mrs. Lewis looked over her shoulder at her daughter.

Deborah just stood there stone-faced, actually fuming inside. "You didn't call first. Everyone knows you don't just stop by someone's house without calling. With cell phones now, there is no excuse." Deborah was talking to Lynox like he was the bug-a-boo guy she'd gone out on a blind date with and now couldn't get rid of.

Under ordinary circumstances, Deborah would have been wooed beyond measure by Lynox's gesture. For a man to be that thoughtful as to bring her lunch in the middle of the day, interrupting his own busy schedule, what woman wouldn't have appreciated that? But these weren't ordinary circumstances. Deborah was living a lie and the idea of being found out instantly put her on edge. She couldn't see past Lynox about to find out, the wrong way, about her son. She couldn't see past all that to appreciate the gesture.

Mrs. Lewis turned slowly from Deborah to face Lynox, slightly embarrassed at the tone her daughter had taken with the surprise caller. "Well, I love a spontaneous man. My husband used to do stuff like that for me all the time. And back then we didn't have cell phones, so the fact that it was indeed a true unexpected surprise was all the better in my book." She shot Deborah a sharp look over her shoulder before turning her attention back to Lynox.

"I'm sorry to catch you off guard. I hadn't planned on staying. I'm actually headed to a doctor's appointment," Lynox explained. "I just wanted to stop by and make sure you were over here eating and not just working yourself to death." Lynox said it in an apologetic tone.

"Well, as you can see, I'm working myself to death. And it still wouldn't have hurt for you to call." Deborah's tone was still snappy. She needed him to leave. Or she needed her mother and son to leave. Someone needed to leave before she had an anxiety attack.

"Actually, I had planned on calling you," Lynox explained, unable to force a smile, enthusiasm, or any excitement whatsoever from his tone. "I was just going to leave the food on your porch, then send you a text letting you know it was there. I don't know. Kind of thought it would be romantic. But I guess I'm not that great at living out romantic gestures personally—just writing about them I suppose. Anyway, my apologies." He looked down at his watch. "I better get going or I'll be late for my appointment." He went to walk away and then realized he was still holding the bag of food.

"Oh yeah." He placed the food down on the porch and then sarcastically said, "Guess I don't need to text you. Enjoy." The wounded puppy dog made an exit off the porch.

"Lynox, uh, wait." Deborah couldn't let things go down like this. Lynox was doing everything right; all the while she was doing everything wrong. If only he knew that her actions weren't personal attacks against him. They were a result of how she was feeling inside. Whenever she got overwhelmed and began to feel anxious, she got snappy and sometimes outright nasty. At the present, she was feeling both overwhelmed and anxious, so there was like a hurricane going on inside of her. She had to calm the storm.

Lynox had heard Deborah call out his name, but he was too furious inside to turn around and acknowledge her.

"Lynox. Hold on, please."

"No, it's cool. I see you're busy—looks like you're about to babysit and all."

"Babysit." Mrs. Lewis chuckled. "Looks like I'm the one who is about to babysit." She stepped outside. "So why don't you two go ahead and share this lunch while me and the little guy here go to get some ice cream." Mrs. Lewis stepped down off the porch. "I'll bring him back in about an hour. Is that enough time?" Mrs. Lewis looked at Lynox and winked.

Mrs. Lewis's kind gesture brought a smile back on his face. "Really, Miss . . ." Realizing he'd never been introduced to the grandmother of the child Deborah babysat for, his eyes asked her to fill in the blank of her last name.

"Mrs. Lewis," Deborah's mother obliged.

Now Deborah wished nothing more than that she had just let Lynox go ahead and leave.

"Lewis?" His eyes got bigger. "Your last name is Lewis too. Is that a coincidence, or are you two kin?"

"A coincidence?" Mrs. Lewis laughed. "I'm—"

"You're just leaving to take the baby for ice cream—remember?" Deborah reminded her mother, making a mental note that this couldn't go on much longer. The close calls were getting closer and closer. Just as soon as she and Lynox were alone, she wasn't going to hesitate to tell him the truth.

"Mrs. Lewis, really, you don't have to leave and come back. I'm sure you have things to do, otherwise, you wouldn't have been dropping off the little guy here for Deborah to babysit in the first place."

Deborah felt the life drain from her body. She could feel eyes of confusion burning on her face. She couldn't return her mother's glare.

"Deborah? Babysit her own—" Mrs. Lewis started.

"Nephew!" Deborah spat. It just came out. Where it came from, Deborah had no idea. But that lie shot out of her mouth like a curse word from a sailor's tongue.

"Nephew?" both Lynox and Mrs. Lewis said in unison.

"You mean this little guy is blood?" Lynox asked. "I should have seen the resemblance." He stared at Deborah's son. "Shoot, he has your nose and your mouth."

Mrs. Lewis stared at her daughter strangely, waiting for her to correct Lynox.

"I guess that explains why you two have the same last name," Lynox said to both Deborah and Mrs. Lewis. Now he looked at Mrs. Lewis. "So you are Deborah's . . ." Lynox was expecting for Mrs. Lewis to say aunt or first cousin or something.

"I'm Deborah's . . . mo . . . ther?" She looked at Deborah to make sure it was okay to tell him that. Because something weird was going on here.

"Mother!" Lynox said in shock. He then threw his shocked expression at Deborah and then back at Mrs. Lewis.

"Yes, that's right." Deborah nodded, letting her mother know it was okay to tell the truth as far as their relationship was concerned. "I guess I never did get to formally introduce you two, huh?" Deborah tried to put an innocent smile on her face, but when she swallowed hard, she must have swallowed the smile as well. "Lynox, this is actually my mother, Mrs. Lewis." She tried with all her might to keep the smile she'd just once again forced to cover her lips. The smile held long enough for her to speak those few words to Lynox, but when she turned to make the introductions to her mother, it quickly melted away. How could it not with the hot look Mrs. Lewis was shooting her daughter? "And, Ma, this is Lynox."

Mrs. Lewis just stood frozen, waiting for some type of explanation from Deborah. She'd be waiting until a cold day in hell if she thought Deborah was going to give her one right then and there . . . in front of Lynox. Explaining to her mother would mean explaining to Lynox. And once again, this was not how the truth was supposed to go down. But something told Deborah that she just might be able to keep the lie going; but would her mother?

Chapter Twenty-seven

"Well, Mrs. Lewis, the pleasure truly is all mine," Lynox said, extending his hand.

"Yes, Mr. Lynox, mine too." Mrs. Lewis was still quite dumbfounded.

"Please, just Lynox is fine." He looked to Deborah. "Honestly, I had no intentions of staying. Really; I just wanted to do something nice for you is all." Lynox was putting his tail back between his legs at the recollection of how Deborah had jumped on him for coming over unannounced.

"And, I'm sorry," Deborah apologized, taking Lynox's hand and looking him in the eyes. "It's just that . . . well, you know how it is when you're flowing in a manuscript."

"Yeah, and not to mention you've got to worry about taking care of little man here, too." He nodded toward her son. "That's awful nice of you to keep your sister's kid for her, knowing you have to work, too."

"Sister?" both Deborah and Mrs. Lewis said at the same time.

"Oh . . . then I guess he's your brother's kid?" Lynox thought for a minute. "But I thought you said you were an only child."

Oh snaps! Deborah felt so cold busted. How in the world was she going to get out of this one? *Think, Debbie. Think. Think. Think.* And so she thought. And she came up with this: "Well, see, he's not really a nephew

. . . nephew . . . blood nephew. His mother is just a real, real close family friend." Deborah needed a coconspirator. It would be taking a risk to use her mother as one, but she had no other choice. "Isn't that right, Ma?" Deborah swallowed again and waited on razor's edge for her mother to reply.

"Oh, yeah," Mrs. Lewis stated, still giving Deborah the evil eye. "The boy's mother is really close to the family." She gave Deborah a sarcastic look. "Why I almost even consider her to be my daughter—almost."

"That's nice," Lynox replied. "Guess next time I'll have to think, and throw a Happy Meal or something in the mix for the little guy." Lynox winked at the toddler. "Anyway, let me get going. Don't want to be late for my appointment."

"I'll walk you to your car," Deborah said, eager to get away from her mother. She did not look forward to being left alone to explain the situation to her. Once the couple arrived at Lynox's car, Deborah took the liberty of apologizing once again for being so snappish toward Lynox. Truth be told, she absolutely loved the gesture. She thought it to be most romantic. She was just caught off guard and didn't know how to respond. Under pressure, instead of being cool, calm, and collected, her emotions kicked into overdrive and she got all fired up. That's how her mother had always reacted to things. Naturally, that's how Deborah reacted to things.

"I'd like to meet your friend, the kid's mother. You never talk about any of your friends. I've only heard you refer to the sisters at church. But you do have a life outside of just the church family, don't you?" Lynox put his hands up in defense just in case Deborah took his comment the wrong way. "Not that there's anything wrong with having a church family and all."

Deborah chuckled. "I hear you. But I guess I'm just so into my writing thing, raising my . . . babysitting my nephew. I just don't have time for the girlfriend thing, you know."

"I hear you. But you have to have a life, too. You gotta get out and live. Otherwise, how do you meet a fine, handsome, successful man like myself?"

"Now that's one thing I didn't miss about you over the years, your cockiness."

"Woman, you know I'm just messing with you." Lynox brushed his hand down Deborah's cheek.

There was something about Lynox's touch that was magic. It calmed Deborah. It made her happy—peaceful. As bad as she felt about not being truthful with him when it came to her readymade family, moments like this almost made it worth it—almost.

"I apologize in advance if this makes you uneasy in front of your mother and all, but I can't help it." Lynox took Deborah's face in his hands and planted the most delicate but, at the same time, sensual kiss on her lips she'd ever had in her life.

For a moment, Deborah forgot about her entire life. It was just her and Lynox. No one else. Nothing else. She didn't know how long the kiss went on as her tongue tangled with his. But what she did know was that when it ended, she could have gone for seconds.

"Apology accepted," Deborah whispered, her eyes still closed. "Now, do you accept mine?" She opened her eyes. She was still nose to nose with Lynox. She could feel his breath like a summer breeze whisking across her face. Thank God they were out in public, in front of her mother, and that he had a doctor's appointment; otherwise, the two of them might have found themselves caught up in an act of sin.

"Apology accepted." He gave her a little peck on the forehead. "But like I said, I'd love to meet your friend. Let's all go out, have some fun. Take the edge off so you won't be so on edge." He playfully began snapping at Deborah's nose like a crab.

"I hear you, and I'll make it happen just as soon as I find the time."

"Make the time. I've learned that you have to make the time or else you'll spend an eternity trying to find it. I've already waited an eternity, it seems, to get with you. I'm not trying to wait an eternity to live life with you . . . really live life."

"Mr. Lynox," Deborah said, mimicking her mother, "you are one amazing man. You have no idea what a woman would do to have a man like you in her life."

"Aww, how sweet." Lynox pulled Deborah in for a hug.

Deborah leaned against Lynox's strong, manly chest while thinking, *No, really, you have no idea what a woman would do to have a man like you in her life.* She pulled away from Lynox and looked over at her son in her mother's arms. *Even deny her own child.*

Chapter Twenty-eight

"Denying your own son, Deborah? Now that's an all-time low," Mrs. Lewis spat as she followed Deborah back into the house after Lynox had pulled off.

"Mom, not now." Deborah raised her hands in frustration. "Besides, didn't you tell your grandson that you were taking him to get some ice cream?"

"Oh, this little fella right here?" She bounced her grandson in her arms. "You mean your nephew?"

Deborah turned with the quickness and they both stopped in their tracks. "Look, Mom, there is a good reason why I had to do that, but you wouldn't understand." Deborah started walking again, heading to her home office.

"The last time I checked, there was never a good reason to tell a lie, and on top of that, the lie that denies your own son—your own flesh and blood. Deborah, how could you?" Mrs. Lewis's tone was laced with disappointment in her daughter. Looking at her grandson's precious face, she couldn't imagine anyone wanting to deny him. She began to tear up.

"How could I not?" Deborah flopped down in the chair at her desk, refusing to look at her mother or the child she was denying. "You spent years with a man who loved your dirty drawers. I end up with men who just want to get in mine. Well, Lynox isn't like that. Lynox is the man of every woman's dreams, and he likes me, Momma . . . a lot. Mr. Lynox Chase is chasing me.

He can have almost any woman out there and he wants Deborah."

"Okay, and I get that. So why does that mean you have to hide the fact that you have a child? This ain't V.C. Andrews's *Flowers in the Attic*."

Deborah ignored her mother's sarcasm and answered her straight up. "Because he's not the type of man who is willing to settle down with a woman who already has kids who are not his. He told me so. He told me before I had a chance to tell him that I was one of those women who already had a kid—who wasn't his."

"Well that's when you should have done either one of two things, tell him the truth, or hightail it on out of there because obviously, no matter how perfect you think he is, he's going to see you as imperfect."

Those words stung Deborah to the core. She stood from her chair. "Imperfect? So now I'm imperfect? You couldn't come up with a word more diplomatic than that?" Deborah's tone got loud. "That's my momma—always there to remind me what a screw-up I am. Always there to remind me how *imperfect* I am." When Deborah enunciated the word, spittle flew out of her mouth, hitting both her mother and her son.

Mrs. Lewis calmly wiped her face, unaware that some had gotten on her grandson. "I'm not saying you are imperfect, what I'm saying is that that's how he is going to see you, so your thinking he is perfect is in vain."

"You need me to go out to the garage and get you a shovel so you can keep piling salt onto the wound?" Deborah yelled at her mother. She was loud. But she was so used to getting loud whenever she got upset that she didn't realize just how loud she was.

"Look, calm down," her mother ordered. "There you go again getting the boy's nerves all rattled." She looked down at her grandson, who was now clinging to her neck, his back facing his mother.

"I don't give a darn. It's because of him I'm in this mess."

Mrs. Lewis remained dead silent. She thanked God her grandson didn't understand the words that were coming out of his mother's mouth. But she understood them and they brought a flood of tears to her eyes. "I can't believe you just said that." Mrs. Lewis snorted.

"Oh, don't go getting all dramatic. I didn't mean it like that," Deborah played it down. "It's just that you are making a bigger deal out of this than it is." Deborah walked back over to the chair and sat down. "I'm going to tell Lynox . . . when the time is right. It's just that the time keeps being all wrong. You pop up, then he pops up, and I'm just never prepared for it to go down like that."

Mrs. Lewis thought over her next words carefully. "Then until you can tell Lynox the truth, why don't you just let the boy stay with me?" she offered. "You know I don't mind." Mrs. Lewis waited with bated breath for a reply from her daughter.

Now that was an idea Deborah could live with. "Really? That would be helpful." She turned around in her chair and looked at her mother. "Just a week. Just give me until the end of the week to plan on telling him." She turned back around in her chair, staring at her computer screen, realizing just how helpful her mother's gesture would be.

"O . . . okay," Mrs. Lewis said nervously, hoping her daughter wouldn't see through to her true intentions. "I mean, even after that, after you guys break up when you tell him, he can still stay with me so that you can get yourself together. Because I know it's going to be hard on you and all." Mrs. Lewis should have stopped talking then, but she made the mistake and kept right on chattering away. "You'll probably be upset and not in too good of a mood. And I just don't want our little guy around to . . ." Mrs. Lewis's words trailed off once she realized Deborah was slowly turning to face her with a knowing look on her face.

"So that's what this is all about? You ain't trying to help me. You're worried I'm going to trip out and snap off or something, aren't you?"

Of course Mrs. Lewis was. She wasn't going to tell Deborah that though. Not with her mouth. But her eyes and the look on her face told it all.

Deborah stood up from the chair and went and snatched her son out of her mother's arms. "Mom, just go."

"No, Deb, wait. That's not what I meant."

"That's exactly what you meant. You think if Lynox leaves me—by the way, thanks for the vote of confidence—that I'm going to take it out on my son."

"Well, you did just say you felt it was all his fault."

"But I told you I didn't mean it like that." Deborah rolled her eyes at her mother. "I can't do this with you right now. Why don't you just go and we'll talk tomorrow or something? This is too much."

"Fine, but why don't you let me take the baby so you can get some work done?" She reached for her grandson. Deborah pulled him away.

"Naw, he's fine."

"Deborah, please," Mrs. Lewis practically begged.

"Mom, why are you doing that? Why are you acting like that—like I'm one of those crazy women who is gonna drown my kid or something?"

"Because I know how you are," Mrs. Lewis said without hesitation.

"You know how I am?" Deborah looked her mother up and down. "Why, Mother, I'm just like you? I'm a hell raiser just like you used to be? I'm nothing like you. And even if that were true, heck, you didn't kill me by drowning, did you?" Then Deborah said under her breath, "I should be so unlucky."

"Yeah, but I had thoughts of doing it," Mrs. Lewis admitted and the room turned stone cold and silent.

Deborah couldn't believe the words that had just fallen from her mother's lips. The look of disbelief was plastered all over her face.

"Yes, that's right. Some days would just be so dark, thoughts of doing really bad things would enter my mind. Thoughts of doing bad things to myself, to other people."

"Me being *other people?*" Deborah clarified.

"I was so miserable. I knew deep down inside I was making you miserable. So, for a blink of a second"— Mrs. Lewis snapped her fingers—"I imagined putting us both out of misery," Mrs. Lewis admitted.

"If you knew you were making everybody so miserable with the way you acted, why didn't you just stop?" Deborah inquired. "I mean, sometimes I know I can get out of hand. But I can always reel things back in. I've never gotten to the point where I feel like I'm losing complete control."

"And I hope you never do. Honestly, I hope you never get as bad off as I did. I screamed, hollered, cussed, and fussed until the day you moved out of the house. And a little bit after that. Heck, your father was pretty much working all the time so he didn't get the full wrath of me like you did." Mrs. Lewis chuckled. "I wasn't stupid, I knew why he was the first on the list when it came time to sign up for overtime at his job. He wanted to hop on any opportunity he could to be out of that house so he wouldn't have to deal with my nasty attitude. I can't even blame him." She shook her head. "But like I was saying, I carried on a little bit after you moved out. Only thing is, no one was there to hear it but me. Yep, that's right, I still ran around the house spewing venom out loud with no ears to hear it but myself. Then I start having those mini strokes."

"Mom! Strokes? What are you talking about?" Deborah was shocked. This was the first she'd heard about her mother ever having mini strokes.

"Yeah, just little ones." Mrs. Lewis shooed her hand. "I brought them on myself. After the first couple, I toned it down a little. After that last one scared me. I knew if I kept things up, I'd kill myself. I just didn't know the damage my actions were causing to my body."

Deborah didn't even realize her eyes were full of tears. "How come I never knew this? How come you never told me?"

"Oh, you were in college. You were seeing Elton. For once in your life—since you were away from me—you were happy. You were free. You were free from me and my behavior—finally. I didn't want to pull you back in."

"But you could have died," Deborah cried. "Then how would that have made me feel?"

"But I didn't die, and that's all that matters. God let me live to see another day and to change my ways. I thank Him for that. Now I just need Him to do a work in you."

Deborah wiped her tears. "I promise you, Mother, He's done a work in me. I'm nowhere near where I used to be. Having a child now has made me want to be better." Deborah smiled at her son.

"And that's good to hear. But the question is, has it? Has having a child made you better? Or, in all actuality, has it made you worse?" Deborah didn't respond quickly enough for Mrs. Lewis, so she continued. "Or has it made you even more on edge? Do you fly off the handle when your son does something that kids do, like make a mess? Like not pick up toys? Like get into stuff?" Still, Mrs. Lewis didn't get an answer quick enough from her daughter. "Do you"—she made quotation marks with her hands—"spank and yell at him for doing what is deemed to be normal for a kid his age?"

Deborah let off a nervous laugh. "Well, yeah, but, don't all parents do that? And you said it yourself a million times, that's how black folks raise our kids. We don't do no time out and all that crap. We have to instill fear in our kids so they don't run around back sassin' and thinking they gon' whoop on us. Do you know I saw a talk show that had parents on it with kids that be putting their hands on their parents? Not nary one of them parents were black. And you know why? Because we ain't having that. We put the smack down from jump."

"Yeah, we teach so much violence, anger, hate, and hurt that we don't even realize that at the end of the day, some of us, who operate under those conditions, are raising pit bulls. We are teaching our kids to be loud, rude, aggressive, to hit. So when I see you and how you are, I can't blame you, but I darn sure can help you."

Deborah shook her head as if she was trying to get a grasp—a clear understanding—of exactly what her mother was trying to say to her. "So do you consider me one of those pit bulls you're referring to? Do you feel as though with how you raised me, you raised me to be a pit bull?"

"If I'm being honest, I see some traits. I really do."

Deborah wanted to fly off the handle. Her mother basically calling her a dog—a female dog—pissed her off to no end. But she knew reacting the way she really wanted to act would only prove her mother's point. "Well, thanks a lot, once again, Mother. That's what every girl wants to hear, her mother call her a female dog. It would have been better had you just come right out and called me a bit—"

"I would never," Mrs. Lewis said, cutting Deborah off.

"Ha, maybe now you wouldn't, but you called me out of my name, including the 'B' word, enough times when I was growing up to last me a lifetime," Deborah reminded her mother. "You know, women on the street have never called me half the names you called me, and you're my mother."

"And I'm sorry, Deborah!" By now, Mrs. Lewis was raising her voice. She was tired of apologizing, but still had Deborah throwing the past in her face. "How many more times do you want to hear me say it?"

"Until it doesn't hurt anymore," Deborah shouted back, startling her son, causing him to cry. "Oh shut up, you big crybaby," she snapped at her son. "Don't nobody want to hear that mess right now." This made the boy cry even harder.

Mrs. Lewis took her grandson from Deborah's arms and snuggled him in her arms. "It's okay. Everything is going to be okay."

"You darn right it will be, just as soon as you quit coming over here, criticizing my parenting like you were this perfect parent."

"I know I wasn't the perfect parent. I'm not using myself as an example of the parent you should be. I'm using myself as an example of the parent you shouldn't be." There was plenty more Mrs. Lewis could have said. There was plenty more she wanted to say. But she knew that, for now, enough had been said. From this point on, she would limit what she said to her daughter. From this point on she decided that her actions would speak much louder than words.

Chapter Twenty-nine

"There's my little guy." Helen greeted him with a smile as Deborah brought her son to children's church. "Oh, no, looks like somebody's been crying," Helen observed, noticing the frown on Deborah's son's face and his tear-stained cheeks.

"He's all right," Deborah said as she glared at her son. "He just almost made us late by pooping on himself right before we were about to walk out the door."

"So I take it the potty training is not quite where it needs to be."

"Hardly." Deborah sucked her teeth and rolled her eyes.

"Well, just hang in there. I hear boys are harder to potty train than girls. I can't even tell you how long it took for my son to catch on."

"Well, hopefully it won't take mine too long. I'll most certainly be needing the patience of Job to keep from hurting that boy." Deborah laughed.

"Now I do remember having to get my son's legs with the switch a couple of times. And if memory serves correctly, it wasn't too much longer after that, that he got it down pat." Helen high-fived Deborah. "You know how black people gotta get things done with their babies."

Deborah smiled in agreement. On the inside she frowned a little, wondering if perhaps this whole "black way" of raising kids was just like an urban myth—an old wives' tale. Just something black people used to justify the way they bring up their children. Just yes-terday Deborah was watching an episode of *Oprah* she had recorded. Joe and Katherine Jackson were being interviewed by Oprah. When Oprah posed the question as to whether Joe Jackson had whooped on the kids, all three pretty much agreed that it was okay for him to answer honestly, because that's how black people raised their children. Deborah could only imagine how many black families had caught that episode and per-haps were now using those very words to justify the way they were raising their children.

That was the only thing that had really set off a red flag in Deborah's mind as to how the yelling and fussing and carrying on was truly affecting her son. It hadn't been her own emotions she'd felt back when her mother used to do that to her. It wasn't even the conversations her mother had tried to have with her in convincing her that there was a better way. Deborah knew firsthand the effect, but it took some icons speak-ing about it to make her look at it in a new light. It took her imagining children all over the world having to be subjected to that type of behavior by their parents, just because they'd watched an episode of a talk show and might have taken from the show that it was okay for black families to raise their children under such condi-tions.

But no sooner had those thoughts soaked completely in, than Joe Jackson said something very powerful. He shared with Oprah that the way he'd brought up his children had kept them all out of trouble and out of jail.

"Amen, hallelujah," Deborah had shouted, and just like that, her spirit was okay with some yelling, fuss-ing, and cussing here and there if it meant keeping her boy out of trouble. If it meant her, and not the system, teaching him a lesson. So this morning, when he went to the bathroom on himself instead of telling her he had to go potty, she laid into him with her tongue real good.

"I bet you you won't poop on yourself anymore," she'd exclaimed to her son, only she'd used the more vulgar word for poop.

"Sister Helen," Deborah said as she handed her son over to the children's church leader, "I know exactly how black people gotta get things done with their kids. So trust me, he'll be potty trained by the end of the month by the time I get done with him."

"And I'll help out while he's here with me. I'll make sure I ask him does he have to go potty and all that good stuff."

"That's cool, but he had me so heated, I just threw a diaper on him so I wouldn't have to deal with it. I'm not trying to be in the middle of getting my praise on and see my baby's number pop up on the monitor for me to come get him."

Helen laughed. "I feel ya. But it still won't hurt for me to ask him."

"I appreciate you," Deborah said before turning to exit.

"Enjoy the service," Helen said to her back and then tended to the children.

Enjoy the service was exactly what Deborah did. Heck, she even broke a sweat getting her praise on. When Pastor asked if anyone needed prayer, or for someone to touch and agree with them, she was one of the first to head down to the altar.

"What do you need prayer for?" Pastor Margie asked her.

"Please pray for me and my mother," Deborah had cried. "I want to be able to forgive her for my childhood. I want to get rid of the anger and not take it out on my own son." Deborah couldn't believe she had said those words. It must have been the spirit talking, because let her flesh tell it, there wasn't anything wrong with the way she acted toward her son. "I don't want to be like my mother. When my son gets older, I don't want him to hold the same grudges against me that I hold against my mother. I need prayer, Pastor."

Pastor Margie began touching and agreeing with Deborah that God would send His comforter, the Holy Spirit, to direct Deborah's path and to fill her heart with forgiveness. That any family curses be broken in the name of Jesus. That God would send a legion of angels to watch over Deborah's son, to protect him and his little spirit. In Jesus' name they prayed and in Jesus' name they touched and agreed with an "amen."

"Thank you, Pastor," Deborah said. "I receive it."

"I hope you mean that, Sister Deborah, because that's the only way you're gonna get it, is to open up your heart and receive it. You know the God we serve ain't in to force-feeding nobody. Either you're going to receive His gifts or not."

Deborah nodded and then allowed an altar worker to aid her back to her seat. She truly felt in her spirit that God was going to do a work when it came to her mother and her own role as a mother.

"Dang it," Deborah said with the snap of her fingers. She'd forgotten to ask her pastor for prayer when it came to something else as well: her and Lynox and the whole thing with her pretending her son was her nephew. Everything in her wanted to stroll right back down to that altar for seconds, but she didn't want to be greedy. *One prayer at a time,* she thought. But by putting the situation off yet again, would she be a day late and a prayer short?

Chapter Thirty

Deborah was excited to be spending the day with Lynox. She'd yet to talk to her mother since their big blowup a few days ago. She intended to though. That was the next thing on her list. First, she needed to take care of the situation that was really stressing her out and was probably the cause uprooting all the tension between Deborah and her mother these days.

Thank God Helen had been willing to do a little baby-sitting for Deborah in her mother's absence. Of course, Deborah did not tell Helen she needed her services so that she could go out on date with Lynox. No matter what Helen said, Deborah felt a little part of Helen still desired Lynox. After all, a big part of Deborah had still desired him and was bound and determined to get him at all cost. The cost: making a fool out of herself several times and then ultimately denying the existence of her own child.

All of that was about to change, though—today. Deborah had prayed on the situation with her and Lynox and she was certain she'd heard God clearly say to her, "Tell him. Tell him the truth." So that's exactly what Deborah was going to do today—at all cost. She had made it up in her mind that nothing and no one would interfere.

In hopes that Lynox wouldn't flip out too much, she decided she'd tell him in a public place. That way, more than likely, he couldn't overreact or anything. After all, he was somewhat of a local celebrity. Even if most authors weren't recognizable, he had quite the female following. He wouldn't want them to see him in a negative light.

This worked out well for Deborah, because if after finding out the truth Lynox decided to leave her hanging, it wouldn't be some huge production. In all the romance novels Deborah had read in her lifetime, public breakups were always less dramatic. All that begging and crying didn't go on.

She thought back to the last time she and Lynox parted ways. That had been in a public place. A bench at Easton Towne Center. This time though, Deborah wouldn't be the one doing the leaving, and if God was on her side, at the end of the day, Lynox wouldn't be doing any leaving either.

"You didn't have to drive all the way here," Lynox told Deborah as they met outside of a designated store inside the shopping center. "I wouldn't have minded scooping you up at all. The price of gas is crazy. Didn't you know carpooling was the new thing?"

"That and biking," Deborah added with a smile. It wasn't even a nervous smile. She was *so* ready to do this. And whatever would be would be.

"So, are you challenging me to a bike ride?"

Deborah laughed. "Tuh—I haven't been on a bike since Columbus set sail. I probably couldn't make it a few pedals without falling on my tail."

"Nonsense. You know what they say, once you learn how to ride a bike, you never forget."

"From the sounds of things, I take it you're some pro or something." The two started walking toward no particular destination. "You ride?"

Lynox thought for a second before breaking out in a chuckle and admitting, "No. My bike would probably end up on top of yours."

Deborah joined him in his laugh. "See, told you. I'd be a fool to try to climb my tail on somebody's bike."

"Yeah, me too," Lynox relented. "So maybe we didn't have to bike it over here, but I still could have come and picked you up."

Deborah just kept walking. No way was she going to have Lynox pick her up. This time it wasn't because she was afraid of the whole situation with her having a son. This time it was because there was a chance if she'd allowed him to bring her to Easton, she'd be needing to hitch a ride home.

"Speaking of bikes . . ." Lynox rushed away from Deborah's side to a display in a window. The mannequins had on biker gear. "Now check out those helmets." Lynox pointed at the snazzy bike helmets the mannequins were wearing.

"Yeah," Deborah said, walking up beside Lynox and staring at the display. "Those must be the Cadillac of helmets. Look at all the colors with that pearly paint and the bedazzled out one for women."

"Yeah." Lynox stared. "Makes you just want to go in that store, buy 'em, go out, buy a bike . . ." At this point, Lynox slid his hand around Deborah's hand. "Get on it with the woman you want to spend the rest of your life with and just take a chance—no matter how many times you fall." He turned to look at Deborah. Her eyes met his in a sentimental gaze.

This was getting too heavy for Deborah. It was like a fairytale coming to life; a fairytale that could be over before it ever even got started. As much as she wanted to just stand there and stare into Lynox's eyes while listening to him say all the right things, she knew she couldn't. The more she did, the harder it would be for her to be able to tell him something that could possibly put an end to things anyway.

"What do you say we head to the food court?" Deborah changed the subject, slipping her hand from Lynox's. The food court, over a plate of chow mein noodles and orange chicken. Or a slice of Sbarro pizza; yes, that's where she'd tell him the truth. If through a man's stomach was the way to his heart, her chances of preserving their relationship would be much better in the food court.

Lynox pulled out his cell phone and looked at the time. "I guess it is after lunchtime, huh?"

"Yes, and I'm starved." Deborah rubbed her stomach for added effect.

"Then to the food court we shall go." Lynox extended his elbow for Deborah to loop her arm through. She did, and the two headed to the food court arm in arm.

They were almost there when they heard, "Is that that Chase guy? The author?"

"Yes, I think so," another voice replied.

The voices were coming from behind them. Never one to pass up the opportunity to acknowledge his reading fans, Lynox turned around and greeted the two women who had been questioning his identity.

"OMG!" one of the women screamed. "It is him." She immediately raced up to Lynox and threw her arms around his neck. "Mr. Chase, you look exactly like the picture on the back of your book."

"And even better than that spread in the Black Expressions catalogue," the other girl added, bumping her friend out of the way so that she could get a hug from Lynox as well.

While the two vied for his attention, they were making such a ruckus that soon others stopped to see what was going on. Before Lynox knew it, he was swarmed with females.

"Are you going to write a sequel?" an eager fan asked Lynox.

"If so, when is it coming out? I just can't get enough of that fine, tall glass of water, Brad."

All the women giggled and blushed at just the mention of Lynox's lead character, Brad. They were acting as if he were a real person and not just some character Lynox had created for a book.

Deborah stood back in awe as she watched Lynox take it all in with pleasure. A smile caressed her face as she thought, *My guy, the famous author. Watch out, Carl Weber and Eric Jerome Dickey!* But no sooner had those thoughts escaped her mind, than a huge knot formed in the pit of her stomach.

"Helen?" The word, in a mumble, came from Deborah's mouth. Could it have been? Was Helen the woman she could barely see far off in the distance over the swarming crowd of fan's heads?

Deborah stood on her tippy toes, but that wasn't working. She still couldn't get a good view of the woman. "No, it can't be," she finally told herself. "She's home babysitting my son," she reasoned. She closed her eyes, took a deep breath, then opened them again, hoping to see things a little more clearly. Hoping to clearly see that the woman was, in fact, not Helen.

The woman had walked a little closer, but had stopped and was now staring through a store window. The similarities between the woman and Helen were uncanny—but it couldn't have been.

Lynox was preoccupied with answering the questions all the reading fans were throwing at him. Deborah couldn't rest until she proved that woman was not Helen. Because if it was Helen, that meant that her son was not far from her.

Deborah began walking sideways, her eyes glued to the woman's every move. Before Deborah knew it, something had stopped her in her tracks. "Oh, excuse me," Deborah said after bumping into a woman.

The woman smiled and nodded, but Deborah could see her true feelings of disdain behind the fake smile. After all, the woman had been nibbling on a pretzel that Deborah practically knocked out of her hand when she bumped into her.

"I'm so sorry." Deborah offered up one final apology without even looking at the woman.

She continued to walk sideways until the woman she'd been scoping out was in full view. And as the woman came into full view, Deborah could see that she was pushing one of those mall rented strollers. Since it was a side profile, she couldn't see the occupant of the stroller, but what she could see were the shoes she'd just purchased her son two weeks ago on the little feet that were kicking from the stroller.

"Oh my God," Deborah said, her body weakening and her having to catch herself from falling. "This can't be. This just can't be." But it was. The woman and the child turned and faced Deborah's direction, and Deborah could say beyond a doubt that the woman was Helen and the child was her son.

Deborah threw her hand over her forehead, which was throbbing, and her other hand over her stomach, which was aching, and not because she was hungry. But when Lynox just happened to look up in search of Deborah, and then landed eyes on her, that's just what he thought: that she was signaling to him that she was hungry. He was reminded that it was after lunchtime and he and his girl had been on their way to the food court before he got caught up in Fandemonium.

"Look, ladies, I'm sorry, but I have to go now," Lynox told the fans. "But if you want to be kept up to date on my future works and what I have going on and where I'm going to be, check out my Web site."

"Oh, I wanna know where you gonna be all right," a woman flirted while others giggled.

Lynox acknowledged her comment with a humble smile and then peeled himself away from the crowd and began to walk away.

"One more thing, Mr. Chase," a woman called out. "Do you have a girlfriend?" Once again, the other women chuckled.

Lynox stopped in his tracks. Staring at Deborah he replied, "As a matter of fact, I don't." He strutted over to Deborah and said, "I have a woman." Once again he extended his elbow for Deborah to grab a hold of. Just as they had been a few moments ago, the two were arm in arm, heading off to the food court.

Deborah would have blushed at Lynox's gesture, but she was too busy trying to keep her eyes on Helen. She deliberately and quickly tugged Lynox toward the food court and away from the direction of Helen.

"Hey, you must be hungry." Lynox laughed as Deborah practically dragged him toward the food court.

She had spotted Helen, but she could not risk Helen spotting her. Once she felt they were safely out of Helen's view, she relaxed and tried to have a civil conversation with Lynox. "You know you left a lot of disappointed, heartbroken women back there." Deborah nodded over her shoulder at the women whose eyes she could feel burning a hole through her back. Eyes envious that it was she who was walking arm in arm with the great novelist instead of them. Deborah loved how it felt. She loved how Lynox made her feel. She loved everything about him. Caught up in his rapture, eventually she'd forgotten all about the fact that Helen, with her son in tow, had been heading in their direction. Lucky for Deborah, though, Helen had stopped off into a store.

"So what do you have a taste for?" Deborah asked as she and Lynox approached the food court.

He looked down at Deborah, giving her the googly eyes. "Trust me, you don't want to know." He immediately turned his attention away from Deborah and began scanning the choices of vendors in the food court.

"Oooh, you bad, bad boy you. Did you forget you're out with a Christian?" Deborah asked while she scanned her choices as well.

"And did you forget that you are out with a man?" he reminded her. "Or don't y'all cover that kind of stuff in that singles ministry of yours."

"We cover lots of stuff. As a matter of fact, you should join us one Friday."

Lynox looked over at Deborah like she was crazy. "Woman, I can think of a lot of better things to do on a Friday night than sit around listening to a bunch of lonely, single women male bash."

Deborah play punched Lynox in his arm. "That is not what the singles ministry is about. It's a support group for singles." Deborah thought for a moment. "Although I do admit that, once upon a time, that's exactly what it used to be." She laughed, thinking back to some of the stories she used to hear from those women. But thank God for taking the ministry to a higher level in Him.

"See there," Lynox quipped.

"But it's not like that anymore. Back then it was just single women. Now there are men in the ministry as well. It's different. It's better. You should really think about joining us one Friday."

"Ah, first it will be a Friday, then a Wednesday Bible Study, then a Sunday or two. The next thing you know, I'll be an usher," Lynox joked on.

Deborah play punched him once again. "And what would be so wrong with that? I know I wouldn't mind following an usher like you anywhere—including hell," Deborah joked. "You know I'm just joking on that one."

Lynox turned and grabbed Deborah by the shoulders. "I know you're joking. But just so you know, I'd follow you to heaven, because I know that's where you're going."

"Oh yeah, and how can you be so sure about that?"

"Because where else do angels go?" He planted a kiss on Deborah's forehead and she thought she would die. Lynox pulled away from her and turned his attention back to the smorgasbord of food choices. "So, have you decided what you'll have?"

"You," slipped out of Deborah's mouth before she could catch it.

Lynox laughed. "Oooh you bad, bad girl you." He shook his head. "But seriously, I think I'm going to have a good old-fashioned burger and fries from that joint right there."

Deborah looked toward where Lynox was pointing. "It's been a long time since I've had a nice greasy burger. I think I'll have the same."

"Great, then could you order for me?" Lynox asked Deborah as he began examining his hands. "I just shook a million hands. I need to go wash mine."

"No problem," Deborah agreed.

Lynox pulled out a twenty dollar bill and handed it to Deborah. He then headed toward the restroom to go wash his hands.

Deborah placed the food order. Once the order was up, she found a table for her and Lynox and sat down. She whipped out a bottle of hand sanitizer, put some on her hands, prayed over her food, and then took a bite of her burger. "Ummmm," she couldn't resist saying out loud. The burger was delicious. She took another bite, then closed her eyes as she melted in the taste. When she opened her eyes, Lynox was standing there with a distraught look on his face.

"What? What's the matter?" Deborah asked with a mouthful of burger.

"I'll bet you a million dollars you'll never guess who I just saw," Lynox said, slowly sitting down at the table.

Deborah thought for a minute, and that's when she remembered that she'd too seen someone who had given her that same reaction. So right then and there, something told Deborah that if she opened her mouth and guessed, she'd be a million dollars richer.

Chapter Thirty-one

"I saw Helen," Lynox informed Deborah as he stood over her, still looking a little stunned. "She didn't see me though. She was coming out of the women's restroom as I was going into the men's. And guess what?"

Deborah braced herself for what Lynox might say next. Perhaps it would be, "And guess what? She was with a kid. She told me it was your kid." In those few seconds, all Deborah could think was why had she just never come right out and told him about having a child? Now, exactly what she didn't want to happen was about to happen. He was going to tell her how he'd found out about her child before she had a chance to tell him. Deborah couldn't let that happen. The clock was ticking, but she was bound and determined to beat Lynox to the punch.

"She was with a kid, I know," Deborah started, then opened her mouth to say the words, "My kid." But that never happened. Lynox interrupted her before she could.

"Yep—a kid. Ain't that something? She's got a kid," he said with a look of disdain as he sat down in front of his food. "Now you definitely don't have to worry about me ever hooking back up with her again." Lynox laughed, but then looked at Deborah to find the most serious look on her face. He grabbed her hands. "Oh, baby, you know I was just kidding. There was never a chance for me and that girl anyway. But her having a kid just drills in my point that much further." He took a bite of his food. "No readymade family for me."

Deborah was now looking at him with disdain. "You know you shouldn't talk with your mouth full." Deborah stood up abruptly. "You know, depending on what you have to say, I suggest that sometimes you not talk at all."

All Lynox's talk that made it seem like single women with kids were like the plague was taking its toll on Deborah. She was one of those women. How could she even think twice about wanting to be with a man who felt that way about women with children? Sure, just like one of the saints in the singles ministry had pointed out, he deserved to have his opinion and it was his choice whether he wanted to date a woman with kids. But did he have to keep drilling in his point and making it seem like the women should be locked up and the key thrown away?

"Whoa, relax." Lynox held his hands up in defense. "I'm sorry. I don't even know why I mentioned her." Lynox took another bite of his food. "Although I can't imagine what type of dude would knock up that nut job. Bet he's sorry." Lynox chuckled.

"I don't even know why I'm putting myself through this," Deborah exclaimed. "Not for a man who talks with his mouth full. Disgusting!" Deborah snatched up her purse and ran off in hysterics.

Poor Lynox sat there dazed and confused with fries in hand all set to shovel in more food to his already full mouth. "Hey, sorry," he apologized, food spewing from his full mouth as he talked. "I didn't know that was one of your pet peeves." He stood, taking one more bite of his delicious burger. "I promise not to talk with my mouth full again." He trailed Deborah, laughing at the irony of him making a promise not to talk with a mouth full of food again while having a mouth full of food.

Deborah stopped in her tracks. "You think this is funny? You think I'm a joke, Lynox?"

Lynox was surprised to see tears rolling down Deborah's face. He swallowed his food in hunks without fully chewing, just to get it down so he could talk to Deborah—without a mouth full of food. "I'm sorry, baby." He put his arms around a weeping Deborah. "Obviously there's something more going on with you." He looked around at all the attention they were attracting. This time it wasn't a crowd of raving fans. It was a crowd of busybodies trying to figure out what was going on. "Come on, let's go outside and walk around. Give you a chance to clear your head."

An emotional Deborah took Lynox up on his offer. As they made their way outside, she felt like a fool. She couldn't turn off the waterworks. She felt awful. Not just because she was lying to Lynox, but what kind of mother denies having a child just because the man she's interested in doesn't want to date a woman with kids? And she called herself a Christian? Surely her actions weren't pleasing to Christ. After all, Christ had been denied by Peter—thrice. She thought she had Peter beat when it came to the amount of times she'd denied her son.

Once outside the mall, Lynox led Deborah to a bench. It just so happened to be the same bench the two had sat on when they'd parted years ago. Deborah saw this sign as an omen. No way would she tell him about her son right there on that bench. If she did, there was a likely chance of a repeat. This time, him walking out of her life. She couldn't do it. She couldn't take that chance. She wanted Lynox. She'd wanted him for a long time, and now she had him. She'd wanted a son, a replacement for the one she'd aborted so many years ago, and now she had him. Would it have been too much to ask God to let her keep them both? But in a matter of days, Deborah would question whether God would even allow her to keep one.

Chapter Thirty-two

"Pastor, I can't thank you enough for approving the Single Shoe event for the singles ministry," Deborah said through her cell phone. "I know some people might think it's kind of out there. But I'm glad I was able to convince you that it's fun and harmless. It's something different, new, and it's something we have never done before at New Day."

Deborah was excited about the event she was planning for the singles ministry. It was given the name Single Shoe, because the women were scheduled to arrive at the affair a half hour before the men. Once they arrived they were to take off one shoe and place it in a pile in the middle of the room and then go be seated. When all the men arrived, they would randomly pick a shoe from the pile, find out who the owner of the shoe was, and go sit next to her and get to know her. Initially when setting up the event, Deborah's only dilemma was the fact that the number of male members in the group heavily outweighed the number of female members. So Deborah opened up the event to other single males of the church. Just enough men RSVPed so that almost every woman in attendance could be paired up with a guy.

"Yes, I think it's quite unique myself," Pastor Margie replied.

"Then perhaps you might consider attending, Pastor," Deborah hinted.

"Oh, no. Now you're starting to sound like your pre-
decessor." Once upon a time Mother Doreen had been
adamant in her attempts to get their single pastor to
join the ministry. It was all to no avail though. "By the
way, how is Mother Doreen doing?"

Deborah felt embarrassed that she didn't know the
answer to that question. Mother Doreen had been like
a second mother to Deborah and the godmother of her
son, yet she'd neglected to check in on her and see how
she was doing. "She's doing fine," she told her pastor.
She hoped she was doing fine anyway. She made a
mental note to call Mother Doreen once she got off the
phone with her pastor.

"That's good to hear. I'm sure she's making a wonderful first lady. I say one Sunday some of us New Day
saints should plan on dropping in on her at her church
in Kentucky to show her our support."

"Ohhh, a road trip to Kentucky? Now that will be
nice. Mother Doreen will be so surprised."

"I'm sure she will." Pastor Margie smiled through the
phone. "Well, I have to get back to my notes for Bible
Study. I was recording some things with one of my cell
phone features when you called me. I hope it saved."

"Oh, me too, Pastor, and I'm sorry I interrupted
you."

"No problem. God bless you, woman of God, and
have a wonderful week."

"Will do, Pastor. Bye-bye." Deborah was going to end
the call and then immediately call Mother Doreen just
to confirm that she was doing fine. She'd hate for her
to be down with a cold or something and here she done
told Pastor the woman was fine. Before she could go
forth with her plan she noticed her son, with a pen in
hand, surrounded by a stack of papers that were scat-
tered everywhere.

Deborah raced over to him. "Nooooooo!" she yelled. "Not the manuscript I was editing!" As she got closer she realized that the entire time she'd been on the phone with her pastor, her son had been marking all over the manuscript she'd been paid to edit. He was merely mimicking what he'd seen her do on numerous occasions.

As luck would have it—as bad luck would have it— the author who had sent her the manuscript had failed to put page numbers within the manuscript, so it was essential that the papers didn't get out of sequence. Now how in the world was Deborah going to be able to put the manuscript in order?

Instinctively, she yanked her son up and began yelling, screaming, and cursing. "Do you know what you've done? Why can't you just sit your simple self down somewhere? Why you always messing with stuff, you little . . ." On and on she went as her son began to roar out in tears.

"Do you think I care if you cry? You ain't worried about all the work I have to do now, so why should I worry about you?" Deborah was on fire as she gathered the papers. She'd stop every now and then and point her finger right in her son's face and scold him a good one. "This is my work. This is what keeps a roof over your head, clothes on your back, and food in your stomach," she ranted as if the child understood. But she couldn't have cared less whether the boy understood. She was just frustrated.

For all the thirty minutes it took for Deborah to gather up the papers and try, to no avail, to put the stack back in order, she ranted on and on. Her son roared the entire time. "That was just stupid. How could you do so something so stupid? Stupid! Stupid! Just plain stupid!"

"I sorry, Mommy," her son cried, wiping his eyes. "I sorry."

"Oh, you don't have to tell me how sorry you are," Deborah raged, as she continued to fiddle with the paper. "You had a sorry daddy, so what else could I have expected?" Frustrated and angry to no end, Deborah just burst out crying. "I can't believe you did this. Now what am I supposed to do?"

"I sorry," her son said again. His voice was so sweet—so innocent. He rubbed his tiny eyes, trying to get that wet stuff to stop coming out of them, but the tears just kept flowing. It was like he couldn't control them, no more than his mommy could control the words that came flying out of her mouth.

Deborah looked over at her fragile son. She exhaled. "No, I'm the one who's sorry, sorry I even decided to have kids. I mean, what was I thinking? How did I think for one minute things would have been different with Elton? I was sorry and stupid to think I could actually get the fairytale—the happily ever after. I ain't even mad at myself for getting that abortion back in the day. In hindsight, heck, it was the right thing to do. Probably should have gotten an abortion the second time too." She let out a harrumph. "Guess God's showing me, huh?"

Deborah let out one last expletive before throwing the mangled stack of papers in the air and walking away. She dragged her drained, tired, and depressed body to her bed, where she'd find it nearly impossible to find the strength to peel herself up off of it again.

"What's happening to me, God?" Deborah cried out, feeling regretful and remorseful for the way she'd just behaved—for the way she'd just behaved to and in front of her son. "This isn't me. It's not me. I don't know who that person is acting like that, but it's not me," Deborah cried. "I need you to help me, God. I need you to bring me through this thing, God. No playing around and no test. As you can see, I fail the tests and I'm tired of taking them over and over and over. I need an instantaneous breakthrough, God. Please," Deborah cried.

Eventually Deborah's bladder forced her out of the bed. It sickened her that she had even contemplated just lying there and peeing on herself. She was just that weak physically, mentally, and spiritually. Life was truly taking its toll on her. From the outside looking in, Deborah didn't appear to have a bad life at all—not one that would cause her such anxiety and breakdowns. But what people couldn't see was the torment, the war, going on in her mind. It was a battle she felt defenseless to fight.

"Jesus," she said before pulling herself up and going to the bathroom. And she knew it had to have been Jesus who carried her there. That's just how weak and lifeless she was. She felt dead.

Since she was up, she decided to go check on her son. Despair and darkness had consumed her over the last couple of hours, so much so that she allowed her son to fend for himself in the house. In her right mind, she knew allowing a toddler free rein of the house wasn't smart. But Deborah was far from being in her right mind.

As she went back to the room where she'd last seen him, she found it empty. She called out his name but got no answer. She proceeded to go from room to room, calling out his name. No matter how many times she called out his name, there was no response.

"Baby, where are you?" Panic began to set in. "What was I thinking?" Deborah said out loud. "What was I thinking not keeping an eye on him?" This time she hit herself upside the head, frustrated and angry with herself.

As crazy thoughts filled her head of what could have possibly happened to her son while she entertained herself at a pity party, she became even madder at herself. *How could I get so caught up in myself and just not care that I let him fend for himself? Stupid! Stupid! Stupid.* With each insult, she knocked herself upside the head again.

"Baby, where are you?" She headed for the front door to see if it was still locked. The entire trek to the door she envisioned her son somehow wandering outside and into the street, and a speeding car taking his life. Those thoughts vanished once she realized the door was still closed and locked. Next she peeked inside the kitchen and called out his name. Nothing.

Deborah went back to her bedroom and checked underneath her bed. Maybe he'd crawled up under there and was hiding or something. When she didn't find him under her bed, she checked her bathroom. She checked closets. She checked inside the washer and dryer. Heck, she checked inside drawers. She couldn't find him anywhere.

The frantic mother realized she hadn't checked the back door. In order to get to the back door Deborah had to walk through the kitchen. She entered the kitchen where the long counter was the first thing that greeted her. She walked around the counter heading to the back door. That's when out of the right corner of her eye she saw something lying in front of the refrigerator. She instantly stopped in her tracks and turned toward the appliance.

There lay her son, lying on his back, surrounded by cookie crumbs, with a half-eaten cookie in his hand. He was sound asleep as his little chest heaved up and down. Hunger had obviously gotten the best of him while he waited for his mother to pull herself out of her funk.

"Oh, God, thank you!" Filled with relief, Deborah ran over to her son and dropped to the floor next him. His little chest went up and down as he made a little snoring sound. Then he made little exhaling sounds like he'd had a long, hard day but was now at peace in a deep sleep. His little round cheeks had dried-up tearstains on them.

"I'm so sorry, son," Deborah whispered as she sprawled out next to her son and lay next to him. "So sorry." She kissed him on his forehead. "I hate myself for this. I hate myself for who I am and what I'm putting you through." Tears dripped out of Deborah's eyes and onto the floor. "I just wish I was dead. I don't want to go through this. I don't want to put my son through this. I'm better off dead." She looked at her son and before closing her eyes said, "He's better off dead with a mother like me . . . We're both better off dead."

Chapter Thirty-three

"Blessed and highly favored," Deborah responded to Helen after Helen asked her how she was doing. Deborah's response was a lie. Maybe it wasn't a lie. Perhaps she really was blessed and highly favored, but she certainly didn't feel that way.

On the inside Deborah was in pain. Her insides hurt. She felt guilt. She felt sorrow. And now here lately she'd felt something that she'd never really felt before: crazy.

One minute she was up, another minute she was down. One minute she was laughing at the things her son did, the next minute she was frustrated, agitated, and aggravated at the things he did. One minute she'd want to call her mother and tell her how much she loved her and that the past didn't matter. The next minute she became filled with rage at her mother. Things felt complicated. Her life felt complicated; too complicated to let anyone in. That's why she hadn't called up her mother and gotten things back on track between the two of them. That's why when Lynox invited her out, she declined, stating she was behind on work. She simply didn't feel like being bothered. She didn't feel like talking. She didn't want to converse with anyone. She didn't have the strength to put up a front and be phony, pretending like everything was kosher. And for the life of Deborah, she couldn't figure out why anyone would want in anyway.

She was in such a cold, dark, dreary place. There appeared to be no light—no hope. No matter how hard she tried to dig herself out of that dark hole, she just kept sliding back down in it. So why would anyone in their right mind want to be a part of that? Unfortunately, her son was left with no choice.

"What happened here?" Helen asked, pointing to the bruise on Deborah's son's arm.

"What?" Deborah asked, curious as to what Helen was referring to.

"This, right here, on his arm." She pointed to a round strawberry-like mark.

"Oh, I don't know," Deborah replied, shooing her hand. "You know how boys are, especially terrible twos."

"Yeah, but it looks like it hurts. I think maybe I better get some ice or something for it."

"I'm sure it's nothing, but ice won't hurt," Deborah agreed. "I'll go to the church kitchen and get some." Deborah exited the room, wishing she had never even bothered to come to church. She didn't feel like all this talking and being fake with all those blessed and highly favored responses. She didn't feel like going to get ice. She just wanted to lie down somewhere and die. She didn't even want to be in church. Obviously, whatever it was that was going on with her, Jesus couldn't fix, because here she was right in His living room, and she felt just as bad as she'd felt in her own. Where was His spirit? Where was all that strength-of-Jesus crap now?

Sure, some time ago, right there in that very house of the Lord, she'd experienced a breakthrough and received deliverance. But look how long that had lasted. She felt worse off than ever. So why come to church and have to keep the lights on with her tithes when she was surrounded by darkness?

"Sister Deborah, my God, I'm so glad I ran into you," Pastor Margie said as she exited the kitchen with a cup of coffee in her hand. "If you have a minute, I'd like to speak with you after service today."

Frickin' great! Deborah roared on the inside. Now her pastor wanted to talk to her. Didn't the world get it? She didn't feel like talking. She didn't even feel like living. "Actually, Pastor, today is not a good day. I've got something going on today and—"

"I promise you, it's very important," Pastor Margie assured her. "You know I almost never meet with anyone right after Sunday service, but you and your son have been in my spirit heavily."

Deborah thought she was going to choke on her spit. Had the pastor sensed something was going on in Deborah's household? The pastor always said how God spoke to her about things—how God gave her a spirit of discernment to be able to know what's going on with her flock. Had God opened His big, fat mouth and ratted Deborah out to Pastor Margie? Those were the last thoughts in Deborah's mind before Pastor Margie spoke again.

"Please, Sister Deborah. It can't wait."

"Okay, Pastor," Deborah reluctantly gave in.

"Good." Pastor Margie exhaled and the two heard clapping in the sanctuary as prayer followed. "We'll go in and head into the sanctuary. I'll see you after service."

"Yes, Pastor," Deborah said, making her way to the sanctuary.

Deborah had given herself a pep talk in an attempt to encourage herself to try to take in today's service, but she did not want to be there. She wanted to be at home in bed. And up until the eleventh hour, that's what she had planned on doing—skipping church and staying home in bed. But she knew better. She knew service wouldn't have been let out five minutes before a New Day member was doing a drive-by to come check on her. She figured the better of two evils would be dragging herself out of bed, putting on her church face, sitting through service, and then going home and going back to bed. Yes, that would be better than some member showing up at her door unannounced and uninvited, fishing around in her business. But now Pastor was throwing a monkey wrench in her game plan by wanting to talk to her after service.

"Lord, get me out of this," Deborah said under her breath as she sat miserably during praise and worship. And just as if God had heard her plea, she looked up and saw her son's assigned number from children's church pop up on the little screen. "Praise God," Deborah said, this time not so much under her breath.

The number method was something a lot of churches used in children's church/childcare. When a parent checked their child in, their child was assigned a number. The parent is given a little ticket with the number on it, just like in dressing rooms or at the deli counter in a grocery store. If that number flashes up on the screen in the sanctuary during church service, that means there is an issue going on with a child and the parent needs to come get them. It can be anything from the child made a mess on himself to the child misbehaving. For Deborah, it didn't matter what the reason. She was just glad to be getting rescued from the sanctuary.

"I saw my son's number show up on the screen in the sanctuary," Deborah said to Helen's assistant once she entered the children's church. She didn't see Helen or her son anywhere in sight.

"Oh, yeah," Unique replied. "Helen put his number in, but she took him to—"

Just then the door opened and Helen entered with Deborah's son in her arms. She had a bag of ice in her hand. "You forgot to bring the ice." Speaking of ice, Helen's tone was a little icy.

"Oh, yeah, I forgot," Deborah replied. "I ran into Pastor right before I went into the kitchen. She got to talking to me, then we heard service start . . . I guess I just got thrown off."

Helen brushed by Deborah. "Well, I really think this bruise is bothering him. He's cranky, whiney, and acting a little mean," Helen said. "And that's just not like our little guy."

"Oh, Mommy's poor baby." Deborah took her son from Helen's arms and began to console him. "Him not feeling well," she said in baby talk. Then, grateful for a way out, she said, "I think I'm just going to take him on home and get him together."

"That might be a good idea," Helen agreed. "And here . . ." She extended the bag of ice to Deborah. "Still try keeping some ice on it. It might make it feel better. But you still might want to call his doctor as well."

"Yes, thank you." Deborah accepted the ice, signed her son out of children's church, and then raced to her car.

It was as if she couldn't get out of that church soon enough. Once she hit the exit doors she exhaled like she hadn't been able to breathe the last half hour. And that's exactly how she'd felt.

As she buckled her son in his car seat she scolded herself for not just staying home in the first place. She was a mess all the other days of the week, so what made her think that on one day she would be okay? Well, she wasn't okay, and she was coming to grips with the fact that there was nothing she could do about it—or God either, for that matter.

Deborah got in the car and pulled out of the church driveway. Hopefully Helen would tell Pastor Margie about how she had to leave church early; that way her pastor wouldn't think she'd stood her up. Deborah had to admit, though, the last thing she wanted was to have a sit-down with her pastor. So she was glad that now she didn't have to. But soon enough, she'd wish she had.

Chapter Thirty-four

"Is everything okay? When you called me on the phone and asked me to come over, it sounded urgent." Lynox stood in Deborah's doorway, genuinely concerned.

"No, everything isn't okay," Deborah replied. "You mind coming in for a moment?" Only seconds after the invitation, Deborah wished she hadn't extended it. Why bother? Just as soon as she told him what she had to say, he would be out the door anyway. Therefore, he might as well have stayed outside. But it was too late.

"I don't mind at all." Lynox stepped inside.

Instead of closing the door behind them, Deborah left it open. At least he'd be able to make a quick exit. Leave, stay; she didn't care anymore at this point. The entire situation was making her crazy. Or more crazy, should she have said? Right now, she just needed to start unloading a lot of things that were weighing her down—things that were making her stressed and tense. Things that wouldn't let her rest and had her mind on edge. There were lots of things, including her relationship with her mother she'd yet to mend. But that was next on her list. Her and her mother's past went deep. Her little secret she was keeping from Lynox would be a breeze to fix compared to that. So she decided to start off in the shallow end of the pool and deal with Lynox first.

"There's something I need to tell you," Deborah dived right in. Enough time had been wasted. If she beat around the bush and put it off any longer, history would probably repeat itself. There would be some interruption—some type of threat of him finding out she had a child from someone other than her.

With her luck, some fairy would probably drop from the sky holding a sign that read, DEBORAH LEWIS IS YOUR KRYPTONITE: A LADY WITH A BABY. And if that didn't happen, then surely her son would wake up from his nap before she had a chance to get the words out.

Within minutes after laying him down in his crib for a nap, Deborah hopped on the phone with Lynox. Her son typically took a two-hour nap. What she needed to tell Lynox would only take five minutes. So when he told her that he could be at her house in a half hour, she knew that Lynox would be there and gone before her son ever even woke up. Or at least he'd sleep until after she got a chance to tell Lynox about him.

"What is it you need to tell me, Deborah?" Lynox was looking more concerned than ever as he went to sit down on the couch. He'd barely bent his knees before he stood back up. "Wait a minute. This isn't déjà vu, is it? I mean, the last time you had something to tell me, it involved you hopping on a plane headed out of the country . . . with another man, might I add." Lynox shot Deborah a worried look. "This doesn't have anything to do with another man, does it?"

"God, no, Lynox," Deborah huffed.

"Thank God." This time he sat down, but on the way down a thought entered his head. "It's not your health, is it? You did say you had a doctor's appointment the other day, that was why you couldn't meet me out for lunch."

"No, yes, I mean . . ." Deborah began to stammer. Yes, she had told Lynox she'd had a doctor's appointment, which was just another lie to add to the collection. There was no doctor's appointment. She just hadn't been up to dealing with him. As snappy as she had been, he was liable to call it quits with her whether she had a kid or not. That's just how ugly and nasty Deborah had been lately.

"Oh, no, Deborah." Lynox stood again. "What happened at the doctor's?" He walked toward Deborah just in case she needed some comforting.

"Nothing, Lynox. The doctor didn't say a thing."

Lynox exhaled. "Then what is it?"

"If you'd stop playing the guessing game, I'll tell you." She was snappy.

"I'm sorry. Like I said, you had me worried when you called me."

Deborah put her hands up. "Please, Lynox, just let me say what I have to say," Deborah pleaded.

"You're right. I'm sorry." Lynox walked back over to the couch. "Go ahead. It's just that, to be honest with you, I was scared to death after I got your call. On the entire drive over here all I kept doing was replaying the last time you asked me to meet you so you could tell me something. I know that's in the past, though, and we said we wouldn't let the past dictate our future. So nothing in the past can affect our future." Lynox plopped back down on the couch, crossed his legs, and opened his arms spread eagle across the couch. "I promise, no more interruptions. Go ahead." Lynox zipped his lips with his fingers.

Deborah's jaws filled with air and then she let it out. "First of all, I apologize for not telling you this a long time ago. I wanted to tell you several times." She laughed and shook her head. "You wouldn't believe how many times. But it seems like every time I went to tell you, I was interrupted."

And this time would be no different as there was a knock on the screen door.

"Are you kidding me?" Deborah groaned those words to no one in particular. She then huffed and turned around to see who in the world was at her door—unannounced at that. Heck, she'd at least shown her face at church on Sunday, so it better not have been a New Day Temple of Faith drive-by.

She held her index finger up at Lynox. "Wait one second, just one second." Deborah turned and walked over to the door. "Yes?" she said to the suited-up woman standing on her porch.

"Hi, I'm looking for"—the woman looked down at the paperwork in her hand—"a Miss Deborah Lucas." She read over the paperwork again. "Deborah Lewis."

"It's both Lucas and Lewis, and I am she," Deborah confirmed. Deborah had already made up in her mind that whatever this woman was selling, she wasn't buying. "But this isn't really a good time." Deborah was going to give it her all to try not to reflect the agitation she was feeling right about now.

"I'm sure it's not, Miss Lucas-Lewis, and I apologize if I interrupted you, but I need to speak with you." The woman reached in her front jacket pocket and pulled out her business card. She held it toward the closed screen door. "My name is Pricilla Folins. I'm with Franklin County Children Services." Next, she extended a badge that she wore around her neck.

Those words and that ID got Deborah's full attention as she wondered why Children Services would be at her door. She slowly cracked open her screen door and took the business card that was being extended to her.

"Miss Lewis, I'd like to talk to you regarding a report we received regarding possible child abuse," Ms. Folins explained to her.

"Child abuse?" Deborah had opened her mouth to say those words, but she was in such shock that nothing came out. So Lynox had asked the woman standing in front of her what Deborah had wanted to ask, but couldn't find her voice.

Deborah looked over her shoulder to see Lynox, who had made his way from the couch, standing there.

"You've obviously got the wrong person here," Lynox said to the woman in Deborah's defense.

"Please, Lynox, I can handle this." Deborah had found her voice.

The woman at the door looked confused. "You did say that you were Deborah Lucas-Lewis, correct?"

"Yes, but—"

"Then I have the right person." The woman looked down at her paper and confirmed the name once again. "I'm here regarding child abuse allegations against you that—"

"Pardon me for interrupting again, but I assure you that you have the wrong person." Lynox chuckled. "She doesn't even have a kid to abuse." Suddenly a thought entered Lynox's mind. "Oh, that's right, your nephew." He looked at Deborah. "Or rather that close friend of the family's kid." He looked back to the Franklin County Children Service caseworker. "But she'd never hurt him." He placed his arm around Deborah. "She wouldn't hurt any kid."

The caseworker shook her head and her blond, bouncy curls did a jig. She took a deep breath, puckered her lips painted in soft pink lipstick, then fluttered her hazel eyes. "Look, Miss Lewis . . ." That was her way of ignoring Lynox. "Can I please talk to *you?* As you know child abuse is a very serious allegation. I'd just like to talk to you for a moment and maybe see your son."

Again, Lynox laughed. "I'm telling you, she doesn't have a son. Don't you get it, lady?" Lynox was trying his best to keep his cool, but this woman was irking him with such nonsense. "You're wasting your time here when it's somebody else's doorstep you should be on right now." Lynox pointed outside. "There's some poor crumb snatcher out there being mistreated as we speak because the system is so messed up that you can't even get paperwork, names, and addresses straight."

"Please, Lynox." Deborah found her frozen voice again. It was beginning to thaw out slowly but surely. Perhaps it was the heat caused from the rising fear inside of her. Child abuse. Children Services at her doorstep. This was heavy. She turned to the woman. "I assure you, no child abuse has been going on here. I'd never hit my sss . . . son." She looked down because she knew Lynox's eyes were glued on her in shock. She could just feel it.

"Deborah?" Lynox said under his breath as he continued to hold a steady stare at the caseworker. "What are you talking about? What's going on here? You don't . . . you don't have a son." He looked down at Deborah. "Do you?"

After taking a deep breath, Deborah was able to look Lynox in the eyes. "Yes, Lynox. I do." She closed her eyes. She didn't want the tears forming to escape. She didn't want Lynox to see the shame and guilt in her eyes. Even worse, she didn't want to see the disgust in his, that same disgust that was in his eyes when he talked about that woman he'd dated who had a kid. That same disgust that was in his eyes when he'd seen Helen at the mall and thought the boy she was pushing around in a stroller was her kid.

"Wha . . . what did you say?" Lynox's hand slowly slid from around Deborah.

Deborah opened her eyes, but she didn't look Lynox in his. "It's what I've been trying to tell you. That's why I invited you over today."

Lynox stepped away and put his hand on his head and cupped the throbbing headache of confusion that was coming on. "A son? But it doesn't make any sense. . . ." Lynox's words trailed off momentarily; then he snapped his fingers. He looked up at Deborah with a gleam of hope in his eyes. "I get it. You're adopting your nephew. His mother—she's the one who has been abusing him. So you're just rescuing him from her. And now the caseworker here needs to talk to you about it. Yeah, that's it," Lynox said as if he'd just come up with a wonderful plot to a story. Shamefully enough, if that woman hadn't been standing at the door to counter the story, Deborah probably would have rolled with it. But she was tired of lying. She was just tired, period. She was tired, but on top of that, anger was starting to form.

"Look, Lynox, this is not one of your stupid books. You can't write everybody's story," Deborah shot at him, "and you dang sure can't write mine. Trust and believe that," she added with a head snap. "I have a son. I don't have a nephew; I have a son. I'm an only child and I don't have any friends, let alone a close enough friend where I'd keep their kid. I have a son. He's mine. Mine and Elton's."

Dumbfounded, Lynox asked, "Why? Why didn't you just tell me?"

"Ha! Are you serious? The way you continuously make it a point to let me know how you feel about women with children? How you don't want the readymade family? How you don't want to be a father to another man's kid?" Deborah brought up everything Lynox had said about women with kids. "And now you ask me that like it should have been the easiest thing in the world to tell you. You made me feel tainted. You made me feel as though something was wrong with me because I'm a single woman with a child. Why didn't I tell you?" she mocked. "That's why!"

The woman at the door cleared her throat to remind the feuding couple that she was still there. As interesting as the soap opera unfolding before her very eyes seemed to be, she had a job to do.

"Oh, yes, I'm sorry," Deborah said to the woman. "Please come in so we can get this straightened out." Next Deborah looked to Lynox. "He was just leaving . . . for good." Deborah stepped to the side and opened the door, for the woman to enter and for Lynox to leave . . . for good . . . forever. It was breaking her heart inside for him to leave, but for the first time since reconnecting with Lynox, there was something more important she had to focus on, and that was her son.

Chapter Thirty-five

"Franklin County Children Services, Mom? Really?" Deborah roared at her mother. "You called the people on me? Seriously?" Deborah could not have confronted her mother about her surprise visitor soon enough. She immediately knew that her mother was behind this nonsense. She didn't know how she did, but she just knew.

Deborah being so sure her mother was responsible for the claims probably had a lot to do with the arguments they'd had lately. Mrs. Lewis had not bitten her tongue about how she disapproved of some of Deborah's parenting techniques. In turn, Deborah had not bitten her tongue on what she thought about her own mother's parenting skills when it came to how she'd raised her. Deborah knew she was somewhat out of line in the way she had come at her mother. Had she known this was how her mother would retaliate, she would have most definitely held her tongue.

Deborah had watched enough episodes of *Judge Judy* and *Judge Mathis* where folks had falsely called Children Services on a person they were beefing with. She just never thought her own mother would do that to her. The people on the court shows had done it out of spite. The judges had seen right through the defendants' vindictiveness, awarding the plaintiffs money for their suffering and loss as a result. Deborah didn't have any plans of suing her mother, but she had every intention in the world of confronting her about it.

Once Miss Folins, the woman from Children Services, had left Deborah's house after over an hour of questioning her and her son, Deborah couldn't wait to get on the phone and let her mother have it. But after picking up the phone and dialing the first few digits of her mother's phone number, she slammed the phone down.

"This requires a face-to-face," Deborah had spat as she gathered together her son and their things and made a beeline out the door—straight to her mother's house. As soon as Deborah's mother had opened the door, Deborah burst through the door in rage.

"First of all, you need to calm yourself down," Mrs. Lewis shot back. "I have no idea what you're talking about. Children Services . . ."

"Oh, so now you're going to act like you don't know what I'm talking about." Deborah rolled her eyes up in her head. "Puhleaze."

Mrs. Lewis tightened her lips. She tried to count to ten, but only made it to four. "Now for the last few years I've been trying to be a different person—a better person. But I'm warning you, Deb . . ." She walked up to her daughter and put her finger in her face. "You gon' make me go old school on you for real."

Deborah was taken aback. For a moment there, she felt like a little kid again. This feeling was brought on by the look in her mother's eyes. There was a hint of the expression she used to wear whenever she used to go on her tangents when Deborah was coming up. Deborah had never met a real, live madwoman. But she'd bet the farm that back in the day her mother bore a close resemblance.

Put in her place, Deborah found a more respectable tone. "Look, Mom, I really don't want to come over here disrespecting you. No matter what, no matter what I think about how you raised me, God only gave me one mother. That is what forces me to strive to want to have a halfway decent relationship with you, but you calling Children Services on me, making accusations that I might be abusing my son, that's kind of hard to look past."

"Deborah, I honestly have no idea what you are talking about," Mrs. Lewis assured her daughter. She said it with such a sincere tone and expression that Deborah knew her mother was telling the truth. Deborah could feel it in her gut that her mother had not been the one to call "the people" on her. Deborah began to soften, preparing herself to apologize to her mother. "But I can also honestly say that I thought about doing it."

Deborah's mouth dropped open.

"I'm just trying to tell the truth and shame the devil," Mrs. Lewis admitted. "Now you know I'm not the praying kind—not on a regular basis anyway—but I even prayed to God about whether to make the call. I ain't too clear on deciphering God's voice, so I don't know what His response was. Obviously He told me to make the call, and when I didn't, He found somebody else to do it."

Deborah threw her hands on her hips. "Now if that just ain't the craziest thing I've ever heard. You're grasping at straws, Momma. But it's all good. I see how you're playing this game."

"I'm not playing any games with you, Deborah. I'm trying, and I have been trying, to be as real with you as possible. When I look back at how I treated you, I don't want that for my grandbaby. That's why I try to give him all the sweet kindness and love that I never showed or gave you. I want to break the cycle with him. But then you counter everything I do with your own hateful actions."

"What I don't get is why you dog me out for acting the same way you did."

"Because I know better now, Deborah! How many more times do I have to tell you that? I was wrong. Dead wrong. But I can admit that I was wrong. Now you need to step up and admit that you're wrong. Because, like the saying goes, you can't quit it until you admit it."

There was a lot of truth to what Mrs. Lewis was speaking and Deborah knew it. But rather than acknowledging that her mother was right, Deborah would prefer to be wrong.

"Just forget it, Ma. I don't have time to stand here and do this with you, my baby is out in the car and the car is running. I gotta go." Deborah headed for the door.

"I didn't call those people on you, Deborah."

Deborah stopped right when she got to the door. She turned and looked at her mother knowingly. "If you say so." Deborah just couldn't bring herself to fully believe her mother; not now. Not after her little spiel about she was going to but she didn't—blah, blah, and blah.

As sincere as her mother had seemed in her earlier comments, the latter comments almost Xed them out. Besides, there was no one else who came to mind who would have done something like that. It just so happened that she and her mother had been disputing over the way Deborah was treating her son. Now out of nowhere Children Services showed up at her door questioning how she treated her son. How Deborah saw it, one plus one equaled two.

"I love you, Mom. God knows I love you. And I'll keep loving you until the day I die. But forgiving you . . . I'm not so sure anymore, Momma. Just not sure." Deborah sighed and then walked out the door.

"Deborah, please," her mother shouted after her. "We can't keep doing this. We have to mend this broken bridge between us." Deborah kept walking as her mother came out on the porch. "You don't even have to meet me halfway. I'm willing to walk all the way across the bridge and meet you where you are. Please, Deborah."

"I love you, Mom," Deborah said, then got in the car and drove off. Tears spilled from her eyes. She was saddened that there was such a huge wedge in her and her mother's relationship. Mostly, though, the tears were of anger. If the person who had called Children Services on her had been anyone other than her mother, she would have done them bodily harm. That's just how angry she was. But the woman was her mother. So she'd have to keep all her frustration sealed up like a can of soda. But it wouldn't be long before, like a soda that had been shaken up, she would explode.

"Thank you, Zelda. The food looks delicious," Debora said to her waitress as she and her son sat in Family Café. No matter what she ordered from Malvonia's local restaurant, she knew it would be delicious. Over the years, she'd tried almost everything on the menu. Her son, on the other hand, had never eaten anything from the diner other than chicken fingers and fries. That would probably go for most kids though.

"Thank you, Deborah. I hope you think it tastes as good as it looks."

"Quit being modest, girl. You know your family makes the best food this side of the map," Deborah complimented her. "And good thing, too, because after the day I've had, the last thing I felt like doing was cooking." And Deborah was telling the truth there. Had her son not begun to beg for fruit snacks, yogurt, and a list of his other favorite foods, Deborah would have forgotten all about dinner. After her conversation with her mother, she'd been way too mad to eat. Hopefully, though, a good meal would relax her mind. Prayer hadn't seemed to be helping her mind, God, church, Jesus—nothing. If food didn't work, she was running out of options.

"We have a new dessert menu. So you and little man need to save room for that." Zelda winked. "Let me know if you need anything else." She walked away to take care of her other customers.

Deborah blessed her and her son's food and they began to eat. Halfway through her meal, Deborah was interrupted.

"The way you smashing that food, I think I'm going to order that," Deborah heard a voice say. She looked up to see Helen standing over her.

"Oh, hey, Sister Helen," Deborah greeted her, wiping her mouth. "How are you?"

"I'm good, but it's my little guy here I'm worried about." Helen pinched Deborah's son's cheek. "That bruise he had. It just stayed in my spirit. Is it doing any better?"

"Yes, he's fine," Deborah said while smiling at her son. "Mommy's baby is just fine."

"Good," Helen replied. "Did you ever figure out how he got it—what the bruise was from?"

"No." Deborah shrugged her shoulders. "Things just happen with kids. You know how that goes." Deborah actually did know how the bruise had gotten there, but she didn't want her food to get cold while she explained all the boring details to Helen. Besides, she didn't have to answer to anybody. Not her mother and certainly not Helen.

"I know. They take a lickin' and keep on tickin'," Helen joked. "But that was just odd. It concerned me. He's always so happy. So it bothered me that it was bothering him so much. It was like he took a lickin' but his tickin' wasn't the same anymore."

Deborah was glad that someone cared about her son just as much as she did. What she didn't appreciate was Helen making it appear as though she cared more than Deborah did.

"Well, he's back to tickin' just fine," Deborah assured Helen.

"You sure? Let me see." Helen leaned in to check the spot where she'd seen the bruise on Deborah's son's arm.

"I said he's fine." The snappiness shot out of Deborah's voice and stopped Helen's actions instantly.

"Oh, my goodness, I'm sorry," Helen apologized. "You two are trying to eat and I'm just interrupting y'all." She laughed. "Forgive me for overreacting sometimes. I'm going to be a mess when I open my own daycare. I'm probably going to be getting on those parents' nerves." She laughed again. "But I don't play that mess when it comes to kids. I'm like Oprah Winfrey when it comes to the kids—very protective and concerned. I can't just let things go."

"Well, the parents should be so lucky to have someone caring for their children who are truly concerned about them," Deborah stated, hoping Helen would keep it moving so that she and her son could enjoy their meal. Let that caseworker tell it, this could be their last meal together.

"Mrs. Lewis," the caseworker had said, "I should inform you of some of the possible outcomes if the allegations of child abuse against your child are found to be true."

"But they won't be found to be true. I do not abuse my child," Deborah had countered.

"So you say, but I should still let you know that not only could your son be removed from your home— temporarily, permanently, or indefinitely—but you could also face criminal charges and serve jail time. And, might I add, having a criminal record, especially against a child, is very, very, very damaging. It will limit you in future career choices, and—"

"Look, I don't mean to interrupt you, but like I said, I do not beat on my son."

The woman stopped and stared at Deborah for a moment before stating, "Mrs. Lewis, do you understand that child abuse involves more than just hitting a child? There are soooo many ways parents hurt and damage their children that do not involve them ever laying a hand on them." To drive her point in the woman added, "You saw that episode of *Dr. Phil* where that woman would punish her son by making him take a cold shower, all the while she's fussing him out?"

"I heard about that." Deborah brushed it off as if sweeping dirt under the rug.

"Then you also heard that she was arrested and charged with abuse." The caseworker swept it right back out.

Those words had really made Deborah think just how serious this situation was. She could go to jail. She could actually go to jail because someone else thought the way she was treating her child was wrong. It was behind that thought that the arguments Deborah had been having with her mother lately had popped into her head. Her mother had made it no secret that she felt Deborah's behavior was damaging to her son. But now, as she sat in the Family Café, she realized that her mother obviously wasn't the only one who thought that. If Deborah didn't know any better, she'd have thought Helen was undercover, trying to hint around that perhaps Deborah could have put the bruise on her son.

A red light went off when Deborah thought back to the caseworker asking Deborah if she could have permission to look over her son. The first place that caseworker went to was her son's arms. That bruise, which Deborah did end up having checked out, had actually been some type of rash and wasn't a bruise at all. With a prescription cream the doctor had prescribed, it went away. So by the time the social worker went to check out her son, it was gone.

What wasn't gone, though, was a fresh thought Deborah was having. It was a thought that now nagged her to the pit of her stomach. She thought back to her mother's reaction, her facial expressions, when Deborah had accused her of calling Children Services on her. Deborah figured she was playing off her ignorance well. But maybe she wasn't. Maybe she truly wasn't the one who had called the people on her. The more Deborah thought about Helen's actions as of late, the more she became certain that her mother wasn't the culprit. No, it hadn't been her mother at all.

"You! It was you!" Deborah stood up so abruptly that she almost turned her plate over. "You called Children Services on me. That bruise . . . You thought I put that bruise on my son's arm, so you reported me. You vengeful, nosey . . ." And before Deborah knew it, an expletive was flying out of her mouth.

"Excuse me!" Helen was in complete shock. Why, all of a sudden, was Deborah all in her face calling her out of her name? She looked around as if the other patrons knew what was going on and someone could clue her in.

"Don't you stand here and try to act stupid." Deborah was all up in Helen's face. She couldn't get any closer. "You making such a big deal out of a little ol' bruise is a dead giveaway. And, just so you know, it wasn't a bruise. It was a rash. So now you can call Children Services back and tell them how ridiculous your claim was." The heat was rising in Deborah. And even though she knew the scripture very well—James 1:20 in the King James Amplified says, "For man's anger does not promote the righteousness God wishes and requires"—she didn't care. The heck with being righteous. The only wish she wanted to fulfill right now was her desire to kick Helen's butt.

"Look, you are tripping," Helen said. "I have no idea what the heck you are talking about here. If you want to calm down and talk about this, then I'm here for you. If I can help you through this situation in any way, I will. But you flying off the handle like some psycho woman all the time is about to drive me crazy." She looked down at Deborah's son. "And if this is how you act on the regular—all bipolar and stuff—then you are probably going to drive your poor son crazy too."

Instinctively, Deborah found her hand planted on Helen's cheek. "Don't you say anything about my son. Don't you worry about my son." Deborah's emotions were at their capacity. It was uncontrollable as she went to hit Helen again.

This time Helen caught Deborah's hand. The two began to tussle back and forth. Deborah lost her balance and slipped backward. The two landed on the table. The food went everywhere as Deborah's son began to cry out.

Zelda came running over and scooped Deborah's son up. "You two stop it! Cut it out." Her pleas fell on deaf ears as Helen continued to tussle with Deborah by holding her wrists.

Deborah managed to loosen one of her wrists from Helen's grip and deck her upside the head. Once again, instead of hitting her back, Helen managed to grip Deborah's wrists and the two tussled more. They fell off the table, onto the booth bench. After tussling some more, they ended up on the floor.

Other patrons stood nearby, trying to figure out what was going on. Zelda encouraged them to assist in breaking up the fight. "Somebody, please do something." Zelda would have done something herself, but her first concern was that of Deborah's son. She wanted to get him away from the drama. She didn't want him to witness his mother engaged in such behavior. As she backed away from the physical altercation, she continued her plea. "Somebody please break them up!"

By now, Deborah had gotten away from Helen and was windmilling her. She was just swinging her arms like a madwoman, not caring whether or where her hands landed.

Finally, a woman encouraged her husband to go break the two women up.

"You are going to pay for this, Helen," Deborah warned once the two were separated. "You done fooled with the wrong one. I knew I should have never let you in my space. You took my kindness as weakness and figured you could pull the same kind of crap on me again. But you got it all twisted."

"You need help," Helen said to Deborah. "I've been there, so I know. You need help, sister."

Deborah went to lunge at Helen again, but she couldn't get past the woman's husband who had pulled her off of Helen in the first place. So, instead, she just continued to hurl insults at her until finally the local police showed up. Seeing the men in blue seemed to be the only thing that settled Deborah down.

"I take it you two are the ones involved in the alter-cation we received a call about?" the officer surmised after seeing Deborah and Helen covered in food with their hair and clothes all out of place.

Neither Helen nor Deborah answered verbally.

The officer shook his head. "I have to deal with grown women acting like they're on a reality show when there are more serious situations I could be taking care of out there," the officer said. "So let's not waste too much time. I'm going to need each one of you to come out to the back of my patrol car while I question you. Then I'll question a couple of witnesses. But please know that be-fore the day is over, someone's going to jail."

Chapter Thirty-six

"Jail?" Deborah spat. "I can't go to jail. My . . . my son is here."

As if on cue, Zelda cleared the corner with Deborah's son in her arms. He was holding a roll. Zelda had given it to him to quiet him down from all the commotion he'd witnessed, which had visibly shaken him up.

"What will happen to my baby?" Deborah began to panic as her eyes darted back and forth from her son to the officer.

"Most likely, he'll end up at Children Services," the officer replied as if he loved being the bearer of bad news. There was just something about this officer that told Deborah that he loved doing his job, that he loved when folks gave him the opportunity to haul them downtown. He wasn't bluffing. Someone was going to jail. That officer was going to make the person who pulled him away from his donut and coffee pay. It would more than likely be the instigator. It would most likely be Deborah.

"Chi . . . Children Services." Deborah swallowed hard and almost stopped breathing.

Children Services had already been at her doorstep today. If her son showed up on theirs, something told her it would be a long time before she got him back. Terror filled her as her nerves began to get the best of her. Her hands started shaking. She looked over at Helen, who had obviously gotten the short end of the stick in the fight. She had scratches, marks, and even a spot of blood in the corner of her mouth. But in that instant Deborah's mind began to conjure up the lie she would tell the officer: how Helen had approached her and thrown the first blow. Deborah had only been defending herself. If the officer still had doubts, Deborah would throw Helen under the bus even further. She would go on to tell the officer that Helen had a violent past and that due to her past, she'd lost custody of her son. He could check the facts on that and find that Helen's mother had custody of her son once upon a time. Yes; Deborah had it all planned out. That's exactly what she'd do. She'd lie now and repent later, but her son was not going to end up in the system.

"Yep, Children Services," the officer confirmed. "Besides, any grown woman who fights in front of her child should be thrown into jail anyway. As a matter of fact, that is the law in some states." He looked at Deborah. "You look like you watch reality TV. That's what happened to the one gal on that reality teen pregnancy show. She was fighting in front of her kid and got arrested—got the kid taken away from her and everything." The officer let out a harrumph. "I don't know why these folks keep going on all these stupid reality shows."

Ironically enough, Deborah did recall hearing about the girl from the reality show to which the officer was referring. It sickened her that she even put herself in this type of predicament.

"So who's first?" The officer sighed.

Figuring she might as well go first in order to get it over with and see where the chips may fall, Deborah decided to volunteer to go first. "I'll go."

The officer started to escort Deborah out of the restaurant.

"Mommy." Deborah's son reached out to her. He'd finished the roll. He wanted his mommy.

"I'll keep him for you, Deborah," Zelda told Deborah as she slowly walked toward the exit.

"Mommy!" her son cried out again.

Deborah turned to face him. "Mommy will be right back, son." Her voice quivered. She didn't sound so confident. The negative, uncertain energy she was producing was being transferred to her son.

"Mommy! Mommy!" He began to cry out louder.

Oh, God, what have I gotten myself into? were Deborah's thoughts, and they were written all over her face. Deborah tried to drown out her son's crying and calls for her as she started her journey toward the exit. It felt like the longest walk of her life. So many actions and so many consequences ran through her head with each step. Why had she made the decisions she'd made? Why had she made them without even caring about the cost? What was wrong with her that she was so out of control that she stopped considering the consequences of her actions? Now not only was there a chance she would have to pay for her actions with jail time, but her son would have to pay as well.

"Wait, Officer!" Helen yelled out with slight hesitation. "There's no need for you to even waste your time with all this. Everybody in here knows whose fault this is—who started it all." Helen looked around at the eyewitnesses with a pleading look in her eyes. "It was me. I started it. I hit her first. She was only trying to defend herself by blocking and holding me." Helen looked at Deborah dead in her eyes. She then looked at Deborah's weeping son. She swallowed and continued. "Isn't that right, Sister Deborah?"

"Sister? You mean to tell me you two are kin up in here fighting and acting a fool?" the officer asked.

"No, not that kind of sisters," Helen replied. "Sisters in Christ. We go to the same church."

"You mean to tell me you two are church folks up in here fighting and acting a fool?" He laughed. "That's even worse. But who am I to judge?" He shook his head in disgust. "Anyway, Sister Deborah," he said sarcastically, "is what she says true?"

Deborah just stood there in utter shock. She didn't know what to say or how to say it. Just moments ago she'd had her own string of lies she'd planned on telling in order to save her own tail, but no, all of a sudden, she couldn't even agree with the one Helen was telling.

"It's the truth, Officer," Helen stepped in. "Her boy isn't going to Children Services because it's not her fault." Helen looked around at the patrons. "Isn't that right?"

At first there was a pause filled with silence.

"Isn't that right?" Helen pressed. "The last place that boy needs to be is down at Children Services." Helen looked over at Deborah's distraught son. Other patrons followed her eyes over to the boy. Just the mere sight broke their hearts, causing a couple of them to nod in agreement with Helen's lie.

Finally there were a few. "Yeah, Officer. That's right."

"So just leave the boy be," another added, confirming that the only reason they were going along with the lie was for the sake of the child.

All Deborah knew was that she was so glad this wasn't a *Primetime: What Would You Do?* episode and that a camera crew wouldn't come out and bust all the folks who had just told the legal authorities an outright lie. They'd feel so embarrassed that they'd all fess up and tell the truth: Deborah was the instigator. Deborah threw the first blow. As a matter of fact, she'd been the only one throwing punches. Helen hadn't even tried to hit her. The only reason she'd had her hands on Deborah at all was to try to keep Deborah from waling on her. Yet here stood Deborah, portraying the victim.

"So like I said, Officer, there's no need for you to waste any more of your time," Helen told him, then extended her wrists in order to sport the metal bracelets.

The officer looked at Helen with uncertainty. "You sure you want to do this?" he asked almost as if he knew deep down in his spirit there wasn't an ounce of truth to the scenario they were trying to get him to believe. But unless someone said otherwise, he couldn't operate on gut feelings alone.

Helen gave Deborah and her son one last look. "Yes, Officer, I'm sure."

The officer proceeded to whip out the cuffs. "Guess you're an okay church folk after all," the officer complimented her. "I mean, you still got no business acting out like this, and especially in front of this woman's kid, but that's what that church business is all about, huh? Recognizing your sins, admitting them, and then repenting for them?" He nodded. "That's pretty noble of you."

The next thing everyone heard was the clinking of the officer slamming the cuffs around Helen's wrists.

"Still gotta take you to jail though," the officer told Helen, then looked to Deborah. "I'm going to go take her statement. Gonna need you to okay it and make one of your own. So, don't go too far." On that note, he escorted Helen out of the restaurant in cuffs.

Deborah just stood there, frozen, knowing that could have been her. It should have been her. But God had spared her. He knew she wouldn't be able to withstand two encounters in one day with Children Services. God didn't want to see her in jail and risk losing her son. At least that's what Deborah told herself to excuse why she wasn't stepping up to the plate and sparing Helen from a trip to the slammer.

"Mommy!" Her son's voice brought her out of her deep thoughts.

"Oh, my baby." Deborah scooped up her son from Zelda's arms. "Thank you, Zelda. Thank you," she said in between kisses to her son's face.

"It's not me you owe a thanks to," Zelda said with venom. "Had that been me, your butt would have been in the slammer and your boy downtown. Because if that's the wakeup call you needed from the Mighty One, then who would I be to stand in His way? And a wakeup call is just what I think you need."

Zelda had been known to speak her mind, even during her days when she used to attend New Day. Deborah had never been on the receiving end of Zelda's lashing though; that was, up until now.

"What's the matter?" Zelda shot. "Ain't got nothing to say now? What, and with all that mouth you got," Zelda seethed. "You should be ashamed of yourself. Acting that way in front of your child, Deborah . . . really?" Even though she wasn't known to, Zelda looked like she was holding back. "There is so much I want to say to you right now, but unlike yourself, I respect the presence of your son." She looked at Deborah's son. "I feel sorry for him."

Deborah was wrong and she knew she was wrong. But she was sick and tired of people judging her relationship with her son. "Look, Zelda, I said thank you— thank you for looking after him. But you needn't feel sorry for him. My son is going to be just fine."

"We'll you can certainly believe I'll be praying for such. Go on and get him out of here. I'll have your bill ready the next time you come back in here." Zelda looked around at the mess in the diner. "For the food and the damage." She then walked around Deborah in order to go clean up the mess.

Deborah just stood there and waited while Zelda cleaned up the mess she'd made in the diner, and outside of the diner Helen covered for her other mess.

Chapter Thirty-seven

"I figured the least I could do was bail you out of jail," Deborah said as she twiddled her fingers. She began inspecting her nails and picking at them. She was doing anything to keep from having to look Helen in the face.

"You're right, it is the least. I can think of a whole lot more you can do, but right now I'm ready to get out of this place, get home, take a shower, and eat a decent meal—since I didn't get to eat my meal at Family Café," Helen added sarcastically as she headed to the exit doors of the jailhouse.

Helen had every right to be upset with Deborah and then some, but Deborah still wanted to make peace with her. She followed Helen out of the jail building. "My car . . . it's parked around the corner," Deborah called out to Helen, then lightly jogged in order to catch up with her. "Pastor was up here to take you home. I told her I would." Deborah chuckled. "You should have seen her face. She said she couldn't believe she was up here having to get yet another one of her church members. She's starting to think someone put a word curse on the members of New Day, or that God's got a strange way of telling her to start a prison ministry." Deborah laughed again.

Helen stopped in her tracks. "You think this is funny? Do you think my going to jail so that your raggedy butt wouldn't have to is funny?" Helen was outraged. She was breathing hard and her eyes filled with tears.

"No, I don't," Deborah said. "I don't think it's funny at all. I think it's brave, courageous, generous, and it was undeserving on my part." She continued, "I know what you did for me and I take it very seriously. I know why you did it. I'd already been spouting off about Children Services being called on me. You knew if they got involved again with this incident, I'd be risking my boy getting dumped into the system. In spite of me and all of my ugliness, you didn't want to see that happen to my boy. I appreciate that. And that means a lot to me, Helen. It really does. And I promise that no matter what I have to do, I'll make it up to you. I've already repented to God, but I need you to—"

"So is that how you get by?" Helen asked, cutting Deborah off.

Deborah wasn't quite sure she knew what Helen was talking about, so she needed clarification. "What do you mean?"

"Is that how you get by with doing the things you do over and over again? You mess up and just run to God and repent and figure since you have a clean slate, you can mess up again, and since God forgave you the last time and all the times before that, it's okay to mess up again because you know that, once again, all you'll have to do is go to God and repent and everything's going to be okay?" Helen had said it all in one breath, confusing Deborah even more as Deborah stood there with a question mark on her forehead. "Just forget it!" Helen threw her hands up and started walking away again.

"Please, I know you have every right to be good and pissed off at me right now, but I'm going to make it up to you—someway and somehow." Deborah walked behind Helen even though they were going in the total opposite direction of where Deborah's car was parked. "I'll help you out in children's church. Heck, when you open up your childcare center I'll write all the press releases, slogans, and—"

"What childcare center?" Once again Helen stopped walking and turned to face Deborah. "I have a record now. Didn't you read the statement on the police report? I attacked a woman who was with her child. I assaulted a woman and endangered her child." The tears that had been frozen in Helen's eyes spilled out. "There won't be any childcare center."

For the first time, Deborah realized the magnitude of what Helen had done for her. She was speechless. "You . . . you gave up your dream for me. You gave up your life."

"Yeah, I guess I did." Helen shrugged in a sarcastic way, downplaying what she'd done for Deborah. "But I'm sure that doesn't mean much to you. You'll be cussing me and fussing me out next week." Helen let out a "tah," and walked off.

"Helen, you've got to believe me, I'm changed. After what you did for me, how could I not be a changed person?"

"Taxi!" Helen yelled out at the yellow car that was driving down the street. The taxi pulled over to the curb where Helen stood. Before getting in the taxi she looked at Deborah. "You're a funny woman, Deborah. I mean you have to be a real comedian if you want me to believe that after what I did for you, you are now willing to change your life."

"It's not a joke, Helen. I mean it," Deborah said with all the sincerity in the world.

"Oh, yeah? Then you're lying to yourself." Helen opened the taxi door, but before getting in and riding away she said to Deborah, "Why would I think for one minute that you are serious about changing just because of what I did for you? Especially when after all Jesus did for you didn't seem to do the trick?"

Deborah didn't know how long she stood on that street, stunned by Helen's final words to her, but she knew she had to get back to Family Café and get her son. Zelda had probably stuffed the poor boy with rolls. Zelda, as a matter of fact, had been the one who suggested that Deborah go bail Helen out of jail. She volunteered to watch her son while she went and did it.

By the time Deborah made it back to the diner, it was closed. But Zelda and a couple other staff members were inside cleaning up. Deborah walked up to the locked glass door and knocked. Zelda was in the middle of wiping down a table when she stopped to go let Deborah in.

"How's Helen?" was the first thing Zelda asked when she opened the doors.

All Deborah could do was put her hand on her forehead and look away.

"Your boy is sound asleep," Zelda shifted the conversation and said. She started walking toward the back of the diner. She turned and nodded for Deborah to follow her.

Once in the back, Zelda led Deborah to a little room off the kitchen. In the small room, there was a little cot, a table with a small television on it, a three-tiered bookshelf with books, a metal folding chair off in the corner, and a shelf with an alarm clock. Deborah couldn't tell whether the room felt like a college dorm or a prison cell.

On the cot was where Deborah found her son sleeping like the sweet, innocent child he was. She didn't know what it was, but just seeing him lying there caused her emotions to just explode as she burst out crying. She tried to hold it in, but she couldn't. Zelda stepped out of the room for a few seconds and then returned with a couple of tissues in hand.

Zelda handed the tissues to Deborah. "You see what you're doing to him, right? God just showed you?"

Through tears, Deborah affirmed with a head nod.

"They said God will meet you right where you are." Zelda looked at Deborah. "Sweetheart, face it—this is where you are. Now the questions you need to ask yourself are, is this where you want to be, and do you want to stay here?"

Prison—that's what the room felt like. It wasn't a college dorm with a youth with a fresh outlook on life about to conquer the world. For Deborah, it was the prison of a girl who had entrapped her own self with the decisions she'd made and continued to make in life. Jesus could have died on that cross a thousand times for her to be made free, but she insisted on choosing captivity. Would she ever choose freedom?

Chapter Thirty-eight

When Deborah heard the knock on her front door, she had to calm the butterflies in her stomach. She'd been expecting her guest, but was still nervous all the same.

She exhaled and looked down at her son. "Well, here it goes, kid." She then went and opened the front door. "Mom, thanks for coming over," Deborah said after opening the door.

"Thanks for calling me up and inviting me," Mrs. Lewis said. "I've missed you. I wanted to call you up and talk to you."

"Then why didn't you?"

"Nah, I knew things had to be on your timing. I didn't want to push. I want a good relationship with you, Deborah, I really do. I don't want to force it on you, though. When I push, it doesn't seem to do anything but push you away. We were far enough apart as it was."

"I agree, and I don't want us to get any further apart than we are now. If this right here is all I'll ever get, then I'll take it. Just don't want to get any further," Deborah said and then continued. "And we won't, Mom. I promise."

Deborah hugged her mother and whispered, "I'm sorry. I'm so sorry." She pulled away from her mother and looked at her. "I'm sorry that I've waited this long to tell you that I'm sorry and really meant it, and I'm sorry that I never accepted your apology, truly accepted it, until now. Mom, I forgive you. Being mad and holding a grudge about my childhood has done nothing but imprison me. It's like poison, while at the same time it's also like a security blanket." Deborah got teary-eyed. "I feel like if I don't have this pain to hold on to, then what else is there? Being angry and holding a grudge is like that old Buddhist saying, drinking poison and expecting the other person to die."

"I know, baby. I know." Mrs. Lewis pulled Deborah in for a hug. "Let's just look toward the future. Please, for once and for all, let's not concentrate on who we used to be, but who we know God called us to be."

Deborah pulled away from her mother. "Whhattt, you preaching? Oh, Lord, God must be in the midst of this reconciliation. Now that I think about it, here lately, you've been doing a lot of talk about God and praying."

"If it took all this to bring me to a better understanding of who God is and who I am, then so be it. Guess it's all been a blessing in disguise."

"I guess it has." Deborah smiled.

Both women laughed and hugged.

"Ganny Ban Banny," they each heard a little voice say. Both women looked to see Deborah's son charging at them.

"What took you so long to come see about me?" Mrs. Lewis asked, scooping her grandson up off the ground. "Give me some sugar."

Upon request, Deborah's son poked out his lips and leaned in toward his grandmother. The kiss grandmother and grandchild shared belonged on a greeting card. At that moment, Deborah honestly no longer cared how her mother had treated her growing up. The way she was now treating her son made up for it. Deborah could see that her mother was sincerely treating her son the way she probably wished she had treated Deborah.

"Thank you, Mom," Deborah said. "I know I've told you a million times that you weren't the best mother to me, and I know that probably hurt you. But I hope what I'm about to say can serve as some type of healing balm." Deborah continued, "You are the best grand-mother my son could ever have. And if I died tomor-row, I'd be resting perfectly in my grave because in my heart, I know you would probably be a better mother to him than I ever could have been." Deborah burst out crying.

"Don't say that, baby," Mrs. Lewis said. "You're not a bad mother."

"And I sure as heck ain't a good one. That's obvious, otherwise, someone wouldn't have called Children Ser-vices on me."

"Speaking of which, did you ever find out who, in fact, did call Children Services?" Deborah's mother asked. "Because I promise, baby, I would never go be-hind your back and do something like that and not own up to it."

"I know, Mom. I know you wouldn't," Deborah told her. "I think I have an idea of who did it though. I mean, she says she didn't. But I still think she did." Even though Helen pretended not to know anything about Deborah being reported to Children Services, Deborah didn't 100 percent believe her. Sure, Helen had jeopardized her own future by taking the rap for the fight at Family Café. Deborah felt it was guilt that had moved Helen to do something like that for her. She figured that Helen felt so guilty about reporting Debo-rah that taking the fall for her was her way of making up for it. That made sense to Deborah, even though there were still a lot of other things that didn't. But

Deborah was willing to forget about it all and just let it go. She was tired of holding on to mess . . . to poison. And she was darn sure tired of drinking it.

"Well, just know that I'm here to support you no matter what," Mrs. Lewis told her daughter.

"Thanks, Mom. Lord knows I'm going to need your help and anyone else's God sends me."

Just then Deborah's doorbell rang. She got up and opened the door. Standing on her doorstep was someone she hadn't expected. She was absolutely surprised. But something told her that God wasn't surprised at all. As a matter of fact, He'd probably hand delivered her guest to her doorstep.

"So we meet again," Mrs. Lewis said to her daughter's unexpected guest.

"And it's so good to see you again, Mrs. Lewis. As much as I adore your daughter, I haven't had the pleasure of really getting to know you. "

"True, but I hear all kinds of good things about you," Mrs. Lewis complimented the guest. "So the three of us will definitely have to get together and have lunch or something. Anybody who has played as big a role in my Deb's life as you have is somebody I might want to take the opportunity to have in mine."

"Well, thank you. The next time I'm in Malvonia, we'll have to make that happen." She turned and glared at Deborah. "But this time I'm only here for a spell. And something tells me I'm going to need every minute I have to take care of why I'm here."

"Speaking of which . . ." Deborah finally joined in on the conversation. "Exactly what is it that brings you to this neck of the woods?"

"Oh, you know me," Mother Doreen replied to her prodigy. "When God gives me an assignment, I don't ask too many questions. I just up and go."

Deborah shot Mother Doreen a knowing look. "Pastor called you, didn't she?"

"Yes, perhaps she did," Mother Doreen said and then leaned in with a serious look on her face and whispered, "But, child, when are you going to realize that God called me first?"

Deborah smiled nervously, unable to detect if Mother Doreen was friend or foe. Was she more help sent from God? Or was she here to perform a verbal exorcism on Deborah? Only time would tell.

Chapter Thirty-nine

"I like your mother. She seems like a wonderful woman." Mother Doreen took a sip of the lemonade Deborah had prepared for the two of them along with a salad. Mrs. Lewis had taken Deborah's son to her house. Since she hadn't been spending as much time with him lately, she wanted him to stay the night with her. Mother Doreen had mentioned that she would only be in town for the night. So this left some time for Mother Doreen and Deborah to catch up on things.

"My mother likes you too," Deborah replied.

"Today was the most I've ever really talked to her. I got to get to know her a little better, and should I say I was pleasantly surprised. She's not what I imagined her to be like after hearing you talk about her for all these years."

"Yeah, I know, but people change," Deborah replied. "And my mother has definitely done some changing. I guess I've just been too selfish to recognize it and give her credit for it."

"Umm, hmmm, I see, and what about you?" Mother Doreen ate a forkful of salad. "You done any changing?"

"What do you mean?" Deborah played stupid, but she knew there was no fooling her confidant and mentor. Mother Doreen had a spirit of discernment that would put any fortune teller or psychic to shame. God shared things with her about a person. She was like this walking piece of confirmation He'd use to set people straight. Well, Deborah was just as crooked as a broken bone. She just wished God had given her a little anesthesia to help limit the pain before He'd sent Mother Doreen to come straighten it out.

Mother Doreen took one last bite of her salad, wiped her mouth, and then pushed her plate away. "Let's not waste any of our time or God's." Mother Doreen dropped her fist to the table. "What in God's creation is going on with you?"

"Nothing," Deborah started, but then remembered who she was talking to. "Just stuff. Everything," Deborah had to admit what she was certain Mother Doreen already knew.

"Oh, I know lots is going on. Even before Pastor called me, child, you were in my spirit something awful."

"Then why didn't you call me?"

"God didn't say call you up. God said to pray for you, so that's what I did. And after that He still didn't have me call you. He had me get in my car and drive here to see about you."

Deborah was touched. Why couldn't she be as obedient to God as Mother Doreen? In her eyes, no matter what anybody said, Mother Doreen was like this perfect Christian. She admired her strength and how she persevered in life. More than anything, she loved the way Mother Doreen loved; the woman loved like she had the heart of Christ. There weren't too many people she got upset with or too many times Deborah had witnessed her even take a loud tone with someone. Why couldn't she be like that, was what Deborah constantly asked herself. Why couldn't she go through life and not let people and things get the best of her?

"Well, thank you for coming, Mother Doreen," Deborah said. "I could really, really use a friend right now."

Mother Doreen, who had initially been sitting across from Deborah, got up and sat in the chair next to Deborah. "Child, don't you know by now that you've always had a friend in Jesus? At least He calls you friend."

"I know, Mother Doreen, but with the things that have been coming out of my mouth, I haven't really been able to find it in my heart to use the same tongue to communicate with Jesus."

Mother Doreen relaxed back in her chair. "Yeah, so I've heard." Mother Doreen looked to Deborah. "And, daughter, I'm so disappointed in you. Acting that way, and in God's house no less. Just flying off the handle, fighting, cursing and things—now that's not how Christian folks are supposed to act."

"And that's just it," Deborah said out of frustration. "Everybody has their different opinion on how a Christian is supposed to act, and then if we don't act that certain way according to their standards, we're supposed to be less of a Christian."

"People's—man's—opinion doesn't matter. It's what God says that matters. It's not about people holding Christians to a higher standard, it's about God holding His saints to a higher standard. Him expecting more out of His children. His wanting us not to sin."

"And I haven't been sinning," Deborah said in her own defense. "So I get upset and cuss sometimes. Let's be real; Christians cuss all the time, Mother Doreen."

"So does that make it all right?" Mother Doreen asked. "Christians lie, get drunk, cheat, steal, kill, all of that; but, my dear friend, does that make it right?" Deborah just turned away with her nose in the air. "Folks, especially folks who claim to be Christians, kill me with all that talk about cussing and drinking not being a sin. So what! Ain't no sin in the clothes I see some of these half-naked women wearing, but just because it ain't a sin to wear a high-cut skirt that shows your butt cheeks and a little top that shows everything but the nipples, why would you want to do it? Just because you can run around with a vulgar tongue, why would you want to? I mean, since when do we need folks to be cussing, drinking, and sexing in order to believe that something is real?"

"That's not what I'm saying," Deborah replied.

"Then by all means, please tell me exactly what you are trying to say, young lady. But keep in mind, I'm old school, so keeping it real means something entirely different to me. Keeping it real means getting your message across with your heart, gut, and passion. I don't need no explicit words or actions for me to know that something is real. Like in the Bible when Jesus turned over those tables in the church when folks were selling stuff, whether He said a few choice words, I will never know, but King James relayed to us that Jesus was mad and went off. But what King James didn't do was use a lot of bad cuss words to convey it. Does that mean King James wasn't keeping it real?" Mother Doreen folded her arms, knowing that there was no way Deborah was going to win this battle. Mother Doreen had had it out with plenty of saints one too many times. She held the championship belt and refused to give up the title.

"Look, just forget it." Deborah shooed her hand, knowing that if she danced around in that ring any longer, Mother Doreen would knock her out cold.

"Oh, no, we ain't gonna forget it." Mother Doreen stood, refusing to allow Deborah to throw in the white towel. "Because this breaks my heart, it breaks my heart to know that my people think that in order to be entertained, in order for them to believe something to be true, in order for them to believe something is real, it has to involve behavior like cussing and carrying on."

"I'm just living in the real world, Mother Doreen," Deborah said, deciding that since Mother Doreen refused to let her out of the ring, she might as well stand there and swing. If she landed a couple of blows, cool. "In the real world, Christians cuss, drink, smoke, have sex with people other than their spouses, et cetera . . ."

"Then therein lies the mistake," Mother Doreen stated. "Instead of worrying about what's going on in the real world, a true Christian after God's own heart should be worrying about what's going on in the Kingdom."

Seven, eight, nine, ten. Deborah had been knocked out cold. Mother Doreen had slugged her with the final knockout punch. There was no getting back up off the canvas.

"Now what was that point you were trying to make again?" Mother Doreen folded her arms, giving Deborah the floor.

But Deborah couldn't get up. She was done. She was done fighting. She was done trying to defend her actions when she knew in her spirit she could do better. God had made her better. She wanted to be better. Honestly, she did. She wanted to be a good person. But she just felt so bad. With all the bad, there was no way she could dig up any good out of her. She wasn't even forty years old yet. She'd only lived half her life at best, which meant she'd have another forty years, at least, of being filled with misery. Just the thought broke her down.

Mother Doreen put her arms around Deborah.

"Mother Doreen, I'm just tired," Deborah cried. "So tired—tired of losing. I fail every test, every time. The Word says Christians are supposed to win this battle, but I keep getting shot up, beat up, beat down, and defeated. And the worst thing about it is that there's not some taunting enemy on the other side. The enemy is in me. I'm my own enemy. I'm in a battle against myself."

"And it's right there"—Mother Doreen pointed to Deborah's head—"in your mind."

"I know. I know." Deborah wept. "And it makes me feel crazy. I mean, sometimes I actually feel like a lunatic—like I'm not myself."

Mother Doreen took Deborah's hands into hers. "Now, look at me, child. Look and just listen to what I'm about to say." Mother Doreen closed her eyes and mumbled in unknown tongues as if she were on *Who Wants To Be A Millionaire* and was calling on her lifeline. After a few seconds, she opened her eyes and said to Deborah, "You ever thought about getting help? Going to maybe talk to a counselor or something?"

Deborah deciphered what Mother Doreen was suggesting. "You mean a shrink? Oh, heck to the naw." Deborah let go of Mother Doreen's hands and stood. She began pacing the kitchen floor. "Black folks don't do psychiatrists, shrinks, counseling, and all that stuff."

"That ain't so. I remember watching *ESPN* with my hubby and them showing a guy winning a basketball championship, he was talking about how his psychiatrist or whatever helped him work through his issues. Why he even gave his doctor a personal thanks, shout out, or whatever it's called."

"Yeah, well, my doctor is Jesus."

"Then if that's the case, how is your doctor supposed to help you if you won't even talk to Him? You said it yourself, right now you can't even talk to Jesus. Well, go find you a Christian counselor or something and speak to one of Jesus' representatives."

Deborah stopped her pacing and looked at Mother Doreen. "You're serious about this, aren't you?" Mother Doreen didn't reply. "Okay, look, I'll call Pastor and ask her if she can set aside some time to start counseling me and maybe—"

"That's fine. I do believe you need some spiritual counseling as well," Mother Doreen interrupted. "The two will go hand in hand. But, Deborah honey, and you know I wouldn't be saying this if God hadn't put it in my spirit to say, you need some professional help."

Deborah threw her hands up. "What . . . I mean, where is all this coming from?" Deborah tried not to sound sarcastic, but that's exactly what she was being. "Oh, let me guess, you are getting this from your spirit. Well, no offense, but your spirit has been all the way in Kentucky. It has no idea what my spirit has been up to."

Mother Doreen didn't take too lightly to folks doubting her ability to hear from God. "Well, obviously your spirit has been up to no good or Pastor wouldn't have felt the need to call me or Children Services."

There wasn't just one, but two huge elephants now sitting in the room. Mother Doreen closed her eyes and internally kicked herself for letting that cat out of the bag. While her eyes were closed—it was a long shot, but—she prayed that God would make it so that Deborah hadn't heard that last comment she'd slipped and made.

"What did you say? Pastor . . . Pastor's the one who called Children Services on me?" Deborah felt like she'd been punched in the gut, so much so that her hand grasped her stomach. "My own pastor?" She looked up at Mother Doreen with hurt and pain in her eyes. "But, why? Why would she . . ." Before Deborah could even get the sentence out, a heat wave of anger flourished through her body.

She instantly stormed out of the kitchen and went and snatched up her purse and keys. Mother Doreen came out of the kitchen, following her.

"What are you doing?" Mother Doreen asked as Deborah opened the front door with keys and purse in hand. "Where are you going?"

"I'm going to get it from the horse's mouth, that's what I'm about to do," Deborah snapped.

Mother Doreen gently grabbed her by the arm before she could make her way out of the door. "Deborah, if you plan on going to confront your pastor, I really believe you ought to think twice about that."

"She should have thought twice about calling Children Services on me," replied Deborah. "And you know what? I would have appreciated her giving me the same respect of confronting me first. But even though she couldn't give me that liberty, I'm about to give it to her. And, oh, am I going to give it to her." Deborah snatched away from Mother Doreen and headed for her car.

"Child, when are you ever going to learn that in the end, yes, the Bible tells us we win, we get the victory, but only if we play by God's rules?" Mother Doreen called out to Deborah, whose head was too full of smoke for Mother Doreen's words to get through. Realizing that it was useless, Mother Doreen closed the door, leaned up against it, then uttered the words, "And, Deborah, honey, when are you going to learn to stop battling the wrong people?"

Even if Deborah had heard Mother Doreen's last statement, it wouldn't have made a bit of difference. Forget about a battle; as far as she was concerned, it was about to be an all-out war!

Chapter Forty

"Sister Deborah, I was expecting you." Pastor Margie stood at her front door, holding the screen open for Deborah to enter. She'd been standing in her living room picture window for the last few minutes. She'd been looking for headlights to pull up in her driveway. Just as soon as she saw them, she turned off her alarm system and went and opened the door.

Mother Doreen had called her a few minutes ago, giving her the heads-up on what had just gone down at Deborah's house. After apologizing for the slip of her tongue, Pastor Margie told Mother Doreen it was okay, the two prayed; then Pastor Margie waited. It was safe to say that the wait was indeed over.

"Let me guess; your tag-team partner called and gave you a heads-up?" Deborah snapped. "Figures."

"I know you are upset," Pastor Margie said to Deborah as she brushed by her pastor, "but I'm willing to talk about the matter with you—like adults. Like Christian adults."

Deborah didn't respond to Pastor Margie's statement. She just strutted in as if she would have whether Pastor Margie had invited her in or not. She headed over to the couch and sat down.

"If you don't mind, can we talk in my office?"

Deborah stood and followed her pastor to the back of her house, where the home office was. Pastor sat behind her desk and went to signal for Deborah to sit in the chair on opposite side, but Deborah had already taken the liberty of sitting down.

"Let me just start by saying that, yes, I am the one who called Franklin County Children Services on you," Pastor Margie admitted. "And I'm sorry. I'm not sorry that I called them, but I am sorry that I didn't talk to you first."

"Pastor, I'm so disappointed in you. How could you bring that agency into my business based on something Helen told you? And for the record, that wasn't a bruise on my son's arm. It was some kind of rash. I have a doctor's statement to prove it."

"I don't know anything about a bruise on your son's arm. Besides, I would never involve FCCS based on hearsay. I called them after what I witnessed, or should I say after what I heard." She shook her head. "Deborah, listening to you on that phone had me scared to death. The way you were going off, I didn't know what you were going to do next. I almost called the police and was going to have them come over to your house."

"What are you talking about, Pastor?" Deborah was clueless.

"That day you and I were on the phone. We were talking about that single shoe dinner or whatever it is you were talking to me about having for the singles ministry."

Deborah recalled the conversation just fine. But what she didn't recall was something that took place during that phone call that would prompt her pastor to report her to Children Services. "I remember," Deborah told her pastor.

"Well, after we got finished talking and said our goodbyes, you must have thought you'd hung up the phone, but you hadn't. I put the phone on speaker trying to get back to the recording function on the phone. The next thing I know I hear this woman's voice roaring through the phone. I hear cursing, yelling, screaming . . ." Pastor paused and reflected. "It was something about a messed-up manuscript. I'm not sure, but I just heard this child crying." She closed her eyes to hide the emotion behind them. Once she'd gathered her composure, she continued. "It didn't take me long to realize that it was you. I can't tell you how shocked I was. But even more so, I was so scared. Sister Deborah, you sounded so angry—so full of rage. I didn't know what you were going to do. I didn't know what I should do."

Deborah couldn't recall every single thing she'd said that day her son had messed up the manuscript she'd been editing. She did know that it wasn't anything she would have wanted her pastor to hear. But even so, it wasn't anything that deemed her being reported to the system. "Well, you shouldn't have called Children Services, that's for sure. And on top of that you exaggerated and told them I was abusing my son."

"But it wasn't a lie. You were abusing him."

"I never laid a hand on my child," Deborah shot.

"Oh but how you tore him to pieces with your words. You said the word 'stupid' more times than I could count."

"Sure, I might have said the word 'stupid,' but I never outright called my son stupid," Deborah reasoned.

"Whether you were calling your child stupid or you were referring to his actions as stupid, all his little mind hears is the word 'stupid.' Do you get what I'm saying here, Deborah?" Pastor Margie asked. "Because I'm not going to sugarcoat this thing for you. What I witnessed through my ears was verbal abuse; verbal abuse that can ultimately have a very negative effect on your son."

"My son!" Deborah pointed to her chest. "My son!" This time she pounded on it. She hated the fact that she was disrespecting her pastor with her loud tone, but she was pissed. This was personal. Her pastor had jeopardized the custody of her son. "I'm sorry, Pastor, but how I see it, how I raise my son has nothing to do with you."

Pastor, as kindhearted and as sweet spirited as she was, was not one to be bullied. With conviction she said, "And how I see it, my nieces and nephews, cousins, whatever, have to grow up with your child. So if you've created this angry little monster, then it does affect me. Oh it affects me tremendously." Pastor Margie rolled her eyes as flesh tried its best to take over. "And parents wonder why there is so much bullying going on these days. The kids are being bullied at home by their own parents. So what do these kids do? Mirror that same thing and come take it out on other people's kids."

"Tsk," Deborah said, brushing off Pastor Margie's comments. "You are being soooo dramatic right now, Pastor. I mean no disrespect, but the black and white cultures are just so totally different. You guys take things way out of proportion. Calling and tattling on somebody because they whooped their child in a Walmart parking lot. That's nonsense. And that's not abuse; it's called discipline."

"I don't have anything to do with that incident. I didn't witness a woman physically abusing her child— or whooping a child at Walmart, as you refer to. And I didn't call it in. What I did witness, and, I repeat, through my own ears, was a woman verbally abusing her child. And that I did call in. Now what?" Pastor shot. She was tired of going back and forth with Deborah. In her heart, she had no regrets. What she heard on the phone made her cringe. She'd bet if Deborah had heard it, she'd cringe too. Then that's when something dawned on Pastor Margie. "Hold on a second," she said to Deborah, then raced over to her cell phone.

"Forget it, Pastor. It's clear we will never see eye to eye on this thing." Deborah stood and picked up her purse.

"No, please wait," Pastor Margie insisted as she fiddled around with her cell phone. She pushed a couple of buttons, and then her recorded voice filled the atmosphere:

"In the Kings James version the scripture says—"

Pastor Margie stopped the recording. "Oh, wait a minute. I'm sorry. That's not far enough." She fiddled around with the phone again, and then it was Deborah's voice that filled the atmosphere:

"Oh, me too, Pastor, and I'm sorry I interrupted you."

"No problem. God bless you, woman of God, and have a wonderful week."

"Will do, Pastor. Bye-bye."

It took a moment to register, but then Deborah realized what she was listening to:

"Do you know what you've done? Why can't you just sit your simple self down somewhere? Why you always messing with stuff you little . . ."

Deborah grabbed her stomach as if someone had just shot her a lethal blow. Her jaw dropped. Her throat was empty as she stared down at the phone. She gasped for air as the vulgarities she heard suffocated the room. They were vulgarities being directed toward a child. Her child. She looked up at her pastor. "You, you recorded it?"

"Not on purpose," Pastor Margie replied. "Remember when I mentioned that I had been recording some

Bible Study notes when you called? Well, I hadn't stopped the recording." Pastor Margie looked down at the cell phone. "I guess the both of us need to learn how to work our cell phones a little better, huh?"

Deborah didn't reply, she just stared back down at the phone and listened to her go on and on and on, fussing and cussing and yelling and screaming and hollering. But then something else seemed to drown out her voice. It was her son, crying. His little wail. He just wouldn't stop crying. And she wouldn't stop her rampage. Eventually Deborah covered her eyes and fell down into the chair.

Pastor Margie raced over to attend to her.

"Turn it off, Pastor, please," Deborah pleaded. "I can't listen to anymore."

"I'm sorry, Sister Deborah, but I can't turn it off. I think you need to hear it. I think you need to hear your-self—hear what you sound like. You need to hear what your child hears."

Deborah just began to cry out and shake her head as if she was being tortured. By the time the record-ing ended, Deborah had no idea how much time had passed. She was drained. She was disgusted. She was humiliated. She was embarrassed. She was . . . she was sorry.

"I'm so sorry, baby," Deborah cried as she rocked back and forth.

Pastor Margie just held her, knowing that the apol-ogy was directed toward Deborah's son.

"Baby, Mommy is so sorry. She'll never do it again. She'll never talk to you, treat you, that way again. Oh, God, I'm so sorry." She sobbed uncontrollably in her pastor's arms. After a while, she cut off the waterworks almost instinctively, looked up at her Pastor, and said, "I need help. I've got some deep-rooted stuff, some generational curse that I need to work through. I'm just so bitter and angry that it's destroying me. I'm like a bad weed and nothing good can survive around me for long. I need help, Pastor."

"Oh, Deborah, honey." Pastor kissed her on the forehead. "I knew there was something going on with you. That day back at my office when I had that talk with you and Sister Helen," Pastor recalled, "I tried to get you to be real with me, but you insisted everything was just fine with you. I should have listened to my gut instincts and pressed harder."

"No, Pastor, you did all you could," Deborah said, thinking back to that day when Pastor had seen right through Deborah's forgiving Helen and Helen forgiving her, and then each of them riding off into the sunset on their merry way. Deborah remembered Pastor telling her that she could confide in her if there were some deeper issues going in her life, other than her issues with Helen. Deborah had assured Pastor all was well. So much had been wrong.

"No, I didn't do all that I could, but I'm going to now." She looked Deborah in the eyes. "I'll be happy to counsel you, Deborah, but the first thing—"

"No, Pastor Margie; I need another kind of help. From a doctor. Yes, I'm going to need your spiritual guidance through all of this as well, but I need clinical help." Deborah shook her head and began crying again. "Something's wrong with me. This losing it and going off, it's like an addiction. It's something I feel like I have no control over and can't stop. It's this pull that I can't explain."

Pastor Margie gave Deborah a sideways glance. "And you said my people were overdramatic," she joked, and then squeezed Deborah close to her.

"I know, Pastor, and I'm sorry. It's just that black women are expected to be so strong—to do so much. But it's killing us. Black women are losing their minds. They are killing themselves and their children. I honestly used to think it was a white thing. 'Black people don't hurt themselves or their children,'" Deborah mocked. "But women, black women, are dying. We are killing ourselves—mentally, physically, spiritually, and literally—and expectations are killing us."

Pastor Margie pondered Deborah's words. No, she couldn't relate to the black woman's plight specifically. But she could relate to the plight of women, period. And she agreed that when it came to women trying to make it in the world, it wasn't a black or white thing. "I hear you, Sister Deborah, and I know it's hard. But please know that I'm here to help you any way I know how. I'll talk to Children Services. I'll be there for you. As your pastor and your friend, I want to see you delivered, healed, and set free. And I want you to walk in that deliverance and healing. Claim it. Own it. Keep it. It's yours, Sister Deborah. If you want it bad enough, it's yours."

"I do want it, Pastor. I do. After hearing myself on that phone . . ." Deborah choked. "Thank you, Pastor."

"For what?" Pastor Margie asked.

"For being loyal to God and not me. For being concerned about my son's wellbeing and not how I would feel. For calling Children Services. If you hadn't, no telling how bad things might have gotten. Children Services being called on me could have been the one thing that really pushed me over the edge. And the devil knew that, too. But what the devil meant for evil . . ."

"God turned it around," both women said in unison, then hugged as they laughed.

God had turned the situation around all right; now the rest was up to Deborah. In the past she'd wanted to change badly. She'd set out to change and had every intention of doing so no matter how hard it would be. But her change had never come. Yes, it might have come temporarily. But Deborah couldn't live off of temporary fixes. A permanent change needed to be made, and this time not making a change could mean losing her son. She couldn't take that risk. This time things would be different. This time, change was gon' come.

Chapter Forty-one

Six weeks after Deborah's confrontation with her pastor, Deborah was feeling better than ever. Before leaving her pastor's house, the two of them had gone online and found a Christian psychiatrist. Deborah had returned home where she and Mother Doreen spent the night praying and reading scripture. Before Mother Doreen returned to Kentucky that next morning, she'd helped Deborah schedule her first doctor's appointment.

Mentally, Deborah had never been in a better place. She'd been going to church, Bible Study, the singles ministry meetings, and counseling sessions with her pastor. All of this had been very beneficial, including her weekly visits with her psychiatrist and the prescriptions he'd prescribed to her. Happy pills was what Deborah called them, but pure joy was what she called what the Lord gave her.

Renewed, refreshed, revived were just a few words to describe how Deborah had felt these past few weeks. Blessed was another word. And one blessing in particular was her case with Children Services being closed without any charges being brought up against her. Pastor Margie and Deborah's mother had joined her at a mediation-type hearing with the woman who had come to her door. If it hadn't been for them being there to support her, God only knows what could have happened. So paying it forward, in a sense, Deborah made sure she showed up at Helen's court hearing to support her. Deborah didn't think twice about going to the state prosecutor's office and telling them the truth about the incident at the diner. Deborah was their main witness, and after her giving them her latest statement, they knew their initial charges wouldn't stick. They ended up dropping the charges and advised Helen as to how to get the arrest expunged.

"That's the least you could have done," Helen had told Deborah with a wink before the two shared a hug outside of the courtroom.

The charges against Helen being dropped meant that Helen's dream of owning her own childcare business was once again a possibility. And Deborah promised Helen her son would be the first to enroll.

Speaking of her son, Deborah had laid him down for a nap of couple hours ago. During his nap, she'd done something she hadn't done for quite a long time. She'd dusted off her book she'd started writing years ago and began working on it again. And it was pretty darn good, if she did say so herself. It would certainly give Mr. Lynox Chase a run for his money. But Lynox was no longer a factor in Deborah's world. The day he stepped out of her door and the social worker stepped in, her only focus became her son. And then she focused on getting herself better with her son. As much as her heart, mind, body, and soul craved Lynox, with as much as she was going through, factoring him in might have only made things worse.

Even though she hadn't wanted to, she blocked Lynox out of her life. Those two times he'd called her cell phone, she'd let the calls go to her voice mail. When she'd checked her messages and heard his voice, she deleted those messages as well. The e-mails he'd sent her had been deleted too. Right now, things were looking too good in Deborah's life for any setbacks. She knew the only reason Lynox was trying to reach out to her was to question her about her lies and then officially dump her. Well, her spirit couldn't handle that, so to avoid the drama, she avoided him until he finally got a clue and gave up trying to reach out to her altogether.

It wasn't easy though, but she managed to work her issues out in therapy, Lynox certainly being one of those issues. It was hard for her to get over him, but with time, distance, counseling, prayer, and God, she was able to see that she needed so much more than just winning Lynox to be happy and secure in life.

Besides, she figured he must have gotten over her real easy. In the past, Lynox had been much more persistent, but this time, he'd given up after only two phone calls, voices messages, and a couple of e-mails. That was proof alone that he was over her but had only been trying to contact her in order to ram the final stake through her heart.

Just as Deborah was about to wrap up her writing for the afternoon, her doorbell rang. She rushed from her office to the door before the person at the door could ring the bell again and perhaps wake her son. She was a second too late arriving at the door as the bell sounded again.

"I'm coming," she whispered so low that whoever was at the door couldn't have been able to hear her. It was a nice summer day, so Deborah had left her front door open with the screen door locked. When she got to the door, words couldn't explain how she felt when she saw Lynox standing on the porch.

"Lynox?" she questioned, rubbing her eyes. She had to make sure they weren't deceiving her; that one of those side effects of her happy pills wasn't hallucinating.

"Deborah," he said, standing there looking as suave and debonair as always, even in the outfit he was wearing, which Deborah recognized as the biking outfit the two had seen in the window of one of the stores at Easton. In each hand he had a cycling helmet. Over his shoulder, Deborah could see the wheels of bikes.

"What are you doing here?" Deborah asked from the doorway.

"What do you mean what am I doing here?" he asked, raising the helmets. "Didn't you get my voice messages?"

"Yeah, I got them," Deborah replied. "I just didn't listen to them." She was going to be honest from this point on, with herself, and with everybody else in her life. But was Lynox still a part of her life?

A crooked smile spread on his lips as he looked down. "I figured as much." He looked back up. "And my e-mail messages?"

"Nope," Deborah admitted.

"I see." He nodded.

"Look . . ." both started. "Go ahead," they both said to one another. "You first," they spoke at the same time and then laughed.

"Okay, ladies first." Lynox smiled.

"I'm sorry," Deborah said. "I'm sorry I hid the fact that I had a son from you. I'm sorry for the charades, the games, the tricks, and the tension it all caused. I'm sorry I wasn't honest with you. You deserved more from me. While you were genuinely trying to establish a relationship with me built on trust, I was one big walking lie. And I hope you can forgive me."

"I certainly can forgive you, Deborah," Lynox said. "But I know I made it easy for you to lie by making all the comments I did about not wanting to date a woman with kids. I was wrong for that. I wasn't wrong for feeling that way, but I was wrong for the way I relayed it; making it seem like the plague or something. It's just that I have friends who have dated women with kids and I heard nothing but horror stories about their dealings with the baby daddy. Not only that, but having a child with another man means that dude showing up at the house to see the kid, and, who knows, maybe with underlying intentions to even see the mother. You know my ego can't withstand that."

Deborah smiled, nodding her agreement.

"But I love you, Deborah. I love every part of you, and your son is a part of you."

"But you walked away so easily that day the social worker came," Deborah reminded him.

"I was in shock mode. You were snapping off. I just didn't see how my being there would benefit either one of us. I was hurt, angry, and confused. I kept asking myself, 'What kind of woman denies having a child?'"

"And the conclusion you came up with?" Deborah was curious to know.

"A woman who loves me so much that she would be willing to put herself through the drama and the stress of doing such a thing." Lynox stared into Deborah's eyes. "I know that had to be hard for you, Deborah. I can't imagine. I almost feel partly to blame. That's why I needed to apologize to you. I hope you can forgive me."

It was as if Deborah could breathe again. No, she hadn't been holding her breath waiting for Lynox to run back to her, but she was glad he had. She was glad that he was even willing to take partial blame for a decision—a wrong decision—she'd made all by herself. "Yes, Lynox. I forgive you." Deborah nodded her forgiveness with a smile.

"Good. Now what do you say that we try this thing—me and you—one more time?" Lynox asked. "I hear the third time is a charm."

Lynox's request was both shocking and music to Deborah's ears. The rejection, the official breakup she was expecting from him didn't happen. Instead, he was still willing, ready, able, and wanting to give the two of them another shot at love. It made her feel really good inside to know that he still wanted her in his life. But the fact also remained that there was someone else in her life.

"But what about Tyson?" Deborah asked.

"Who?" Lynox had a confused look on his face.

"Tyson—my son."

"Oooooohhhh," Lynox replied while nodding with a smile. "So the little guy does have a name."

Deborah nodded as tears filled her eyes. Tears that displayed the hurt of ever denying her son just because she wanted to be with a man.

Lynox took a step toward Deborah. He placed her helmet in the same hand as his was in, then took his thumb and wiped away her tear. "Don't cry. Tyson has a helmet too." It was at that point that Lynox stepped to the side. There Deborah saw two bikes: a hot pink one and a royal blue one. No doubt the hot pink one had been purchased for her. And on the back of the hot pink one was a special seat made just for a toddler the size of Tyson.

"Lynox?" Deborah said in both surprise and shock. But she had a question mark all over her face as she looked back and forth from the bikes to Lynox. The unspoken question was asking him what all this meant. "Does this mean . . ." She couldn't even get the words out she was so choked up with hope. Could—would—the God she served, after all the mistakes she'd made, some twice (heck, others over and over again), really give her the fairytale? Would God really give her another chance at her heart's desire?

Lynox looked from Deborah to the bikes. "This means . . ." He left Deborah's side and walked over to the hot pink bike. He pulled something out of the toddler seat. It was a mini version of the helmet that matched the one for Lynox. "That we all have to take a chance—together. That includes Tyson. If one falls, then we all fall together."

Lynox quickly and intensely walked back to Deborah's side. "But we'll all get back up together again. But you never know . . ." His eyes and his index finger pointed at the bike. He then looked back at Deborah. "We may never even fall. Who's to say we can't ride this thing out? But we'll never know unless we try. I mean"—the excitement in Lynox's voice picked up—"so what, neither one of us hasn't done something like this in forever. Something in my gut . . ." He touched his stomach. "Something in my spirit tells me that I can do this." He walked up as close as he could to Deborah. "That we can do this. I mean, so what if it's not true— that once a person learns how to ride a bike they never forget? But what I do know to be true, Deborah Lewis, is that once a person learns how to love, now that, they never forget. And after all this time, no matter how many miles away you were, I never forgot how to love you. I'll never forget how to love you. All of you—and that includes Tyson. Like I said, and maybe you missed it. But Tyson is a part of you." He looked Deborah up and down while licking his lips. "And I want all of you, woman."

Lynox wiped a falling tear from Deborah's eye as she listened intently to Lynox's words. "Your son is a part of you—the woman I love. Any man who loves you, how could he not love that big a part of you? And God knows I love you. This entire situation . . . it's taught me something about myself and made me face an issue I'd just assumed I couldn't deal with. And that's the issue of being with a woman who had a child. I'd never given it a chance. I just had all these preconceived notions about baby daddy drama that I knew I didn't want to deal with. I know your situation is different, but I can honestly say from the bottom of my heart that even if Tyson's father were alive, I'd still want you as my girl."

Lynox placed his hand on Deborah's cheek. "So, baby, will you be my girl?" And that was the end of Lynox's spiel, which he couldn't have written any better for a lead male character in one of his novels. This was straight from his heart.

Deborah wanted to pinch herself to make sure this was all real. So she did. And then she pinched Lynox.

"Ouch! What was that for?" He rubbed the spot on his arm that she'd just pinched.

"My pinch was to make sure I was awake and not dreaming all this. Your pinch was to make sure you were real—that I wasn't imagining all this. Because you do know those pills my doc prescribed me have some side effects that—"

"Pills?" Lynox was puzzled until Deborah went on to explain about her counseling, therapy, and her happy pills. "Forget about those pills. Those are just temporary. The same way a person never forgets how to ride a bike or how to love, they never forget who they truly are inside. Or as you church folks would say, who God called you to be." Lynox pointed to Deborah's heart. "She's in there, and with God's help, and mine, and Tyson's, you aren't going to need a pill to be that person. You got that?"

"I do," Deborah cried, trying not to break down. But she was just so moved. "And yes, yes, yes, yes. I will be your girl." Deborah threw her arms around Lynox's neck.

Suddenly she heard her son crying. "Oh, my. Tyson must be awake from his nap."

"Good, because he's got a helmet to test out!" Lynox exclaimed. "Why don't you go get him and I'll adjust these helmets and make sure everything is all good with these bikes." He pointed to his Hummer. "I literally carried all this stuff straight from the store to your doorstep. So I'm going to test things out. Wouldn't want perhaps my future readymade family to get hurt," he smiled, winked, and then turned his attention to the bikes and began poking around at them. He looked so serious, so intent on making sure her and her son were safe. On making sure their hearts were safe. Lynox Chase was a man who would never hurt her. That much she knew. That much she could tell just by watching him now.

And Deborah could have stood there and watched him forever, but when Tyson let out another loud wail, she raced off to get him. A few minutes later she and Tyson joined Lynox for a bike ride. As he got their helmets on them and Tyson buckled in the seat, they headed off down the sidewalk. And "they" had been right; once a person learned how to ride a bike, they never forget, and Lynox, Deborah, and her son rode off toward the sun.

With each and every pedal, Deborah couldn't do anything but thank God. He'd given her the fairytale. No, the man of her dreams hadn't shown up like a knight in shining armor on a horse. He'd shown up in biker gear on a Schwinn. And that was good enough.

Readers' Guide Questions

1) Do you feel a woman who has had an abortion in the past should tell her new mate about it? Why or why not?

2) Do you have any friends like Deborah, who you feel act nasty sometimes, but have not confronted them about it?

3) How do you feel about the idea that black people raise their children by yelling at and spanking them? Do feel that it is a cultural thing so that makes it okay?

4) Neither Helen nor Unique told their pastor about Deborah's outburst. Do you think they should have or did they handle it correctly in your opinion?

5) Do you think people like Deborah are rare: those who can be holy and full of the spirit in church, but act like the devil outside of the church?

6) What did you think about Deborah keeping the fact that she had a child a secret from Lynox? Did you agree or understand where she was coming from?

7) Did you get the significance of Deborah's son's name not being revealed until the end of the book?

8) Do you think Pastor Margie was wrong for reporting Deborah to Children Services? Do you think Deborah was correct in her assumption that white people overreact to certain situations more so than black people?

9) Did the main character's not-so-likeable actions make for an awkward read, or do you feel it was good to see such a severely flawed main character?

10) What is your take on Deborah taking prescribed pills to help her cope? Do you feel it was much needed? Or do you feel it was a copout and she should have leaned more on God in hopes that He pulled her through without the use of medication?

UC HIS GLORY BOOK CLUB!

www.uchisglorybookclub.net

UC His Glory Book Club is the spirit-inspired brain-child of Joylynn Jossel, Author and Acquisitions Editor of Urban Christian, and Kendra Norman-Bellamy, Author for Urban Christian. This is an online book club that hosts authors of Urban Christian. We welcome as members all men and women who have a passion for reading Christian-based fiction.

UC His Glory Book Club pledges our commitment to provide support, positive feedback, encouragement, and a forum whereby members can openly discuss and review the literary works of Urban Christian authors.

There is no membership fee associated with UC His Glory Book Club; however, we do ask that you support the authors through purchasing, encouraging, providing book reviews, and of course, your prayers. We also ask that you respect our beliefs and follow the guidelines of the book club. We hope to receive your valuable input, opinions, and reviews that build up, rather than tear down our authors.

What We Believe:

—We believe that Jesus is the Christ, Son of the Living God.

—We believe the Bible is the true, living Word of God.

—We believe all Urban Christian authors should use their God-given writing abilities to honor God and share the message of the written word God has given to each of them uniquely.

—We believe in supporting Urban Christian authors in their literary endeavors by reading, purchasing and sharing their titles with our online community.

—We believe that everything we do in our literary arena should be done in a manner that will lead to God being glorified and honored.

We look forward to the online fellowship with you. Please visit us often at *www.uchisglorybookclub.net*.

Many Blessing to You!

Shelia E. Lipsey,
President, UC His Glory Book Club

Author Bio

BLESSEDselling author E.N. Joy is the author of *Me, Myself and Him,* which was her debut work into the Christian fiction genre. Formerly a secular author writing under the names Joylynn M. Jossel and JOY, when she decided to fully dedicate her life to Christ, that meant she had to fully dedicate her work as well. She made a conscious decision that whatever she penned from that point on had to glorify God and His Kingdom.

The "Still Divas" series is a continuance of the "New Day Divas" series, which was incited by her publisher, Carl Weber, but birthed by the Holy Spirit. God used Mr. Weber to pitch the idea to E.N. Joy; sort of plant the seed in her spirit, which she prayed on and eventually the seed was watered and grew into a phenomenal series of books that she is sure will touch readers across the map.

"My goal and prayer with the 'New Day Divas' and the 'Still Divas' series is to put an end to the church fiction/drama versus Christian fiction dilemma," E.N. Joy states, "and find a divine medium that pleases both God and the readers."

With the success of the "New Day Divas" and the "Still Divas" series thus far, it is safe to say that readers agree this project is one that definitely glorifies God in every aspect, but still manages to display in a godly manner that there are "church folks" (church fiction) and then there are "Christian folks" (Christian fiction) and come Sunday morning, they all end up in the same place.

E.N. Joy currently resides in Reynoldsburg, Ohio where she is working on future "Divas" projects as well as writing songs for and artistically developing the girl group, DJHK Gurls.

You can visit the author at:
www.enjoywrites.com

E-mail her at: enjoywrites@aol.com to share with her any feedback from the story as well as any subject matters you might want to see addressed in future "Divas" books.

Coming Soon

"Always Divas"
Three Book Series

Book One: *I Ain't Me No More*—Helen's Story
(November 2013)

Book Two: *More Than I Can Bear*—Paige's Story

Book Three: *You Get What You Pray For*—Lorain's Story

Be sure to pick up your copy of *A Woman's Revenge* featuring E.N. Joy's "Best Served Cold" April 2013.